SINCE
SHE'S
BEEN
GONE

SINCE SHE'S BEEN GONE

A NOVEL

SAGIT SCHWARTZ

CROOKED
LANE

NEW YORK

Copyright © 2024 by Sagit Maier-Schwartz

Published in the United States by Crooked Lane Books, an imprint of The Quick Brown Fox & Company LLC.

Crooked Lane Books and its logo are trademarks of The Quick Brown Fox & Company LLC.

Library of Congress Catalog-in-Publication data available upon request.

ISBN (hardcover): 978-1-63910-627-1
ISBN (ebook): 978-1-63910-628-8

Cover design by Crooked Lane Books

Printed in the United States.

www.crookedlanebooks.com

Crooked Lane Books
34 West 27th St., 10th Floor
New York, NY 10001

First Edition: February 2024

10 9 8 7 6 5 4 3 2 1

For my mom, Penina (1950–1997),
who believed in me,

and

For anyone suffering from an eating
disorder and for their families.

There is hope for recovery.

AUTHOR'S NOTE AND CONTENT WARNING

SINCE SHE'S BEEN Gone offers an unvarnished look at what it's like to live with an eating disorder. The novel includes graphic descriptions of disordered thoughts, the competitive nature of restrictive anorexia, exercise compulsion, feeding tubes, scale/weight numbers in pounds, and one act of self-harm. An eating disorder-related heart failure death and an eating disorder-related miscarriage also occur in the book.

Although I'm a licensed psychotherapist who has been impacted by an eating disorder, this book is *not* a roadmap to recovery. Rather, it's an honest account of what it can or may feel like to live with an eating disorder—with a hopeful message that recovery is possible.

Other content warnings in the book include parental loss and opioid addiction.

Please read with care.

PART I
Presenting Problem

Being entirely honest with oneself is a good exercise.
                                    —Sigmund Freud

1

Day One

THE NEW PATIENT called yesterday.
"Can you get me in today?" she asked. "It can't wait."

I've gotten calls like this before. Sometimes people are in deep emotional pain, desperate for immediate help. Other times I learn, after the fact, that they lack boundaries. I told her I had no openings and offered to squeeze her in at seven this morning.

"That's even better," she said. "Fewer people will be around then, right?"

Her question made me wonder if she's self-conscious about being in therapy—I've had my share of patients who are. Or maybe she's famous and doesn't want to be recognized.

As a therapist with a private practice in Beverly Hills, I've had a few celebrity patients, some of whom I didn't know were famous until I Googled them.

It's 6:42 AM, and I'm tired. I sip my coffee, trying to wake up, regretting offering up the 7 AM time slot.

Eddie and I stayed up until one thirty in the morning, having the same conversation we've been having for the last few months. He wants me to move in with him, and I've been waffling.

On paper, it makes sense. We've been together for almost two years. He's a wonderful guy—loyal, funny, and a dedicated father. But I know moving in together will be the final step before he asks me to marry him. And I already went down that path a decade ago, unsuccessfully.

I also worry it'll be hard on Sarah, his seven-year-old daughter, if things don't work out between us. Eddie's late wife unexpectedly died when Sarah was just four years old. If I step in as her mother figure and our relationship falls apart, Sarah will lose another mom. And this time, it'll be worse, because she'll have memories with me, ones she doesn't have with her own mother since she was so young when her mom died. I know that pain all too well.

And what if I don't measure up as a day-to-day mom? Eddie says Sarah adores me, but I don't tuck her in every night and wake up with her every morning. The three of us spend weekends together and see each other a couple of times during the week for dinner. Moving in with them will mean being there for her *all the time*—from nursing fevers to planning birthday parties to taking her to the dentist.

I take another sip of coffee, trying to swallow down my thoughts. I Google the new patient's name. Nothing of note comes up for an Audrey Gladstone in Los Angeles.

The call light turns on. She's fifteen minutes early. Left to my own devices, I'd bring her in now. Setting boundaries is something I have to continually work on. I remind myself that if I do it this time, she'll expect it the next, and next time I might not be able to if I have a patient before her. I scroll through the news on my cell phone instead.

After fifteen minutes, I leave my office to get her from the waiting area. She's seated on a chair wearing a nondescript, black baseball cap with her head facing down. Both of her knees are nervously bobbing up and down. And one of her hands is wound tightly in a fist. *Anxiety disorder?*

As soon as she notices me, she jumps up. She looks like she's in her early twenties, but there's a worry on her face that ages her.

I bring her into my office, close the door behind us, and motion for her to sit on the couch.

"Please take a sea—"

"I only have a few minutes," she interrupts, still standing. "I'm not here for therapy."

What? I came in early because she made it sound like she needed to be seen as soon as possible.

"I don't understand," I admit.

"Your mother's in danger."

"I'm sorry?" I've heard a lot of things over the last decade between the walls of this two-hundred-and-fifty square-foot office, but this is a first.

"You need to find her to let her know," she implores.

"My mom died twenty-six years ago," I tell her, though I don't owe her an explanation.

The woman shakes her head. "No, she didn't."

My chest feels like it's starting to burn. "This isn't funny."

"I risked my life by coming here." She bites down on her lip nervously. "The people after her will come after me too if they find out I met with you."

"Who are you?" I demand.

"It's not safe for either of us, if you know. You need to find Irene and warn her. But don't go to the police, FBI, any type of law enforcement—that'll put her in more danger. I heard she's somewhere in the Bay Area. You need to tell her she's in trouble again."

Again? My mother is *alive* and in trouble *again?*

I don't know who put this woman up to this, maybe a former disgruntled patient, but it feels like the cruelest, sickest joke anyone could tell, and I want her out of my office. Now.

"Leave," I say.

"I didn't think you'd believe me," she says, opening her tightly wound fist. That's when I see it—a gold bracelet with a Tiffany lima bean charm, just like the one Mom wore. The one the police told Dad had been stolen after the hit-and-run accident.

My chest is on fire. I'm unable to form words. I feel like I might pass out. I try holding onto the side of the couch to steady myself.

" . . . Where did you get that?"

"I gotta go," she says, dropping the bracelet on the floor as she bolts out of my office.

Before I know it, I'm chasing after her down the hallway. My legs understand what my brain hasn't registered yet. If what she just told me is true, this woman may be the only way to track down my dead mother.

I slip in my heels, coming down hard on my left ankle, but I pull myself back up and keep going.

She ducks into the stairway exit and runs down the stairs. I hobble after her, the distance between us growing as she reaches the first floor and swings open the door to the lobby.

By the time I reach the ground floor, she's already outside. A black-tinted Cadillac Escalade with an obscured license plate screeches up to the front of the building. She jumps in the back seat and speeds away.

I'm left standing alone on the corner of Wilshire Boulevard and Rexford Drive at 7:04 AM on a Tuesday morning, surrounded by palm trees and sunshine like nothing ever happened.

CHAPTER

2

My COLLEAGUES AND I keep an ice pack in the communal office fridge. I sit at my desk, icing my throbbing ankle.

For twenty-six years, all I've wished was for my mother to somehow still be alive.

Dad and I went through the unimaginable after we lost her. She'd been my rock, my cheerleader, my everything, and I found life without her unbearable.

All the things I'd previously taken joy in as a teenager, like hanging out with friends at the beach, going to concerts, and playing on my high school soccer team, I struggled to do. Life was marching on for everyone around me, while I was slowly withdrawing from it.

Dad had his own challenges as a new widower and single parent. In addition to her career as a therapist, Mom had been in charge of everything in our house, from grocery shopping to paying bills to calling a plumber whenever a sink was clogged. After she passed, Dad had to shoulder all of it alone, along with his job as a partner at a law firm in downtown LA.

He was barely keeping his head above water, so he didn't notice when I started rationing my food, skipping breakfast, and barely touching my dinner. It was only when I flat-out refused to eat at all and my clothes began hanging on me like I was a Halloween skeleton that he realized I had a problem.

He tried everything in his power to get me to eat, and I was horrible to him. I threw bowls of food, accused him of abusing me by forcing me to eat, and even hit him on several occasions. My brain was so deformed from months of starvation that any will I'd had to live had all but disappeared. I was on a death march, and he was in my way.

The stress was too much for him to bear, so he started smoking again, a habit Mom had helped him quit when I was a toddler. He died of lung cancer over a decade after she passed. I've spent the better part of the last twelve years blaming myself for what I put him through, even questioning if I was responsible for his death.

Now, hearing that Mom could still be alive, however unlikely it is to be true, how can I not wonder if Dad and I might've been spared all the suffering we went through? If she's really alive, does she know anything about what happened to us after she disappeared? Did she keep tabs on us from a distance? Or did she orchestrate her death to cut us off for good?

Maybe she was secretly unhappy in her life with us. She didn't act like it, but I've read enough novels about unhappy housewives who one day decide to pick up and leave, to their families' great surprise.

And what about what the fake patient said—how Mom is in trouble? *Again.*

Was she leading a double life while married to Dad? Was she in some kind of trouble?

No. She can't be alive. We buried her. We held a memorial service at a family friend's funeral home. Though, Dad and I never did see the body.

He told me the police said it was too mangled after the hit-and-run accident for viewing. Instead, he said he gave them her dental records, and they identified her that way.

But what about the bracelet the woman dropped on the ground before running out of here? Everyone who knew her knew she wore a bracelet with a lima bean charm—she never took it off. It's in every picture of her for the fifteen years after I was born. Someone trying to get to me who knew that specific detail about her could weaponize it to hurt me. But who would that person be?

The ice pack is thawing. Wet droplets drip onto my ankle. I focus on them instead of the bracelet staring at me from the white carpet. The sunlight from the window catches on the gold chain, making it sparkle.

I memorized every centimeter of Mom's bracelet when I was little. Dad bought it for her after she held me for the first time at the hospital and dubbed me her "little bean." My name and birthdate were engraved on the lima bean, and there was a small scratch on the top left-hand corner.

I can't tell from my desk whether the engravings or the scratch are there. And I'm scared to check. Because a sense is taking hold that this may be the last moment before everything I know to be true about my life is turned upside down. Before I find out that the person I thought loved me more than anyone else on the planet possibly abandoned me.

Courage, I tell my patients, is not the same as fearlessness. Courage is action in the face of fear. I close my eyes, take a deep breath, and stand up.

I limp over to the carpet, my throbbing ankle providing little distraction from my thumping heart pounding so forcefully that it feels like it might break my chest wide open right here, right now.

I close my eyes and pick up the bracelet, first holding it tightly in my fist and then slowly opening my eyes and the palm of my hand.

My name, birth date, and the small scratch in the left-hand corner are all there.

My head suddenly feels heavy. The room starts to spin. I collapse on the couch to buffer myself, clutching Mom's bracelet, and trying to calm down by taking a deep breath and exhaling slowly.

Could she really be alive? And, according to the fake patient, living in the same state as me? My mind can't wrap itself around this possibility.

I reach for my cell phone with a shaking hand and cancel all my morning sessions. I can barely form thoughts, let alone give anyone advice.

I don't know what to do next, but I know I don't want to do it alone.

* * *

I'm standing in front of Eddie's house off Pico Boulevard, pounding on his door. He opens it, clearly confused to see me here on a weekday morning at this hour.

"Everything okay?" he asks. "We're about to leave for school."

Sarah appears behind him, holding her pink and purple tie-dyed backpack. "Hi, Beans!"

"Wanna join us?" he asks me.

I'm temporarily pulled back into the reality of my life. If I accompany Sarah and Eddie to her school, he might think I'm getting closer to saying yes to moving in together. I don't want to mislead either of them, but I'm struggling to find an excuse for why I can't.

Sarah looks up at me with her wide, blue eyes. "Triple please," she says.

Her words tug at my heart. Whenever Eddie and I take her to get ice cream, we get a triple scoop cone and share it because of a story I once told her about the last trip I took with my parents before Mom died. Mom, Dad, and I had gone to Italy for the summer, and whatever town or city we were in, we would order a triple scoop of gelato, which the three of us shared.

Mom used to carry a picture in her wallet of the three of us sitting on the Spanish Steps in Rome, sharing a cone. Her purse was stolen along with her bracelet after she was killed, so we never recovered that photo. And I haven't looked at any others from that trip since she died. They are memories of before times, when my family was complete and I still wanted to eat ice cream.

Sarah's still standing in front of me, waiting for an answer.

"Sure," I say.

She slips her hand into mine, and we walk to Eddie's car together.

We drive along Pico Boulevard until we reach her charter elementary school. Eddie pulls up in the drop-off line, gets out, and walks around to the back to open Sarah's door. She climbs out of her car seat, and he hugs her goodbye.

"I love you," he says.

"Love you, Daddy," she says back.

She waves at me through the window, and I wave back.

Eddie gets back in the car and turns to me. "What's going on? Why aren't you at work?"

"Something happened," I say.

"With a patient?" he asks.

"Not exactly." I pause. My ankle is still throbbing and everything that happened this morning is starting to catch up with me. "I'd rather talk at your place."

When we return to his house, I fill him in on everything—the fake patient, how she said Mom might still be alive and in the Bay Area, and the bracelet.

"Whoa," he says, taking it all in. "Do you know who the woman was?"

"She didn't give me her real name," I say. "She said it was too dangerous for me to know because the same people after my mom would go after her if they knew she came to see me. I tried to chase her, but she was too fast. I have to find her, Eddie."

"Are there cameras in your office building, like in the lobby?" he asks.

"I never noticed before," I admit.

"Because if we can get an image of her, we could try using a facial recognition app to find out who she is," he says.

Eddie knows about all things tech. He's a software engineer who creates, designs, and develops computer software that companies use to run their organizations, like operating systems, business applications, and network control systems. He's fortunate in that his job allows him to work from home, which has been a godsend since he became a single dad.

"Even if there are cameras, she was wearing a baseball cap that covered her face," I say.

"You never know," he says. "There might be an angle where her face is exposed. Let's find out. I'll drive." He picks up his car keys.

"Don't you have to work?" I ask.

"I'll make it up later," he says.

"Thank you."

I'm grateful for his kindness. He knows how much losing my mom impacted me and about the eating disorder I struggled with in high school after she died. One time I even confessed to him that I felt guilty about Dad dying of lung cancer because of what I'd put him through, and Eddie only showed me compassion.

"Something I've learned through my support group is that everyone grieves differently," he told me.

He still meets with a group of widowers once a month, the same support group he started going to after Sarah's mom died. He said they were instrumental in helping him make the right choices for Sarah. And his primary focus has always been to do whatever's best for her. That's how we met.

A couple of years ago, I was on my way to work and stopped at a local bakery to grab a birthday cake for one of my suitemates. When I stepped inside the bakery, a man in his thirties with brown hair and kind eyes was trying to order a cake, and I could tell he was struggling.

"So, white frosting with pink writing?" a young store clerk with a short, blond ponytail asked him.

"Yes," he said. "Wait, I'm not sure. Maybe chocolate frosting and purple writing would be better."

"We can do that," she told him. "Do you want any decorations on it? Edible flowers? Animals? Sprinkles? Balloons? We do themes too."

He stood there looking at her like a deer in headlights.

"I'm not sure," he said.

"Do you want to think about it, and I can help this other customer?" she asked him, pointing to me.

"Okay," he said.

When he stepped to the side, I noticed tears in his eyes.

"How can I help you?" she asked me.

"Hang on," I said to her and walked over to the man. "Are you all right?"

"Sorry, I didn't mean to make a scene," he said. "It's my daughter's fifth birthday, her first since my wife died. Her mom was always the one in charge of her birthdays. I don't know what little girls like."

"I'm so sorry for your loss. Can I help you?" I offered.

He nodded. "Okay."

We walked back to the counter and stood side-by-side. "Before I pick up my cake, I'd like to help him finish his order," I told the store clerk.

"So far, he has a rainbow-shaped cake with chocolate frosting and purple writing on top," she said.

"My daughter likes rainbows," the man told me.

"Is there any way to do rainbow-colored frosting on the rainbow cake?" I asked the woman.

"Sure, we can do that. How about toppings?" she asked.

I spotted some cakes inside the refrigerated glass counter below with long rainbow-swirled lollipops.

"I think those lollipops would be great on top of the cake to keep with the rainbow theme," I told the man. "What do you think?"

"Okay," he said.

She totaled his bill, and he paid her.

"Thank you," he said to me.

"I'm sure her mom would be happy you're celebrating your daughter's special day," I said.

He nodded, the tears still in his eyes, and left.

Later that day, I checked my phone for messages between sessions and saw one from a number I didn't recognize. I figured it was a prospective new patient. But it was the man I'd helped at the bakery. His name was Eddie.

He'd gone back to get my name from the bakery clerk, Googled me, and found my therapy website. He asked if he could take me out for lunch to thank me.

I wouldn't characterize that first lunch together as a date, since he had asked me out to thank me. So it felt pressure-free, and we got to know each other without all the usual dating stressors.

I remember leaving the lunch thinking I liked him, not romantically, but as a person. He was hurting, in pain, and trying to do right by his daughter, just like Dad had tried to do with me, and I admired him for it.

When he asked me out again, I thought it was the beginning of a friendship. It wasn't until a couple months later, when he kissed me for the first time in front of my house, that I realized he felt something more.

The truth was that I had wanted him to kiss me for a while but wasn't going to go there since he was grieving his late wife.

In the middle of the kiss, he pulled away from me.

"I'm sorry," he said. "I'm not sure I can do this. It feels like I'm cheating on Helen."

"It's okay," I told him. "We can take things slowly or just be friends."

"Thank you for understanding," he said. And then he pulled me in close again, kissing me for a long while. We've been together ever since.

When we arrive at my office in Beverly Hills, I knock on the building manager's office door.

"Coming," the manager shouts before opening the door. He only has a few strands of white hair left on his head. I notice a couple of dated security television screens behind him.

"Yes?" he asks.

I take out my driver's license and show it to him. "Hi, I'm Dr. Beatrice Bennett from suite 301. I saw a new patient today who didn't give me her last name or contact information, and I need to call her. It's an emergency. I'm wondering if you have any footage of her," I say.

He looks confused. "I might," he says. "But how's that gonna help?"

Eddie holds up his phone. "We can scan her face using a facial recognition app to figure out who she is."

"I'm not sure I'm allowed to do that. You're not the police. What kind of danger are we talkin' 'bout?" the manager asks.

"A danger to herself," I say.

He raises his eyebrows. The hairless skin on his scalp bunches up in surprise. "Okay . . . but do it fast. Don't want trouble if the owners come by," he says.

"I'm a software engineer," Eddie explains. "If you allow me to scroll through the footage, I can do it quickly and leave it exactly as is after we're finished."

The manager motions for us to proceed. We walk over to the dated security screens, and Eddie takes control of the panels.

"What time do you think she arrived?" he asks me.

"Sometime between six thirty and six forty-five," I say.

He scrolls back through the footage of the first screen, which covers the exterior of the building. A couple of people walk by the entrance, someone walking their dog, another holding a Starbucks to-go coffee cup, and then at the 6:44 AM mark, I spot a woman with a black baseball cap.

"That's her," I tell Eddie.

He goes slowly through the footage of her approaching the building. We watch her enter, but her hat obscures her face. No luck.

Eddie moves to the second screen that covers the lobby and scrolls back to her entering it. She steps inside the building with the cap still on, presses the elevator button, and disappears inside—still, no luck.

At 7:03 AM, we watch her run out of the stairwell back into the lobby as I chase after her. And then it happens—for a split second, her baseball cap falls off.

Eddie zooms in on the moment the hat drops and grabs a screenshot of her face on his phone. It's not a great image, but it's something.

"Got it," Eddie says.

"Time to get goin'," the manager tells us.

"Thank you," I say.

"No need to thank me 'cause this never happened," he says.

3

THERE'S ONLY ONE thing about losing my mom at fifteen that I have ever felt lucky about: I wasn't younger when she died. Had I been, say, five years old, I probably wouldn't have any memories of her, but because I was a teenager, and my brain was more fully formed, thankfully, I do.

Eddie and I are upstairs in my office. He's busy downloading facial recognition apps on his phone while I'm methodically going through every memory I have with my mom, especially from the year before she died, to see if there was any sign that she might've been in *trouble*.

The problem is, when I think about her, the last thing that comes to mind is trouble. Dad used to tease her for being a goody-two-shoes. She once got a parking ticket, and he jokingly announced at the dinner table, "She's going to prison, Beans."

They were graduate school sweethearts who met at UCLA in their first semesters. He was in law school, and she was getting her PhD in psychology. He said when he saw her in the cafeteria, laughing with a couple of her girlfriends, it was love at first sight for him.

"She was so full of life, so luminous, I knew I had to introduce myself," he told me.

They married after each of them finished their respective graduate programs. I was born shortly after that. My dad never lost his marvel of my mother. As far as he was concerned, she walked on water and could do no wrong.

When I entered adolescence and began acting out at times, he always defended her. "You've got the best mother in the world. Listen to her," he told me.

I only ever heard them fight once. A couple of months before she died, it was late at night, and they thought I was asleep, but I wasn't. The fight was so unusual that I got out of bed to see what was happening. I remember approaching their bedroom quietly, placing my ear on the closed door to hear what they were arguing about.

"Don't we matter?" Dad asked Mom.

"It has nothing to do with you," she said.

"It has everything to do with us!" I had never heard him raise his voice with her before.

"I'm spending the night at Pearl's," she announced. Pearl was her oldest friend in LA. As Mom approached their bedroom door to open it, I quickly ran back to my room before they could discover me eavesdropping.

The following day, when I woke up, she wasn't there. Dad told me she'd left early for work due to a patient emergency, but I knew that was a lie. When I came home from school later that afternoon, she was in the kitchen unpacking groceries. I told her I'd overheard her and Dad fighting the night before.

"I'm sorry you heard it, but everything's fine now," she said, trying to reassure me, even though she looked worried.

"What did Dad mean when he said, 'Don't we matter?'"

She looked at me, taken aback. She hadn't realized I'd heard what they were saying to each other.

She paused before responding. "Your father would prefer if I didn't work as much and were home more, but I love my job. Please don't bring it up to him. It'll just upset him more."

At the time, I remember what she said struck me as odd for two reasons. First, I was well into my teenage years, about to start taking driving lessons, and even thinking about college, not a toddler who needed my mom around all the time. Second, she had never asked me to keep anything from my father before. But she looked upset, so I let it go.

Now, thinking back on that fight, I can't help but wonder if it was really about her staying at home or whether it was about something else. Did she want out of her marriage? Was she unhappy with her life? Was she thinking of leaving us?

At her funeral, her friends, colleagues, and relatives came up to me and told me how no parent had ever loved their child more than she loved me.

If she's still alive, how can that be true? Who abandons a child they supposedly love? The burning in my chest from earlier returns.

"The image quality isn't good enough for these apps," Eddie says. "We need more sophisticated software. I'll call Paul. He'll be able to help us."

Paul is Eddie's best friend. They met at the University of Michigan as roommates freshman year and quickly bonded as fellow technophiles. He was Eddie's best man at his wedding with his late wife, and he's also Sarah's godfather.

Paul works in some capacity for the FBI that he's not allowed to disclose and lives in New York with his husband, Anthony, a professor at NYU. I haven't met them because Anthony has been ill over the last couple of years, and they haven't been able to travel. Eddie has talked about Sarah, him, and me making a trip to the Big Apple now that Anthony is doing better.

"Do you think contacting Paul is safe?" I ask Eddie. "The woman warned me to stay away from law enforcement, that it would be dangerous."

"It's Paul. If I explain the situation to him, he won't tell a soul," he says.

"But what if the FBI tracks what he's doing?" I ask.

"He knows how to cover his tracks," he says.

I quickly mull it over. What other choice do I have?

"Call him," I say.

* * *

Eddie left Paul a phone message and then went home for a Zoom work meeting.

I have an hour and a half before my first afternoon session starts, and something's gnawing at me. If Mom's truly still alive, she couldn't have staged her disappearance alone. We buried her casket—doesn't that mean there was a body involved?

I argued with Dad at the time, saying I didn't care if her body was in bad shape. I still wanted to see her one last time. But he was adamant that I couldn't.

"I'm your parent, and it's my responsibility to keep you safe," he told me. "Seeing your mom's disfigured body could traumatize you for the rest of your life. I won't allow it, Beans." So that was that.

Now I'm wondering if maybe he didn't want me to see it because there wasn't a body at all. That's why I'm parked in front of Frank Esposito's funeral home, where we held Mom's memorial service and where I also held Dad's service a decade later.

Frank is the undertaker and was the husband of one of Mom's colleagues, who has since passed away. He presumably would've seen Mom's body.

I remember how at her service, he came up to me and said, "Just because people are gone, doesn't mean they leave us." When I returned a decade later to bury Dad, he repeated it. I haven't seen him since Dad died, but I still get a yearly holiday card from the Esposito family.

When I step inside the funeral home, a dark wooden casket is prominently displayed in the entryway. Dated red-and-white flower arrangements are everywhere, like a sad Christmas.

"Hello?" I call out since nobody's around.

Frank walks out from the back, older than I remembered him. "Beatrice?" he asks. "Is that you?"

"Yes," I say.

"Everything okay?" he asks, which is understandable considering the last two times I was here was to bury my parents.

"I'm okay," I say. "I have a question for you."

"All right . . ."

Might as well be direct. "Did you see my mom's body after she died?"

He shifts his weight from one leg to another. "Why do you ask?"

I don't respond, but I clock his discomfort.

"Are you wondering if she could have been saved?" he continues. "Because that's a common response after losing someone we love, holding onto the hope that things might've turned out differently."

I note that he didn't answer my question and instead responded with one of his own. I decide to keep quiet. In therapy, pregnant silences can often lead to profound patient revelations. "Irene was my friend. I couldn't stomach seeing her body, so, no," he finally replies. "An employee dealt with her body."

He seems a bit hedgy.

"Can I speak with them?" I ask.

"Oh, they're long gone," he says.

"Can I have their contact information?" I ask.

He narrows his eyes. "What's going on?" he asks me.

"Nothing," I say.

"To be honest, I don't remember who was working back then," he adds. "And even if I did, we deal with so many funerals. They wouldn't remember one from twenty-six years ago."

I nod, even though I'm not sure I entirely believe him. It took him a while to tell me he never saw Mom's body, and he was visibly uncomfortable when I first asked him about it.

"I wish I could talk more," he says. "But we're getting ready for a memorial service now. I hope everything's okay with you."

I nod.

"Remember, just because people are gone—" he says.

"Doesn't mean they leave us," I say.

4

I'M IN SESSION with my patient, Tom, putting on an Academy Award-worthy performance, acting as though a woman didn't barge into this office a few hours ago to tell me my dead mother is still alive.

"I told her I got the promotion," Tom says about his mother. He's thirty years old and has spent the last year in therapy coming to terms with having a narcissistic mother.

"How did it go?" I ask.

"She made it all about herself, like usual. Barely acknowledged it and then asked if I knew she was leaving for Sedona next week."

As he's speaking about his mother, I can't help but think about my own. If Mom is still alive, deserting Dad and me twenty-six years ago is whatever comes after narcissistic.

Could she *really* be alive?

"The good news is I didn't expect her to react any other way," Tom continues. "Something clicked in our last session when you told me to think of her narcissism as unchangeable, just like her eye color. It helped me not take her response personally—"

My cell phone buzzes on my desk, interrupting him. I usually silence it before seeing patients, but with everything that happened this morning, I forgot.

It buzzes again and again and again—it won't stop.

"Excuse me," I say. "I forgot to turn my phone off. My apologies."

As I lift my phone, another text blooms, adding to the stream that's already there:

LIE

LIE

LIE

LIE

LIE

LIE

LIE

LIE

LIE

LIE

LIE

LIE

Lie? My palms immediately clam up in a sweaty panic. Who's sending me these texts? I don't recognize the number.

Who is this? I text back.

Message undeliverable.

"That light just went on," Tom says, pointing to the call light next to the door, alerting me that my next patient has arrived, even though my next session isn't supposed to start for forty minutes.

"Do you have another patient now?" Tom asks.

"I'm sorry," I say. "I think there might've been a mix-up with scheduling today. I'll be right back."

I leave my office, confused by the texts and the call light. A police officer stands by himself in the waiting area.

"Are you Dr. Bennett?" he asks me.

My heart pounds like I've done something wrong, even though I haven't done anything.

"Yes . . ." I say.

"Detective Thompson," he says, showing me his badge. "Do you have a minute?"

"I'm in the middle of a session now."

"It's important," he says. "Based on street camera surveillance, apart from the janitorial staff, only two people entered this building before seven this morning. One of them was you, and the other was a young woman wearing a baseball cap . . ."

He's here about the fake patient?

"Did you meet with her?" he asks pointedly, meeting my eyes and not letting go.

LIE, the texts said.

Is she the one that sent all those texts? Did she mean I'm supposed to lie to him about her being here, or what she told me about my Mom, or both? But how would she even know he's here?

"I need to know what she said," he presses.

Part of me wants to tell the officer that the fake patient told me my mom is still alive, to ask him if a police report exists about the hit-and-run that killed her, since Frank admitted he never saw her body. But I remind myself of the woman's warning to stay away from law enforcement—that it could put Mom in more danger if she's still alive.

"I'm not allowed to reveal who my patients are or discuss what they tell me. Patient-therapist privilege," I say.

"Thing is, the woman that entered this building at 6:44 this morning is the primary suspect in a murder," he says.

Good thing I have years of practiced stoicism under my belt so as not to look shocked during patient revelations.

"We can do this the easy way or the hard way," he continues. "If she told you about a felony crime that she committed, and is trying to work through a way to escape punishment, you could be charged as an accessory after the fact."

I stand up straighter. "Without a court order, I'm only legally allowed to tell you if I believe a patient may hurt themselves or somebody else. I'm not required to report past crimes. And in this case, I know nothing about any crimes committed in the past, present, or future."

He nods, unconvinced.

"I'll find out one way or another what she told you," he says. "You're just making things harder for yourself by not cooperating with an officer."

"I have a patient waiting for me in my office," I remind him. "I need to get back to work."

When I return to my office, Tom continues talking about his mother for the rest of the session, but it's hard to focus. What the detective said sounded like a threat.

I've only had the police visit me one other time in my life, and it wasn't a good experience back then, either.

5

January 1998

A FEW MONTHS AFTER Mom died, when I was deep into restricting my food, I came home after school and locked myself in the bathroom. It was the first thing my ED—eating disorder—made me do as soon as I stepped through the front door each day.

I methodically examined myself in the full-length mirror on the back of the bathroom door, beginning with my head, moving down to my toes, disgusted with every inch of my body.

All that existed was this.

Not the grief of losing my mother. Not that I had gone from being a straight-A student to failing all my classes. Not that earlier that same day, I'd felt like I might pass out during soccer practice when I ran twice the number of laps the coach had asked us to do.

ED had given me a way out. A way to focus all of my energy and attention away from the pain I was in.

I was bent over in front of the mirror, my head hanging between my legs, busy studying the space between my thighs, trying to figure out if it was bigger or smaller than the day before, when there was a loud knock at the front door.

After Mom died, Dad had started working from home a couple of days a week to be there for me. I listened as he opened the door. "What's going on?" he asked.

I couldn't hear the response, but I heard a couple of people walking inside our house, and then there was a knock on the bathroom door.

"This is Officer Sandra Cho. I need you to come out, Beatrice," a woman told me.

I had never dealt with law enforcement before. "I didn't do anything wrong," I told her through the door, my voice wobbly with sudden fear.

"Didn't say you did, but you still need to come out," she said.

I slowly opened the door. She was petite, with black bangs, and dressed in uniform.

"This is Officer Reynolds," she told me, pointing to a large man standing next to her. "We need to speak with you and your father together." Dad was standing next to both of them in the hall.

I walked out of the bathroom and followed everyone into the living room. Dad and I sat on the couch, and the officers took a seat on chairs across from us.

"We understand you made a child abuse complaint to a counselor at your high school today," she said. "We're here to investigate your claim."

I had reported Dad because my starved, scrambled brain actually believed he was abusive for trying to make me eat, and that if I reported him for it, he'd be too scared to do so again for fear of getting in trouble.

Dad raised his eyebrows so high they nearly reached his hairline. He turned to me, deeply worried. "Is someone hurting you, Beans?" he asked me.

I stared at him in disbelief. ED was in my ear, reminding me that this was why Dad was an *evil* guy—he was trying to push his abusive behavior onto others.

"It's you," I told him.

He looked at me, stunned.

"You make me eat food because you want me to gain weight so I can be miserable like you. I know you're sad Mom died, but that's not my fault."

The officers looked confused.

"You reported your father for abusing you because he makes you eat?" Officer Cho asked me.

"It *is* abuse when I can't fit into clothes that all the other girls at my school wear," I answered.

She gave me a once-over. "I'm sure you'd be able to wear any of the clothes your classmates wear," she said.

"I'm 5'3" and weigh ninety pounds,' I said, waiting for the officers' shocked responses, which never materialized. "That means I'm clinically obese. I should weigh eighty."

"Eighty pounds?" she said in disbelief.

She was wearing my last nerve.

"I know how big I am, and I know he's the one responsible," I said, pointing to Dad. I stood up and returned to the bathroom, locking myself inside.

Dad continued to talk to them. I could hear their conversation. He was telling them how every day after school, I'd lock myself in the bathroom for hours at a time, how he was worried I might hurt myself, and that he didn't know what to do.

"You need to remove her bedroom and bathroom doors," Officer Cho told him. She also said he should throw out our scale, which he'd already done when I began obsessively weighing myself countless times a day.

After they finished speaking, Dad thanked them for their time, and they wished him good luck. He needed much more than that.

Because a couple of days later, I was hospitalized.

6

My patient, Tom, just left, and I have a ten-minute break before my next session starts, so I rush to call Eddie.

"After you left, I went to the funeral home where my mom's memorial service was held. The undertaker was a family friend. He told me he never saw her body and was hedgy when I first asked him about it," I tell him. "And a detective was just here. The woman that came to my office this morning is a primary suspect in a murder."

"She's also a fugitive," Eddie says.

"What?" I say.

"Paul just called me. He has a contact in the FBI's facial analysis eval unit who ID'd her. Her name's Cristina Cadell."

Cadell . . . why does that name ring a bell?

"Wait . . . as in the TriCPharma billionaire Cadell family?"

"Yes," Eddie says. "She's William Cadell Jr.'s daughter."

"He's one of the brothers the Feds are targeting in their case against TriCPharma," I say.

"Exactly."

I know about TriCPharma because it's one of the biggest companies responsible for the opioid epidemic in this country. Last month the justice department announced fraud charges against William Cadell Jr. and Quentin Cadell, the brothers who inherited the company from their late father, William Cadell Sr., for misbranding one of their addictive pain drugs—which had only been meant to be used in short-term hospital settings—for everyday use by the masses.

Many in my field who've witnessed firsthand how TriCPharma drugs have destroyed patients' lives and their families feel these charges are a long time coming. When the charges were first announced, I immediately thought of my mom, who specialized in treating addiction in her private practice. The year before she died, she lost a patient to an accidental overdose who had suffered a sports-related back injury and was prescribed pain medication that led to a pain pill addiction.

As laid back as my mom was, I remember how his death hung over her. After she went to his funeral, I overheard her talking with Dad about it. "It didn't have to be this way," she said, choking up. Treating patients who suffered from addiction impacted her deeply. I never saw her drink alcohol in my life, not even once.

What in the world could Mom possibly have to do with Cristina Cadell from the billionaire TriCPharma Cadell family? Cristina didn't look old enough to have been born yet when Mom supposedly disappeared.

"Cristina is the primary suspect in her mother's murder," Eddie continues. "The two went sailing for a few days near Catalina Island a month ago, and her mother fell overboard. Cristina said it happened one night while she was asleep, but authorities think she was involved."

"Jesus." Christina may have come across as a bit unhinged, but she didn't strike me as a sociopath, let alone someone capable of killing their own mother.

"They were planning to arrest her and hold her without bail because she was considered a flight risk due to her family's wealth, but someone tipped her off that they were onto her, and she fled before they got to her—right after visiting your office."

"Where did she go?" I ask.

"Right now, it looks like she's on a private plane to Barcelona," he says.

"Will they extradite her after she lands?"

"She's too high profile. Think Roman Polanski. Spain won't let the Feds do that without going through the Spanish courts first, and who knows where she'll be by then. They assume she won't stay put."

"Do they really think she killed her mother?" I ask. "Why would she do that?"

"I have no idea. There's no known motive yet. Paul mentioned that her mom was a pharmaceutical rep for TriCPharma before she married William Cadell Jr. They divorced a few years ago."

As upset as I am at the thought that my mom might still be alive, and might've abandoned me, a sense of despair takes hold, watching my one chance of locating her disappear. Cristina was my only hope of finding out where Mom might be, and now she's a fugitive on her way to Europe.

"Are you okay, Beans?" Eddie asks me after a long silence.

"Not really," I say.

"We'll get through this," he says. "I promise. You're coming over tonight after work, right?"

"Yes," I say.

"Good, we're looking forward to seeing you," he says.

After we hang up, I go to the bathroom and splash cold water on my face. It dawns on me that I haven't eaten anything since breakfast, so I quickly walk to the kitchenette.

When I open the door, I find two of my colleagues, Rona and Owen, eating their lunches.

We exchange hellos as I microwave an Amy's Mac & Cheese meal that I stored in our communal freezer early this morning.

They're focused on a small television we keep on the counter next to the coffee maker, watching the breaking news about Cristina Cadell.

"Guess she's figured out how to run away from the law too," Owen says.

"Like father, like daughter," Rona says. "Do you think the brothers will finally get what they deserve with the new charges?"

"I'm not holding my breath," Owen responds. "They've managed to skirt the law this long."

The microwave beeps loudly, startling me. I pull out my meal and join them at the table.

"Did you hear?" Owen turns to me. "One of the Cadell brother's daughters allegedly killed her mother and fled the country."

I shake my head, pretending I haven't heard the news, let alone had the alleged murderer fugitive visit me in our office suite hours ago when she informed me my dead mother might still be alive.

I stick my fork into the mac and cheese and take a bite. The pasta feels like sand in my mouth. I struggle to swallow and stand up, about to throw the entire meal away. But I stop myself. This could turn into a slippery slope, and not one I can afford to go back down. So I sit back down and finish eating.

CHAPTER

7

January 1998

A COUPLE OF DAYS after the police came to our house, I
passed out on my high school soccer field during team
practice.

When I woke up, I was in the hospital after being admitted for a low heart rate, and a nurse was inserting an NG
feeding tube through my nose. The pain of it making its way
up my nostril was unbearable.

I could feel it passing the back of my throat until it
reached my stomach, and I had the urge to gag and spit it
out. But I was too afraid that I'd have to withstand the painful insertion process again if I did. After the nurse finished,
she taped the tube on my face and marked it so she'd know
if I tried to move it.

"When will it be taken out?" I asked her with begging
eyes.

She explained the hospital policy required me to eat all of
my meals for seventy-two hours before removing it, and liquid meal replacement like Ensure didn't count. That meant
I had to eat three meals and three snacks daily for three con-
secutive days. I had no interest in recovery because I had no

interest in living without my mom. But I did what I was told because it was the only way to get the tube out.

After three days, I was ready to be discharged. Dad was terrified of me returning home. He knew I wasn't well, and I'd fall back to restricting. He pleaded with the hospital to keep me, and when they told him they couldn't, he asked the staff to help transfer me to a residential center.

This was the nineties, and the Malibu coast wasn't lined yet with rehabs and treatment centers. Eating disorders were even more amorphous than they are now. The nurse told him there was only one local place, but it had no beds available, and there was a three-month waitlist. He had no choice but to take me home.

When we returned, he made dinner for us—hamburgers with tater tots and broccoli. He put the plate of food in front of me, and I threw it on the ground, watching it crash into a dozen ceramic pieces. Our small rescue dog, Rascal, ran over to gobble the burger up, but Dad quickly put him in his crate before he got to it.

Dad then returned to the dining room table, put his face in his hands, broke down, and cried. It was the only time I'd ever seen him cry. Even at Mom's funeral, when he held my hand as her casket was lowered into the ground, and I saw he was about to, he bit his lower lip to stop himself. He was old school and believed he needed to exude strength so that I knew I still had one parent there for me.

As I watched him sob at our dining table, a tiny part of me that ED hadn't completely taken over hated myself for what I'd done to him. But ED roared back, reminding me that Dad was a monster who secretly wanted me to gain weight.

I angrily got up from the table, stormed to my bedroom, and locked the door.

Later that night, I heard Dad talking to someone on the phone, saying he couldn't manage me on his own anymore and didn't know what to do.

The following day, when I woke up expecting him to drive me to school, I found him seated in the living room.

"Beans," he said. "A bed opened up at the treatment center. I'm taking you there now."

Not another place where I'd be forced to eat again. "I'm not going," I said defiantly.

"It's not a choice," he told me.

"Well, you can't make me," I dug in.

"Either you come with me in my car, or the police will escort you there," he said.

ED was cornered, so I stomped back to my room and packed a small bag to go to the stupid treatment center. I wasn't planning on staying there long. I'd gotten myself out of the hospital in three days. I'd quickly find a way to get out of there too.

As we drove through the San Fernando Valley toward the center, I wanted to know who was responsible for ripping me away from my home and Rascal and, most importantly, interfering with ED.

"Who were you on the phone with last night?" I asked him.

"Uh . . . Rose," he stammered.

I'd never heard that name before.

"Who's that?"

"A friend of your mom's . . . a former colleague," he said.

"Is she the one that got me into this place?"

He nodded.

It struck me as odd that I'd never met or heard of this Rose friend before, and yet she was the one responsible for this. Whoever she was, I didn't like her.

When we finally reached the center, Dad pulled up in front of a sprawling ranch in Hidden Hills. The exterior somehow looked familiar, as if I'd been there before, but I couldn't place it. When we got out of the car and walked up to the front door, I spotted a red barn next door. And that's when it hit me—Mom had shown me a picture of this place.

About six months before she died, we discussed where I might want to go to college and what I might want to do with my life, and she took me through her academic and professional history. She showed me a picture of her graduating from NYU, photographs of her at the UCLA psychology graduate program, and the various places she'd interned before becoming a licensed psychologist.

"This is where I did my first clinical internship," she told me, pointing to the ranch. "Next door was a red barn filled with horses that the girls used for equestrian therapy."

As I stepped inside the ranch for the first time as a patient, I imagined Mom greeting me, telling me it had all been a bad dream and that she was here, and everything was going to be okay.

But she was long gone, and I would have to face being there alone.

8

"In high school," I tell Eddie on the phone while driving, "after Mom died, I went to a residential treatment center for eating disorders in Hidden Hills. After I got there, I realized my mom had done her first clinical internship there—she'd shown me a picture of her standing in front of the place. The strange thing was that at first, there were no openings for me at the place, but suddenly, overnight, a bed became available."

"So you think if she's still alive, she might've had something to do with getting you in?" he asks.

"I don't know," I say. "After I was admitted there, I asked some employees if they had known her. A few had and told me they were sorry for my loss, but nobody mentioned her helping me get in. I figured my dad must've known about the place because she had worked there and contacted them to see if he could leverage her connection to help me get in."

"That makes sense," Eddie says.

"But now I'm wondering if maybe she *had* been involved with my admission. The place still exists, so I'm going there now. I want to see if any people from back then still work there. Maybe one of them knows something."

"If you can wait until tomorrow, I'll take you," he says. He's with Sarah, who's home from school now.

"I don't want to put you out any more. You helped me enough this morning," I say.

"Helping you doesn't put me out," he says.

"I also can't wait," I admit.

"I understand," he says. "Just wish I could be there with you."

"Hi, Beans!" I hear Sarah shout in the background.

"Tell her I say hi and give her a hug from me," I say.

"I will," he says.

When we hang up, I think about how, up until now, the only thing that's helped quell my fears about whether I'll measure up as a mother to Sarah is that I had a wonderful mom who loved me. It's the same reason that made me believe I would be a good mother a decade ago when I was married to my first husband, Jay.

I was always terrified of becoming a mom because I knew what it meant to lose mine. The fear of tragedy striking again and potentially leaving a young child motherless loomed large.

The thing about bad things happening to you when you're young is—unlike people who are afforded decades of life before tragedy strikes—you learn early on that you're not immune. You understand that bad things don't just happen to other people, they can happen to you, and they can happen anytime.

Despite the burden of this knowledge, the one thing that helped propel me to take the leap to become a mom was knowing what an amazing one I had had. Her example made me believe that I could rise to what the role demanded and also helped drown out the noise of the ticking clock measuring however long I might have with a child.

But once I became pregnant and the hormones kicked in, I felt nauseous, and eating was difficult. I started losing weight, which triggered ED, which I thought I'd put behind me over a decade prior.

Not everyone who restricts food develops an eating disorder—the cause is genetic, the same way that not everyone who drinks alcohol will develop alcoholism. For those biologically vulnerable like myself, experiencing any energy deficit, whatever the root cause is—like when I was pregnant, nauseous, and struggling to eat—presents a relapse risk. And I relapsed.

How was I possibly going to parent a child when both of my own parents were gone? The fear and loneliness made it easy to fall back into restricting—to avoid feeling the magnitude of my losses.

When Jay first noticed I wasn't eating much, he chalked it up to the nausea and first trimester hormones, but at a certain point, it registered that I was restricting again. Being a psychologist himself (we had met in our graduate school psychology program) and knowing my teenage history of anorexia, he insisted I meet with a psychiatrist and a therapist. He wasn't just concerned about me—he was also worried about my pregnancy, and he had every right to be.

By the time I got the help I needed, it was too late—I'd miscarried at seven weeks. Our marriage didn't survive. There was a lot of finger-pointing, and the situation made Jay have second thoughts about being with me long-term. Like me, he assumed I had long tucked ED away, but we both learned the hard way that ED is a formidable, slippery foe, and one should never count him out.

Eddie knows I was married before, but I haven't told him the specifics of what happened in my first marriage. I've been nervous about how he might react, scared he might not want to be with me anymore. Who'd want a woman who'd miscarried due to an eating disorder to be in charge of raising their young daughter?

That's the real reason I've always kept just enough distance between us, so I wouldn't have to tell him the truth. But things are coming to a head. Although he's been patient, I'm not sure how much longer he's willing to wait.

I don't want to lose either of them, but I also know Eddie needs to have all the facts about me to decide whether he still wants to be with me. Continuing to withhold the full truth from him isn't fair to either him or Sarah. He wants her to have a mother, and if I'm not that person, I don't want to close doors for him to find someone else.

My recovery group has been supportive, helping me summon the courage to have the big talk with him. The thing I've always returned to, which is the very thing that I'd planned to tell him, is that although ED resurfaced during my pregnancy, I've recommitted to my recovery, and he can count on me to be a wonderful mom to Sarah because I had the best mom imaginable.

But now, I can't help but wonder if maybe I never really knew my mother. I've spent so much of my life imagining who I am through the lens of who I thought she was. If she isn't that person, where does that leave me?

* * *

I arrive at Better Horizons, the treatment center where Dad dropped me off twenty-six years ago. In some ways, it feels like ten lifetimes ago. I became a psychologist. Dad died. I got married. I relapsed. I miscarried. Time is devious, the way it silently accumulates before bearing down all at once.

I'm standing in the entryway underneath the same sign that greeted me when I was fifteen years old: *Free of Judgment*.

I didn't understand what it meant until years after I'd left here, when I was more recovered and the pain of what

I'd put Dad through began to sink in. The shame and self-loathing of how I'd treated him when I was in the thick of anorexia have been painful to grapple with.

Being in an environment—like my recovery group—that is free of judgment, proved vital in helping me own my behavior and forgive myself. In the group, we've talked about how making amends should be part of eating disorder recovery the way it is in twelve-step recovery programs for alcohol and drug addiction.

I'm so thankful that I had the chance to seek Dad's forgiveness before he died. I told him how sorry I was for everything I'd put him through, and he assured me that he knew my behavior was due to the disease and not me.

I approach a red-headed receptionist sitting behind a desk at the entrance. A group of teenage girls is behind her in the cavernous living room, sitting and writing in their journals.

I remember when Dr. Larsen, the psychologist I met with daily during my stay here, handed me a journal for the first time. I defiantly laughed in her face, but she patiently smiled at me and said, "It's nice to meet you, Beatrice."

"Do you have an appointment for a tour?" the receptionist asks me. She probably thinks I'm here for my child.

"I'm not here for a tour," I let her know. "I was a patient here twenty-six years ago."

"Wow!" she exclaims. She doesn't look much older than twenty-six herself.

"I'm wondering if any of the same people still work here, like Dr. Larsen," I say.

"She died last year," she says.

The words hit harder than I expect. I feel sudden, deep regret for not coming sooner to thank Dr. Larsen for everything she did for me.

"Don't be sad," the receptionist says. "She was old."

That provides little comfort.

Suddenly one of the girls in the living room runs toward the fireplace. She starts tapping the top of the mantel repeatedly, alternating with each of her hands, engaging in a repetitive OCD ritual.

Psychiatrists consider obsessive-compulsive disorder, delusional disorder, and anorexia the most difficult mental illnesses to treat, and anorexia has features of the first two. It also has the second-highest mortality rate of any mental illness, more lethal than depression, bipolar disorder, and schizophrenia, only outranked by opioid use disorder due to the deadliness of fentanyl. In the field, overcoming anorexia is likened to "slaying the dragon."

A counselor walks over to the girl and intervenes, moving her hands away from the fireplace mantel, trying to talk her through it.

"I don't think anyone's here from twenty-six years ago," the receptionist tells me. "That was a *long* time ago."

"Are you sure?" I ask.

"Wait," she says, scrunching her nose, looking up at the ceiling like she's thinking really hard. "Was Joan here when you were here?"

"Joan?" I ask.

"The riding instructor," she says.

I'd forgotten about her. "Yes, she was," I say.

"She's at the stable," she says. "You can talk to her if you want."

"Thanks," I say.

I exit the ranch and walk next door to the red barn. As soon as the smell of horses hits me, I feel nauseous.

I think I hated the horses more than anything about this place, apart from having to eat. Their smell always made me want to gag. The other girls loved being around them because they were animals, but I found them too large to form any attachment to. All they did was make me miss Rascal at home.

When I step inside the barn, I find Joan brushing one of the horse's manes. She must be near seventy and has gone entirely gray since I last saw her.

"Joan?" I say.

She looks up, trying to place me.

"I'm Beatrice Bennett. I was a patient here twenty-six years ago."

"Oh, yes . . . I remember you," she says.

"You do?" I ask.

She nods her head. "Hard to forget. You hated the horses. Most girls love 'em—a break from having to eat. What brings you back?"

"I have a question for you. My mom worked here years before I was admitted. I'm wondering if you knew her."

"What's her name?"

"It was Irene Bennett," I say. "She passed away."

"Sorry to hear that," Joan says, her voice softening. "I remember her."

"Really?" I say.

She nods. "She also hated horses."

I smile, thinking about Mom and me sharing this in common. I never spoke with Joan about Mom when I was here—I almost always avoided the barn.

"Do you, by any chance, know if she used her contacts to get me in here?" I ask.

"I've never had anything to do with admissions," Joan says.

"Do you know who might know?"

"We've probably had about half a dozen admission directors and hundreds of interns since she worked here. And nobody keeps track of interns after they leave."

Like that, I watch my only lead vanish.

"Okay," I say, defeated. "It was nice seeing you again."

"Likewise," she says.

I walk away feeling deflated when she calls back out to me. "Did your mom end up with the guy from New York?"

"What?" I say, turning back around again.

"Is that your dad?" Joan asks.

"My dad was a native Angeleno," I say.

"Guess you got lucky," she says. "That other guy sounded like a real piece of work."

Who's Joan talking about? When Mom was working here, she and Dad were an item.

"You probably have him confused with someone else," I say.

"Nope," she says emphatically. "Your mom talked about him *all* the time. He drove around in a VW with a surfboard on top like he was born on the beach, but he had the thickest New York accent I'd ever heard. Your mom said he wanted to be a director."

CHAPTER

9

January 1998

WHEN I WAS first admitted to Better Horizons, I was placed with a roommate, Emily, who was all of sixteen and on her seventh stint at the treatment center.

She had been battling ED since she was eleven, and her body was a portrait of battle scars. She had never gotten her period because she had stopped producing estrogen due to severe malnourishment, which negatively impacted her bone density, leading to osteoporosis. She'd end up with a broken bone with the slightest wrong movement.

When I first met her, she was wearing a cast on her wrist after trying to twist open a jar in the kitchen during a cooking lesson, which happened regularly at the ranch to get girls used to being around food again.

She was markedly short due to her stunted growth. Her thinning hair was nearly gone, with patches of bald spots on her scalp, and she had large purple, blackish circles under her eyes.

Even though she was only sixteen, she looked like an "after" portrait in a then-and-now series of photographs of people aging over a century.

She filled me in on the ins and outs of the place since she was well-versed in them. Lights out every night at 9 PM. Bedroom doors needed to be left open. Someone would check in on us hourly throughout the night.

If we needed to use the bathroom, we had to press a button for someone to escort us, and the bathroom door always had to remain slightly ajar. The staff set a one-minute timer when girls were inside because of the ones that purged. Emily didn't know if I was a purger (I wasn't), so she also let me know they checked the toilet bowl after, looking for sprinkles underneath the seat, not just inside the bowl.

Purging wasn't an issue for Emily, who refused all food and had a feeding tube. I noticed that during the dark hours of the night, between the hourly staff check-ins, she took her earrings off and used them to poke tiny holes in her feeding tube, letting the liquid food dribble out, which she wiped down with tissues to flush the evidence.

Emily's trick wasn't the only ED trick I was exposed to at Better Horizons. Some girls hid food at the bottom of their bras because nobody ever felt them closely enough to know what they were hiding there. Others sported messy buns so they could hide food in their hair.

Some pretended to want "more" hot chocolate when they just used it to spit up chewed food (food sunk well into hot cocoa).

Some of the girls that purged stole fabric softener sheets from the laundry room to pad themselves with to help cover the smell of throw-up on their clothes.

Many girls water-loaded before weigh-ins, drinking a ton of water to appear to weigh more than they did.

My tactic was different. It was the same one I had used at the hospital—I ate every bite on my plate so I could get out of there as quickly as possible and return home to ED.

After a week of complete eating compliance on my part, Dr. Larsen sat me down for our daily therapy session and said, "I think you're doing a little too well."

"Too well?" I asked.

"I think ED is telling you to eat everything on your plate because the sooner you get home, the sooner you can return to restricting," she said. "I'm here to make sure he doesn't win."

I was surprised because I didn't think anyone had noticed.

"Why do *you* care? You're not my mom," I shot back at her.

"I'm not, but I knew her. I started working here a month before she finished her internship."

Wait, was Dr. Larsen *Rose?* Mom's supposed friend, who Dad said got me in here?

"Are YOU the reason a bed opened up for me? Because you knew my mom?" I seethed.

"Uh, no . . ." she hedged. "But I want to honor her by helping you. Your dad told me your mom would've given anything to be here with you. He loves you very much and wants the best for you too."

ED didn't care about any of Dr. Larsen's platitudes. He was in a rage because she'd figured out his plan to get me out of there, so he lashed out.

"Maybe you should focus on the girls here who actually have a problem, like Emily," I said.

"What do you mean?" she asked me.

"Emily pokes holes in her feeding tube, and none of you have a clue," I said.

Dr. Larsen tried to hide her surprise, but it was apparent this was an ED trick she'd not yet come across. She gathered herself before responding. "We're extending your stay here."

"But that's not fair! I've been eating everything I'm supposed to!"

"Then it shouldn't be an issue for you to stay a bit longer," she said.

ED was cornered without any chess moves left. Eating my way out of the place hadn't worked, and not eating wasn't

going to work either. I would have to stay at Better Horizons
however long Dr. Larsen saw fit.

"What do you want from me?" I asked her.

She paused before meeting my eyes.

"What do you want for yourself, Beatrice?" she asked.

I glared at her before angrily stomping away.

Later that night, when Emily and I were lying in our
beds, I noticed she was no longer wearing earrings.

"That bitch figured out my trick," Emily told me.

She hadn't, actually, but I wasn't going to tell Emily that.
Dr. Larsen *had* figured mine out though, and ED was beginning to wonder if he'd met his match.

10

I GRASP THE STEERING wheel tightly to stop my hands from shaking, not just because of what Joan told me about Mom and the New York surfer guy, but because of what it made me remember.

A couple of months before Mom died, around the same time she and Dad had that fight, she had a visitor. She told me the man was her second cousin once removed, with whom she'd grown up in a suburb outside Chicago.

Dad was working late that night, so he didn't meet the guy when he arrived to pick Mom up. Beforehand, she had pulled out all the stops to look as good as possible—makeup, perfume, and blew out her hair, curling it at the bottom.

I only vaguely remember meeting the guy, but I remember how Mom lit up when she first saw him standing in front of our door. They hugged, and when they walked away, I watched her thread her arm in his, laughing as he spoke, before they got into a VW with a surfboard on top.

I didn't think anything of it at the time—this was her relative, after all. But now, after visiting Better Horizons, Mom's "cousin" sounds a lot like the guy Joan described.

When Mom returned home from that dinner, Dad was back from work, but Mom's visitor didn't drop her off. She returned in a taxi. And when she stepped inside our living room, her eyelids were puffy like she'd been crying and there was black mascara streaked all over her cheeks.

When I asked her why she was upset, she started crying again and said that her second cousin had told her his mom, her first cousin, was dying. I was surprised to see her so sad because she'd never spoken much about her cousins in Chicago.

But I was even more surprised by Dad's reaction, who kept his distance from her as she sobbed.

I finally went up to him and whispered, "Why aren't you comforting her?"

"There's nothing I can do to change the situation," he said flatly.

If Mom's visitor was the New York surfer guy Joan said Mom was seeing while she worked at Better Horizons, was she really crying that night because he'd broken up with her? Did Dad know about them, or did he believe Mom's lie that this man was her second cousin?

*　*　*

"How do you stop the butterflies from going into your stomach?" Sarah asks Eddie and me that night while slurping a spaghetti noodle into her mouth, coloring her lips red in tomato sauce. She has a spelling quiz tomorrow that she's nervous about.

"When I was in school, I'd think about my teacher only wearing underwear," Eddie says.

She giggles and turns to me. "Did you do that too, Beans?"

"I don't remember," I say. "What usually works for me is taking a couple of deep breaths through my nose and letting them out through my mouth."

"That's probably a better idea," Eddie says to Sarah. "You're lucky. You're getting free advice from a professional psychologist."

"Are you sleeping over tonight?" Sarah asks me.

Her question surprises me, because I've never slept over on a weeknight.

"Oh, um . . ."

"Will you help me practice my spelling words?" she says.

Eddie smiles. "I'll clean up the table, and you two can get to it."

I guess he's decided for me.

* * *

The clock reads 3:03 AM. I ended up sleeping over at Eddie's, but I haven't been doing much sleeping. I've been tossing and turning all night in Eddie's bed. My ankle is still sore from chasing Cristina out of my office, but that's not what's keeping me up.

She's in trouble. Again.

Cristina Cadell's words about Mom swirl around in my mind like a spinning top.

The burning in my chest returns. It feels like anger.

What if she's still alive and got herself into some kind of trouble with that guy? Why should I, the child she abandoned for someone else, be the one who has to extricate her from whatever mess she got herself embroiled in? I suffered so much in the aftermath of losing her as a teenager. And for what? So she could carry on an affair?

Cristina is gone. Nobody at Better Horizons could direct me to Mom. I have no idea how to find her to warn her, if she's still alive. Why am I the one tasked to solve this impossible riddle?

I pick up her charm bracelet off Eddie's nightstand, staring at it, the engravings, the small scratch in the corner, trying to remind myself that I don't know for sure if anything Cristina or Joan said is true.

I wish there were someone who could help shed light on what happened. And then it comes to me—Pearl, Mom's oldest friend in LA, who still sends me a birthday card every year. When Mom first moved here to go to UCLA for graduate school, she and Pearl were roommates. Pearl might know if Mom was seeing someone other than Dad back then.

Sarah appears by Eddie's bedroom door, startling me.

"I had a nightmare," she says. "I'm scared to go back to bed."

Eddie is passed out and snoring next to me.

"Want me to go with you?" I ask her.

She nods. I get up and follow her through the hall to her room. She lies down on her lavender sheets, and I squeeze in on her twin bed.

"I'm scared I won't know how to spell the words tomorrow," she says.

"Try taking a deep breath through your nose and letting it out of your mouth slowly," I say.

She takes my hand in one of hers, holding her blanket with the other, and closes her eyes.

I watch her take a deep breath in, her tiny chest going up and down, and think about how my mom used to lie next to me in bed when I was a scared little girl.

Tears begin to swell in my eyes, so I also take a deep breath. And for just a second, the butterflies disappear.

11

January 1998

MEALS AT BETTER Horizons took place in a large dining room at a wooden, rectangular table. All the girls had assigned seats with name cards and were sandwiched between counselors to help them get through the meal. Even Emily, who refused all food, was still required to attend.

Eating in front of others is one of the most feared rules to break for those who suffer from eating disorders. Normalizing this process through exposure therapy lessens the anxiety surrounding it. To achieve complete recovery, one needs to be comfortable eating around others.

At Better Horizons, each girl's meals were prepared based on their particular caloric needs. Some girls needed more food than others because their bodies were in a hypermetabolic state. This happens after someone has restricted food for an extended period, and their body becomes used to rationing energy for life-saving functions like pumping the heart to stay alive.

When that same person suddenly begins to increase their caloric intake, their metabolism speeds up in response to the flood of energy. During this period, their metabolism may go into overdrive, and they often need far more food than they did before just to maintain their weight, let alone gain weight.

The first meal I went to after Dr. Larsen told me she had extended my stay was different from the ones before when I'd eaten every bite on my plate. ED was enraged that compliance hadn't worked to get me out of there and gave me orders not to eat any food at all. The alternative was liquid meal supplementation. If I refused that for twenty-four hours, I'd have a feeding tube inserted, which I never wanted to go through again after my hospital stay.

"Here you go, Beatrice," Iris, a kitchen staff member, said as she placed my dinner plate in front of me—two fish tacos, rice, beans, and a scoop of guacamole on top. She may as well have asked me to swallow a plate of daggers.

"Ensure," I said.

"You're not eating your dinner tonight?" Iris asked.

"No," I said, glaring at Dr. Larsen, who was sitting directly across from me at the table. Emily, with her feeding tube, was seated at the opposite end of the table, watching the scene unfold.

Iris took my plate away and returned with two bottles of Ensure, which I had to drink, or a feeding tube awaited me. After I finished, I felt bloated and sick from all the liquid inside my stomach. But ED felt like he'd achieved a small victory against Dr. Larsen.

Later that night, Emily and I were lying in our beds in the dark, with the moonlight and stars shining through our windows providing the only light.

"So you're not eating food anymore?" she asked me.

"No," I said.

"Well, you still have a long way to go to catch up to me," she said, lifting her feeding tube. "Do you know Dr. Larsen told me she's never seen anyone more dedicated to their eating disorder than me?"

I looked over at Emily. Even in the dark, I could make out the smile on her face. Her scant translucent skin tightened over her cheekbones. Her ocean-blue eyes, the only physical attribute that had remained intact from before ED had gotten ahold of her, sparkled. She was proud, carrying Dr. Larsen's words like a badge of honor.

"I guess that makes me the best anorexic," she said.

12

Day Two

A FTER A FITFUL night of sleep, I cancel my patient sessions for the day, citing a family emergency, and call Pearl to see if I can stop by.

"Of course, Beans," she tells me. "I'm always here for you."

When Mom first arrived in LA after graduating from NYU, she looked for a place to live and found a notice Pearl had put up on a corkboard at a local coffee shop. Pearl was a make-up artist whose musician roommate had picked up and left, leaving her in the lurch for next month's rent. She decided she wanted a non-artist as a roommate, someone more stable, and was thrilled when Mom, a psychology graduate student, responded to her note. It turned out to be the beginning of an enduring friendship.

When I arrive at Pearl's house, she hugs me and leads me to her living room. As I walk through her hallway, I pass pictures of her, her husband, her children, and her grandchildren on the wall, and my heart sinks, thinking about everything that Mom, Dad, and I have missed out on. She picks up on my sadness and directs me away from the photographs toward her sofa.

After I sit down, I spill everything that's happened over the last twenty-four hours. It's a relief to get it all out to someone who knew Mom.

"I don't know what to say . . . it seems inconceivable, all of it," Pearl says, shaking her head in disbelief. "Especially the idea that your mom might've been unfaithful to your father and got caught up in some kind of trouble with another man. She's not the type that would've strayed. She wouldn't have gotten married if she wanted to be with more than one person. I know how loyal she was to your dad and you. She would've never betrayed either of you like that."

"But the woman at the treatment center asked if Mom ended up with this other guy, and Mom and Dad were together by the time she interned there," I say.

"Well, maybe, this man was interested in her, but that doesn't mean your mother was with him. Also, your parents weren't married yet when she was in graduate school. Maybe she was trying to figure out who she wanted to be with and, in the end, chose your dad."

"Did she ever mention this New York guy to you? Do you think she knew him from college?"

"I don't know. She never mentioned him. After she moved in with me, she told me how relieved she was to be in LA and to have put New York City behind her. When I asked her why, she didn't want to talk about it. So, years later, when she told me she was going to her college reunion, I was surprised because I'd gotten the feeling she hadn't had a good experience there."

"It doesn't make sense," I say. "If she was happy to put New York behind her, then why did this guy visit her before she died, and why did she lie to me and say it was her second cousin?"

"I wish I had answers for you, Beans," Pearl says. "But I do know one thing. Your mother always said she was unabashed when it came to her love for you. Everyone that knew her knew how much she loved you and how proud she was of you. If she's really still alive, she would've never left you unless she had to."

"Then she should've owned up to whatever trouble she'd gotten herself into—faced it like a grown-up," I cry, Pearl's words hitting a nerve. "Even if she had to go to prison, she would've at least been in my life."

Pearl shakes her head. "I wasn't referring to her needing to protect herself."

"What?"

"I was talking about you," she says.

It dawns on me—the question I haven't asked myself in the thick of my anger.

Could Mom have left because *I* was in danger too?

* * *

A month before Mom died, she went to New York for the reunion. Before she left, I remember asking her if she was excited.

"I'm excited, but also nervous," she told me.

"Why nervous?" I asked her.

"It's been so long since I've seen most of these people. Some have gone on to become big theater actors. I hope we'll still have things to talk about," she said.

Mom had gone to the NYU Tisch School of the Arts with dreams of becoming an actress, only to realize it didn't suit her. The conversation made me wonder if she had ennui about her past and how her life had ended up unfolding.

Dad didn't join her on the trip because someone had to stay back and take care of the house, Rascal, and me, so she went on her own.

While she was away, she called and I overheard Dad on the phone with her.

"Are you okay?" he asked her, sounding panicked.

I ran up to him. "What happened?"

"Your mother was mugged," he said.

"Is she hurt?" I asked.

"I don't think so."

But when Mom returned to Los Angeles, the entire left side of her body was black and blue. She said the guy who stole her purse was on a bike and had crashed into her.

"That's so scary," I said. "Did you have to go to the hospital?"

"Yes, but I'm fine now," she said, trying to reassure me.

"Are you sure?" I asked her.

She nodded and picked up her cup of coffee; her hand was shaking. "You can go to college anywhere, Beans," she told me. "Just stay away from New York."

* * *

Every news channel is covering the Cristina Cadell fugitive story. *Heiress on the lam! Billion-dollar runaway!* are just a couple of the chyrons scrolling on the bottom of the screen. The public can't seem to get enough of this sensational schadenfreude story—a wealthy heiress to a billion-dollar fortune accused of murdering her mother Maria Cadell, William Cadell Jr.'s ex-wife, while they were out sailing. There's still no known motive, even though Cristina is now a wanted fugitive in Europe. For the life of me, I still can't comprehend what she has to do with my Mom.

I'm standing in front of my hall closet, staring at the boxes on the top shelf. Mom's boxes, filled with all of her remaining possessions.

After she died, I draped myself in her clothes, smelling her perfume, putting on her jewelry each day, desperately trying to cling onto any piece of her. All I wanted was to have her waiting for me in the kitchen after school, for her to hug me, and to feel her presence in our house again.

But after I returned home from Better Horizons, I packed up all of her belongings that Dad had left untouched, and I never went through them again. They reminded me that I'd lost the person who loved me more than anyone else, and I couldn't bear to look at them.

Although I haven't opened these boxes in decades, they have moved with me everywhere, from college dorm rooms to various apartments to my first house with my ex-husband to my new home in the aftermath of my divorce. They have been my constant, silent life companion, a mirror to her absence.

I pick up a box labeled *Letters* and open it. Inside are dozens of cards that people wrote Mom through the years, including ones that Dad and I gave her and a bunch of letters she wrote me.

On top of the pile is a copy of the eulogy our family's rabbi gave after she passed. I was in a daze at her funeral, too heartbroken to hear his words. To this day, I have no recollection of what he said.

I pick it up and start reading:

This is a day of many feelings. Irene has died, and we have come to bury her. Death is always too soon. We yearn for one more moment, one more smile, one more confiding conversation to bear our hearts, one more bit of wisdom, reassurance, one more moment of intimacy. Although it is all too soon, Irene is now in eternal peace.

Irene was a mother, wife, beloved friend, and colleague of so many. And she was someone who so loved the world, and people, that she would want your memories of her to be filled with fun, humor, good times, and love. She was a woman of basic pleasures. The profound simplicity of this was that though she had an appreciation for all the luxuries life can bring, she knew at their core they didn't matter if you didn't have good relationships. Her relationships are what defined her, and although she enjoyed hiking, reading a good book, taking a walk, or a good joke, it was in her family and her friends that she saw God and felt blessed.

As an only child who had lost both of her parents in high school, her pillars were her pride in Beans and her love for Carl. She gained in their enjoyment her own contentment. Once on a plane flight with them, there were two first-class tickets and one in coach. Irene insisted that Beans and Carl sit together in first class. And in her excitement to know what they had to eat and how they were being pampered, she was both the adoring mother and wife.

No matter your station in life, she cared about you, and in her concern, you always felt better for having been around her. She dedicated her life to working with those grappling with alcohol and drug addiction, some of whom are here with us today and with whom I've had a chance to speak. In their words, a clear portrait emerged of a psychologist who never judged them and instead helped them become the best versions of themselves so they could lead meaningful lives.

Today and in the future, as we recall Irene, speak about her, tell stories, laugh, and cry, she achieves immortality. For as long as she is alive in the hearts, minds, and souls she loved, she has eternal life. May her life be a blessing.

I grab a box of tissues and weep in a way I haven't in years, maybe since my miscarriage. Then I do the unthinkable, something I know will cause me immeasurable pain—I begin reading the letters she wrote me.

Happy birthday, my darling Beans.

It is hard for me to believe that you are already nine years old. But it is so exciting, Beans, because as you get older, life gets even more interesting. I am so grateful you are my child—I am so proud of the wonderful girl you are. I love you and can't wait to share 4th grade with you.

Millions of hugs and kisses,
Mommy

Dear Beans,

Just a little note to cheer you up. I know you were upset, but you are a very conscientious student, and I am proud of you. It's a new day. I hope you are feeling better. Things don't always happen in life as we may want. But the main thing is to learn and to go on and enjoy the next day. I love you no matter what your grade is. Have a nice day, my little girl.

Tons of xxxxs and ooooos
Mommy

My dear Beans,

Today is Mother's Day. Thank you for being such a special daughter and for making me such a happy mother. Thank you for all the joy and happiness you've given me. I can't wait to spend today with you. I'll love you forever and ever.

Millions of kisses and tons of hugs,
Mommy

Dear Beans,

I could burst, I'm so proud of you and the person you are. I remember your first day of preschool, kindergarten, first grade, etc., etc. Okay, I'll stop. I've so cherished being with you as you've continued to grow. Good luck on your first day of high school!

I love you beyond words.
Mom(my)

Beans,

I know there is nothing I can do or say to make you feel better, but I just wanted to tell you again how proud I am of you. It takes a lot of courage to try out for something and a lot of strength to deal with the disappointment of not having your hopes realized. You have such a great personality and inner strength that even with the rough times, you'll come through smiling. Just know that Dad and I love you and that you're the star in our home—that's for sure!

Zillions of kisses,
Mom

Dear Beans,

It's New Year's, and I feel like getting sentimental. I always have a hard time explaining to you why I love you so much—part of it is because you're my child, and I'd love you no matter what. And it's not just that I'm proud of you for being so pretty and smart. I really like you for who you are—you're sensitive, loving, have a good heart, have such a great personality, and are fun to be with. I have always loved you, and now that you're in high school, and even though you might not believe this, I'm enjoying you more than ever! Have a wonderful 1997, my Beans. The coming years as you

*finish high school and go to college will be an incredible
time of growth for you and new experiences. Enjoy it!
And remember, always feel my love <u>deep inside of you.</u>*

*Zillions of kisses and hugs,
Mom*

* * *

I stop reading when the fountain of tears blurs my vision.
I breathe deeply, trying to calm myself, but I can't stop
crying.

I think about the last letter—1997 was not a wonderful
year for me. I lost her, and then I lost myself. But mainly, I'm
crying because I can feel how deeply she loved me in these
letters, and it makes me realize how much I've missed her.

I needed to read these letters, not just for my sake but
for Eddie's and Sarah's too. I needed to know that I did
have a loving maternal role model and that I can love a child
unabashedly, the same way Pearl said Mom loved me.

I'm struck by how well Mom *knew* me in these letters.
She could tell I was a perfectionist prone to anxiety, which
I'd later learn are specific risk factors for developing an eating
disorder. She knew I needed reassurance that things would
always work out.

She also seemed happy with her life with Dad and me.
There's no hint that she wanted to leave him or knew she
was going to have to, which means that either she was the
best liar ever or that what Pearl said must be true—if she's
still alive, she left because she needed to. To protect us from
something—but what? What could she have been running
from?

I assemble the letters back into a pile. I feel a sudden,
desperate urge to hug both Eddie and Sarah.

As I place the stack inside the box, an unopened letter drops out. It has a *Return to Sender* stamp—the return

address is Mom's old office in Santa Monica—and is dated
August 27, 1997, a couple months before she died.

I flip the envelope over, and swallow hard when I notice
the name on the outgoing address:

Margot Cadell Davis
424 Paulina Street
Malibu, CA 90265

13

January 1998

"I MISS YOU," I told Dad over a yellow landline phone while standing in the nurses' station at Better Horizons.

The truth was I didn't miss him at all. I was furious with him for forcing me to be there. But ED was busy scheming how to get me out, and since eating my way out of the place hadn't worked, he told me to try to manipulate my father instead.

"I miss you too, Beans," Dad told me.

"Then come and get me," I said.

"That isn't possible."

"Why not?" I asked.

"Because you're not ready."

"You don't understand what they're doing to me here."

Dad got quiet.

"They're abusing me," I said, forgetting that I'd falsely accused him of the same thing.

At first, he didn't respond. I thought I had him. ED was a hell of a manipulator. Grade A.

"I don't believe you," he finally said. "It's the eating disorder talking."

Dad was now sounding like Dr. Larsen, and ED wasn't having it.

"If you don't come and pick me up right now, I'll kill myself," I threatened.

He got quiet again. I imagined him wincing on the other end. "If you feel like you might kill yourself, you're safer there than at home," he said, anguished.

"Just get me out of here!" I screamed. "I'll eat anything you want me to. I promise."

"I don't believe that either . . . yet."

"Fuck you," I said and hung up.

The nurse raised her eyebrows as I stormed out of the station.

I returned to the living room, where all the girls wrote in their journals while Dr. Larsen walked around overseeing them. As I sat on the ground next to the fireplace, she handed me my journal, smiling.

I drilled her a look and wrote about how much I hated, literally despised, Dad and his cult leader, Dr. Larsen. They didn't understand a damn thing about me. They were the reasons why my life had gone to hell.

* * *

Later, in the middle of the night, I was lying silently in my bed in the dark, biding my time. After a staff member came by to do the hourly night check-in, I got out of bed and put on my gym shoes, the only shoes I'd brought to Better Horizons.

"Where are you going?" Emily asked me. I'd thought she was asleep.

"I need to get out of here, and my dad refuses to pick me up. They always talk to us about personal responsibility," I said. "So I'm taking matters into my own hands."

I tiptoed out of the room. The front door was at the bottom of the staircase, so it would be an easy escape as long as no staff member was guarding it.

When I got downstairs, it was clear, so I quietly unlocked the front door and made a run for it. I ran as fast as possible toward the Santa Monica mountains in the distance.

If I had actually thought about the fact that I had no money, nowhere to go, and no one to run to, I might not have left. But there was no reasoning with ED. He was in complete control, telling me that I needed to continue running as far away from Better Horizons as I could to swear my allegiance to him.

I must have reached the mountains at some point because I was running up and down steep inclines. After it felt like I had been running for miles, I stopped to catch my breath, wiping the sweat off my brow, taking in the sounds of nature surrounding me.

The Santa Ana winds tussled the branches and leaves on the trees. Animals howled and cooed. But then I heard a different kind of sound.

At first, it sounded like an unrecognizable animal in the distance. As it got closer, I realized it was a car.

Before I knew it, headlights flashed into my eyes, and a white van screeched to a halt right in front of me. Two men, dressed in black clothes like ninjas, jumped out, one from the driver's side, the other from the passenger side, and grabbed me.

As they strapped me into the backseat with a rope, I tried to fight them off, kicking and screaming. My futile calls for help echoed into the empty mountain valleys.

"Where are you taking me!?" I shouted.

They didn't respond.

After they finished tying me, one of them sat next to me in the back seat while the other returned to the driver's side, turned on the engine, and drove us away.

I couldn't see anything out of the windows because we were in the middle of the mountains, and it was pitch black outside.

But I already knew how this story ended—rape, murder, discarding my chewed-up body into a river. I started to cry, alternating between loud and soft sobs until the rage kicked in. Rage at my father, who should've picked me up from Better Horizons, who I had *begged* to pick me up. The last thought I had before the van abruptly stopped was that I hoped my demise would make him feel guilty for the rest of his life. It would serve him right.

"Time to get out," the man sitting next to me said.

When the driver got out of his seat and walked around to my side to untie me, I saw we were parked in front of Better Horizons.

As conniving and manipulative as ED was, the folks at Better Horizons seemed to be a couple of steps ahead of him.

I was about to step out, but the man sitting next to me stopped me with his hand. "Not so fast," he said. "I need your shoes."

"My shoes?" I asked.

"Yup."

"No, I only brought one pair here, and I'm not walking around barefoot."

"You're a flight risk now," he said. "Harder to run away without shoes."

He put out his hand, waiting for them.

I looked at him and considered my options. He was at least a foot taller than me, muscles popping out of his chest and arms, and could easily snap my spine in half, not to mention the driver who was still blocking my door with his body. I could only get out if I handed the shoes over.

I begrudgingly took them off and gave them to the guy, shaking my head at the indignity of having to go barefoot, too sick to understand the real indignity of what had just happened.

14

I HAND EDDIE THE letter I found, which he reads out loud:

Dear Margot,

If I did or said something that upset you, I apologize. I'm here if you want to pick up the conversation.

Sincerely,
Irene

"Who's Margot?" Eddie asks me.

I have my cell phone ready with her obituary pulled up:

Margot Cadell Davis
August 30, 1967—December 1, 1997

Margot Cadell Davis of Malibu, California, beloved daughter of George Brian Davis and Cynthia Cadell Davis, was a cherished daughter, niece, cousin, and friend to many. She graduated from Loyola Marymount University and dedicated her life to wildlife conservation. Despite her challenges, she loved helping

people and animals. In lieu of flowers, the family kindly
asks that you send donations to the National Alliance
on Mental Illness (NAMI) or the World Wide Fund for
Nature. Memorial to be announced.

"Margot's mom was Cynthia Cadell, William Cadell
Sr.'s younger sister. Cynthia and her husband died in a small
plane crash over ten years ago," I explain.

"So Margot was first cousins with the Cadell brothers,
William Jr. and Quentin . . ." Eddie says, connecting the
dots.

"Yup," I say.

"What do you think she had to do with your mom?" he
says.

"My guess is Margot was my mom's patient. The return
address on the envelope is my mom's old office address, and
my mom's letter sounds like Margot terminated treatment
because she was upset with her. I've had patients project
anger that they have toward other people in their lives onto
me, get overwhelmed by it, and abandon treatment."

"Interesting," he says.

"And Margot was only thirty years old when she died,
but the obituary didn't include the cause of death. But it did
cite her 'challenges,' and the family asked for donations to
be sent to NAMI, which makes me think it might've been a
suicide or drug- or alcohol-related. My mom specialized in
treating addiction."

"So you think your mom might've gotten caught up with
the Cadell family through a patient?"

I nod. "What if, during treatment, Margot told her
things that the family worried would get out?" I say.

"Can you find out if Margot was her patient?" Eddie
asks.

"I looked through all of my mom's things, but unfortunately, I didn't find anything work-related. I want to go to

Malibu to see if the people living in Margot's old house or any neighbors on the block knew her and possibly anything about my mom. I know it's a long shot, but it's my only lead. Maybe I'll get lucky, and there will be older neighbors there who knew Margot."

"Let me take you," he says. "I don't need to pick Sarah up from school for a few hours."

I'm grateful to have him accompany me and thankful I don't have to drive since I didn't sleep very much last night.

"Thank you," I say, kissing him on the cheek.

"No, thank *you*," he says.

"For what?" I ask.

"On the way to school this morning, Sarah told me you helped her fall back to sleep last night," he says.

The vulnerable look in his eyes says what his words don't—how much he wants me to be her mother.

I wonder if the look in my eyes also says what my words don't—how scared I am that I won't measure up.

*   *   *

Eddie and I stand in front of a Craftsman house deep in the Malibu hills. I ring the doorbell and hear a dog barking and footsteps approaching.

A young woman with huge gold hoop earrings, dressed in a crop top and short shorts, opens the door. "Hello?" She looks confused.

"Hi, I'm trying to find out information about Margot Cadell—"

"You have the wrong address," she cuts me off.

"I don't think I do," I say.

An athletic, shirtless guy walks up behind her holding a small white Shih Tzu dog.

"What's going on?" he asks her.

She whirls on him. "Who's Margot?" she demands.

"I have no idea who—" He pauses, thinking. "Wait, you mean the woman that lived here before my parents bought the place?"

"Yes, exactly," I say.

"Ohhh!" Hoops looks relieved, like she thought he was cheating on her.

"Did they know her?" I ask him.

"No, they bought the place from her family after she died."

I nod. "I know this may sound strange, but do you know how she died?"

"Heard it was an overdose. My parents said that's why they got a deal on the place."

"Someone *died* in this house?" Hoops asks, horrified.

"Who cares?" he responds defensively. "It was decades ago."

"That's still really creepy," she says, adjusting her earrings.

The dog starts squirming in his arms.

"We're going to the beach. Anything else?" he asks, annoyed.

"No, thanks for your time," I say.

He closes the door.

"Let's try that house next door," Eddie suggests.

We walk over and ring the doorbell.

A man with curly black hair opens the door. There are construction workers behind him rehabbing the place.

"You're late," he says.

I blink. "I think you have me confused with someone else."

"Are you here for the appraisal?" he asks.

"No," I say.

"Dammit." He shakes his head, frustrated.

"Are you the owner?" I ask him.

"They're in China and selling. I'm their realtor. Wanna take a peek?"

"I'm not looking to buy a home. I'm trying to get information about a woman that lived next door—Margot Cadell."

"No idea who that is. This place has had a revolving door of tenants for the last two years. That's why my clients are selling."

"Ven aquí!" someone shouts from inside the house.

"I gotta go," he says and closes the door.

I look at Eddie, officially discouraged.

"Let's try the house on the other side," he says.

We walk over to a dated-looking house with a yellow intercom box from the eighties. I try buzzing, but nobody answers.

"Maybe it's broken," Eddie says. He tries knocking loudly. Still, nothing.

I try hiding how defeated I feel, but Eddie picks up on it. "Don't worry, Beans. There are a lot of houses on this block we can still try."

We begin walking away when a frail old lady slowly opens the door.

"Hello," she says, steadying herself on the frame. "Sorry, it takes me a while to get anywhere these days."

"No worries," I say, my hope lifting. "I don't mean to bother you."

"It's no bother. It's nice to see a smiling face," she says.

I make sure to smile extra wide before asking her about Margot.

"I'm wondering if you know anything about a woman who lived next door back in the nineties. Her name was Margot Cadell Davis."

The elderly woman shakes her head in disapproval. "A Greek tragedy."

"What do you mean?" I ask.

"All the money in the world and addicted to everything you can imagine."

The kind of patient Mom would have had.

"That's very sad," I say. "Did you know her personally? Do you know if she saw any therapists for her problems?"

"Too many to count. She was in and out of every rehab in town, but nothing ever stuck, even when she was pregnant. Lost a baby because of her addiction a couple of days after it was born. Still couldn't get her act together and ended up overdosing. Who are you, by the way?"

"We're friends of the family. They want me to write a profile for her for the National Alliance on Mental Illness to help raise awareness." I'm surprised by how quickly I make up the lie.

The old lady nods her head. "Don't tell them I said this, but I was relieved after she wasn't my neighbor anymore. I wasn't happy that she died, but she wasn't easy to live next to."

"What do you mean?" I ask.

"I can't count how many ambulances came barreling down this street to whisk her away because of overdoses. She also had a horrible boyfriend. They'd have loud screaming matches in the middle of the street."

"That sounds very unpleasant," I say.

She nods again. "One minute, she'd shout profanities at him. The next minute they'd be back to the hugging and I love yous. But it never lasted long before the fighting started again. I think he used her for her money. He was a bit older than her, maybe a decade—a beach bum and not even good at it. A neighbor across the street said he'd always wipe out whenever she saw him surfing. Didn't stop him from driving around in his VW with a surfboard on top. Like he was the king of Malibu, even though he had the thickest New York accent I'd ever heard."

15

January 1998

F IELD TRIPS AT Better Horizons happened once a week and ranged from movie outings to the local mall. They were also earned. Girls who ate food were allowed to participate, and girls who chose liquid supplementation had to stay back.

I had been allowed to go on field trips the previous two weeks, visiting a photography museum and a botanical garden, because I had eaten food. But I hadn't cared about those trips.

A few days after I began my strike against food and tried to run away, the field trip van was parked in front of the ranch again, ready to take the girls to a rescue shelter for dogs—*this* trip I wanted to go on.

I missed Rascal desperately and wanted to be around other dogs who didn't ask anything of me and who I felt understood me more than anyone, apart from ED.

No indoor pets were allowed at Better Horizons because a common ED trick is dropping food crumbs and letting dogs and cats eat them. So this trip was my only chance to be around dogs while I was there.

We were seated at the dining room table, waiting for breakfast before the van departed for the shelter.

Iris approached me with my plate of food—scrambled eggs, potatoes, and toast with butter.

"Ensure," I said, snarling at Dr. Larsen, who was once again seated across from me.

"We're going to the dog shelter today. If you want to join us, you'll need to eat your breakfast," she told me.

I looked down at my bare feet.

"I can't go anywhere without shoes," I shot back.

"They'll be returned to you for the trip if you eat breakfast," she said.

I wanted to eat it so I could go to the shelter, but ED's voice was too strong.

It wasn't until I was in graduate school, enrolled in an eating disorder treatment class and reading *Biting the Hand That Starves You*, that I finally learned why. When it comes to eating disorders, ED's voices typically fall into one of two categories—a mean girl or an abusive partner.

The mean girl constantly criticizes how you look and act, letting you know you're not good enough but making you believe that if you're self-disciplined enough to lose weight, you'll finally be accepted by the popular crowd. If you ever dare question her, she lashes out at you, reminding you why you're a worthless reject, which perpetuates your self-loathing and solidifies the delusion that the only way out of your hell is by listening to her.

Then there's the abusive partner who at first appears like a comforting friend, telling you seductive lies about how he'll always be there for you as long as you swear allegiance to him by following his orders to lose weight. If you dare stray, he tears into you, blaming you for being dumb and undisciplined. And if you ever dare recognize his voice as abusive, he deftly shifts gears, returning to a comforting tone, telling you he understands you, unlike everyone else, using a similar tactic to what an abusive partner might do if you question whether you should leave them after they hit you.

Both ED voices—the mean girl and the abuser—have the same goal: to isolate the eating disorder sufferer from their loved ones and support system so they have complete control over them. My ED voice fell into the abusive partner category. After Mom died, I felt nobody understood me the way she had until he came along, telling me lies that he did.

When Dr. Larsen said that I needed to eat breakfast if I wanted to go to the animal shelter, ED told me that she was trying to manipulate me and that if she really cared about me, she would let me go without making me eat anything, reminding me that he was the only one on my side.

"Ensure," I told Iris, who was still holding my plate of eggs.

"Are you sure?" Dr. Larsen asked me.

ED was enraged—*how dare she challenge him, who had my best interests at heart?*

"What part of *no* don't you understand!?" I asked furiously.

I stood up, accidentally bumping into Iris, who dropped my plate of food. Yellow bits of egg flew in the air and landed on the ground, leaving oil marks on the wooden floor. There were no ceramic plate pieces to pick up like there had been at home when I threw plates of food on the ground. These outbursts were common at Better Horizons, so meals were served on plasticware.

"Well, then, Ensure it is," Dr. Larsen said stoically.

Later that day, Emily and I were in the living room tasked with doing a writing exercise in our journals while the other girls were at the dog shelter.

"They're so weak," Emily said. "Can you imagine choosing a dog over ED?" she asked.

I didn't respond. I'd been ignoring her for a few days, mad because I was sure she had ratted me out when I tried to run away.

"Hello?" she said.

I still didn't respond.

"Hello—" she said again when her face suddenly turned beet red, almost purple. She started coughing uncontrollably and couldn't stop. I'd gotten so used to the plastic feeding tube hanging out of her nose that I hardly noticed it anymore, but she was frantically pointing to it.

"It's clogged! It's clogged!" she shouted between coughs. "I need help! Get the nurse!"

I ran out of the dining room to the nurses' station, telling the nurse there was a problem with Emily's feeding tube. She grabbed a syringe filled with liquid and quickly ran back to the living room as I followed her from behind.

While the nurse connected the syringe to the middle of the feeding tube to flush out whatever had clogged it, I looked over at Emily, whose eyes were bulging with fear. She was not the portrait of assured confidence and swagger as ED had made her and me believe.

I stared at my bare feet, thinking about the other girls who were probably at the shelter by now, petting the dogs, while I was stuck at the treatment center with a nurse, Emily, and her feeding tube.

For the first time since I'd arrived at Better Horizons, I heard a whisper of a voice inside of me, *my* voice, a voice that dared to question if ED really understood me . . . before he quickly shut it down.

16

"I DON'T KNOW HOW to piece together everything I've learned over the last day," I tell Eddie once we're back at his place. "I keep hoping something will click so I can figure out what happened."

We spoke to a few more neighbors on Margot's old block in Malibu. An older couple that lived across from Margot echoed what her elderly neighbor said, that Margot was in a turbulent relationship with an older man who appeared to be using her for her money—a man who sounded a lot like the guy Joan said Mom was seeing. But none of Margot's neighbors knew about specific therapists she saw or could directly connect her to Mom.

"This may sound silly, but would making a list help?" he asks.

I shrug.

"Let's try," he says. He grabs a pad and a pen and writes LIST at the top. "I'll be your assistant. Tell me everything you've learned, and I'll write it down."

So I do just that:

1. Mom is supposedly alive and in trouble again, according to Cristina Cadell.

2. Cristina is a wanted fugitive in Europe for allegedly murdering her mother on a sailboat.
3. Frank, the undertaker at the funeral home where we held Mom's memorial service, never saw her body.
4. According to Joan at Better Horizons, Mom was involved with a New York surfer guy while doing clinical work there, even though she and Dad were a couple by then.
5. The New York surfer guy visited Mom a few months before she died, but she lied and told me he was her second cousin.
6. Margot Cadell Davis was likely Mom's old patient who could've told her damaging secrets about TriCPharma.
7. According to Margot's neighbors, Margot was dating a New York surfer guy who sounded eerily similar to the man Joan said Mom was involved with.

As I'm saying everything aloud to Eddie, a thought occurs to me.

"What if my mom was in a relationship with the New York surfer guy and realized her patient Margot Cadell was too? Or maybe it was the other way around. Margot discovered her therapist was seeing her boyfriend. Either way, it would've been very upsetting for Margot, especially if she was pregnant with his baby. Maybe that's why she terminated treatment with my mom, and that's what the unopened returned letter that my mom sent her was about."

"Could be," Eddie says.

"Margot's neighbors said her boyfriend was using Margot for her money. If she was insecure and settling for someone who didn't love her, maybe she wanted Mom out of the picture to make the threat of another woman disappear."

"Enter her cousins, the Cadell brothers," Eddie says.

"Exactly. What if she told them she'd disclosed some of the family's business secrets to her therapist so they'd go after my mom? It would've been a perfect way to do away with her boyfriend's other girlfriend for good."

My cell phone buzzes. I slip my hand inside my pocket to get it, feeling Mom's charm bracelet scraping against the palm of my hand.

I look at my phone. A new text awaits me:

I'm being framed. I didn't kill my mom.

Your mom's running out of time too.

My heart starts to pound. The burning in my chest returns.

WHY IS MY MOM IN TROUBLE? I text Cristina back.

Message undeliverable.

I tighten my grasp on the phone, hoping to squeeze out another text, another clue . . . but nothing comes.

"What is it?" Eddie asks me.

I hand him my phone, and he reads Cristina's text.

"Holy shit," he says.

17

January 1998

IT HAD BEEN a week since I had run away from Better Horizons. My only interaction with Emily was when I got the nurse to help her when her feeding tube was clogged.

She kept trying to talk to me, and I kept giving her the silent treatment. Finally, one night, when we were getting ready for dinner, she had had enough.

"I'm not going to stop talking to you for the rest of the night until you tell me why you're so mad at me," she said. "What did I do?"

I turned to her and finally spoke my mind. "You told them I ran away."

"No, I didn't," she said defensively.

"I don't believe you," I said.

"They check in on us every hour during the night, and you weren't here," she said.

"I don't believe you," I repeated.

"Why would I tell them you left when they'd find out anyway?" she dug in.

"Because I didn't 'leave.' I ran away. Something you've never done. Something you've never even had the courage to try."

Her lips narrowed. Her brows furrowed. She looked angrier than I'd ever seen her.

"Are you fucking kidding me?" she seethed. "I have nine hospitalizations under my belt, and this is my seventh time here. You're not in the same league as me. Not even close!"

I was too ill to register how warped this conversation was. Both of us clinging to our disease like it was our greatest accomplishment, in competition for who was the best anorexic, unable to comprehend how sick we were.

Anosognosia is one of the defining features of anorexia—the medical term for when a patient is unable to understand that they are sick, stemming from anatomical changes to the brain due to starvation. It's incredibly problematic because, without an awareness that one is sick, the patient has no desire to get better, which makes the disease so confounding and difficult to treat.

Families of ED patients and clinicians who treat them often hear things like, "I don't have a problem. You're the one with the problem!" even when often there's ample and serious physical and medical evidence, including heart problems and organ failure, demonstrating otherwise.

With virtually any other illness, from cancer to depression, people understand that they are sick and want to get better. But the vast majority of the time, with anorexia, that understanding doesn't exist, at least at first, which is why waiting for a sufferer of an eating disorder to have insight into their illness and be ready for treatment doesn't work. If you keep waiting, they'll keep restricting, suffer more brain damage, and risk dying in the interim. The saying goes: *Treatment first, insight later.*

So how do you get a person who doesn't believe anything is wrong with them to change their behavior? By using external motivations, making them earn things that they want, whether it's material possessions, video games, or time with friends, *through eating.*

Dr. Larsen tried doing that with me when she told me I needed to eat to go to the dog shelter. And she was about to try this technique again.

Emily and I were still arguing when Kyle, a staff member, appeared at our door. "What's all the shouting about?" he asked us.

"Did Emily tell on me when I ran away?" I asked him.

"Yes, she let the staff know," he said.

"I knew it," I said, staring her down.

"You owe her a debt of gratitude," he added. "She probably saved your life."

I thought about my mom and the car that had barreled down the street, killing her, and how often I had dreamt about what would have happened had someone been there to push her out of the way in time to save her.

Kyle suggesting that what Emily had done for me was akin to this didn't mesh with what ED's thundering voice told me—Emily had ruined my only chance of escaping Better Horizons. Who knows how far I might've gotten had she not ratted me out?

"Your dad's coming tomorrow," Kyle told me.

"I already know," I snapped back at him. It was going to be Dad's first visit, and I wasn't looking forward to it at all.

"He's supposed to bring your dog," he said.

"Rascal?" I asked, surprised.

"Yes," Kyle said. "But not if you keep shouting up here and not unless you go downstairs for dinner."

I immediately jumped up, solely focused on the prospect of seeing Rascal. Emily was now an afterthought. I quickly ran downstairs to the dining room.

When I got there, I was the first girl at the table. Dr. Larsen was already seated, directly across from me like usual.

"Good evening, Beatrice," she said.

I didn't want to speak with her, but I was worried she'd tell Dad not to bring Rascal if I was rude.

"Hi," I said.

"Are you looking forward to your father's visit tomorrow?" she asked.

"Yes," I said.

"I heard he's bringing your dog," she said.

I nodded.

Iris came out with my plate of food—hamburger with fries, a small side salad, and ketchup—the dreaded ketchup. Once I started restricting food, condiments became toxic, unnecessary calories that needed to be avoided at all costs.

"Ensure," I said.

Dr. Larsen met my eyes. "Rascal won't be able to come tomorrow when your dad visits unless you eat your dinner tonight."

How the fuck does she know my dog's name? I thought.

I despised this woman with every fiber of my being, the busybody of busybodies who micromanaged my every move. I wanted her out of my life so badly. I took a deep breath in, trying to stop myself from screaming.

"It's your choice, just like choosing not to go to the dog shelter was," she reminded me.

The other girls began filing into the dining room and sat down. Some of them ate. A couple drank Ensure. I sat for an hour with the plate of food in front of me, not touching it but not asking for liquid supplementation either. I could feel Emily, at the other end of the table, staring at me, wondering if I'd cave.

After all the girls finished, I was left alone, sitting with a cold plate of food and Dr. Larsen still seated in front of me.

I considered if I did eat the food where I might be able to hide some. There were no napkins with meals at Better

Horizons because they could be folded in half and used to spit food into discreetly.

We weren't allowed to wear hoodies, jackets, or anything with pockets that could hide food either. There was a shorts-only policy during meals because it was easier to hide food in long-leg pants while the food dropped right out with shorts.

I wasn't a purger, so trying to throw up after eating wasn't an option. After I became sick, I believed that if I tried to purge food, and it didn't come up all the way, it would go back down again, and it would be like eating twice, meaning double the calories. And even if I wanted to purge, it would be a challenge. We weren't allowed to use the bathroom for one hour after meals or snacks for this reason.

The bottom line is I either had to eat the meal or forgo seeing Rascal in the morning.

"What'll it be, Beatrice?" Dr. Larsen finally asked.

I angrily picked up a fry and ate it. For a split second, I enjoyed the taste—but immediately felt guilty. ED was on me, reminding me this was another example of why I was the biggest failure of all time. I stuffed the rest of the fries in my mouth to get the meal over with as quickly as possible.

"Easy does it," Dr. Larsen said.

"Isn't this what you want me to do?" I said, nearly choking, my mouth filled with fries.

I inhaled the hamburger too, like someone might try to steal it from me. I needed to finish because I knew ED's wrath awaited me, and I wanted that over with too.

The dangle was seeing Rascal. As I swallowed the last couple of bites, I feared I'd made a colossal mistake. Would the few moments I'd have with him in the morning be worth it?

It didn't matter now. My plate was empty.

18

EDDIE IS STILL holding my phone when his phone vibrates on the coffee table in front of us—it's Paul. He quickly picks it up and reads the text.

"Paul pulled up your records and has a question about the car break-in last week," Eddie says.

Last week, I was in the middle of my workday when Eddie called me to tell me his mom had fallen and his dad had just taken her to the ER. She was okay but needed X-rays, and he wanted to meet his parents at the hospital. He's very close with them and is their primary support in LA since he only has one sibling, a sister who lives in Seattle.

Eddie asked if I could pick Sarah up from school since I'm listed as one of her emergency contacts. I took her to her favorite boba place on Sawtelle. While we were sipping our drinks outside, a car alarm went off nearby, and after a minute I realized it was mine. I didn't think anything of it— that occasionally happens when someone walks too closely by my car.

"That's my alarm," I told Sarah. "I better go turn it off."

As we got closer to the car, though, I noticed the doors and trunk were slightly ajar.

"Did someone break in?" Sarah asked me.

"Looks like it," I said calmly, not to scare her.

When I opened the front passenger side door, I saw they had rummaged through my glove compartment but had left the $20 bill I keep hidden underneath a pile of old CDs for emergencies. I assumed they were after electronics like Air-Pods, which I don't keep in my car.

Even though they hadn't stolen anything, I still reported the break-in to the police because they had damaged my glove compartment latch, which was surprisingly expensive to repair, and I wanted reimbursement from my car insurance company. Paul must've read the police report I filed.

"Paul's wondering if you ended up finding anything was stolen," Eddie continues.

I shake my head. "Not that I know of. Why?"

"Because he doesn't think it was a regular break-in."

My stomach drops. "Really?"

"He thinks it had something to do with your mom," Eddie says in an ominous tone.

"*What?* Why?"

"He says that since nothing was taken from the car, who-ever broke in likely had a different motivation than theft. It was probably someone looking for information—possibly someone hired by the Cadells to follow you and find out if you've been in contact with your mom." He swallows in apparent fear. "Paul says to be careful at home too. If they want information on you, they're not going to stop at break-ing into your car."

My mind is racing.

If the Cadells broke into my car last week, that means they were watching me well before Cristina showed up at my office yesterday.

She's running out of time.

The words from Cristina's text send a chill down my spine. If they've been watching me, do they know she visited me?

I look at Eddie. Visibly worried, he glances down at his watch.

"I need to pick Sarah up from school," he says.

I nod, swallowing the sudden lump in my throat. "Okay."

We say goodbye in front of his house and avoid discussing the unnerved look in his eyes. But I know what he's thinking—Sarah was with me when the Cadells broke into my car. Until all of this is over, he's not going to want me around her. I don't blame him.

It's clear what I must do—get as far away from here as possible.

CHAPTER

19

February 1998

"COME WITH ME," Dr. Larsen said. She led me outside to a large wooden deck off the ranch where girls met with visitors, mainly family members and occasionally friends. Dad was already there, seated on a chair with Rascal, who was leashed by his side.

As soon as Rascal saw me, he ran my way, jumping on me, his tail wagging in a dizzying spin. I picked him up, and he started licking me uncontrollably.

Before I was admitted to Better Horizons, I was scared of him licking me, terrified there were calories in his saliva that could be transmitted to me. I had also feared touching his food and treats for the same reason, making Dad feed him whenever he needed to eat.

But at this moment, ED couldn't stop me from hugging him as tightly as I could and letting him lick me.

"It's nice to see you smiling again," Dad said.

I hadn't realized I was smiling and made sure to drop it quickly and scowl at him.

"Can you leave?" I said. "I don't want you here. I want to be alone with Rascal."

"No," Dad said.

I rolled my eyes at him while Rascal kept licking my face.

"I brought you something," he told me.

"It better not be food," I said.

"It's not," he said, handing me a large handmade card that all the girls from my former high school soccer team had signed. I quickly glanced over at the various messages: *Get better! We miss you. Hope you feel better soon!*

I was livid. There was nothing wrong with me. The problem was Dad, Dr. Larsen, and everyone else.

"How do they know I'm here?" I interrogated Dad.

"They don't know where you are. They just know you're not feeling well," he said.

"I'm feeling fine," I said. "You're the one with the problem. I can't believe you made me come here. They won't even let me wear my shoes." I pointed to my feet which only had socks on.

He didn't respond.

"Well?" I said. "You don't care that I'm walking around barefoot? Because it's abuse. If I had access to a phone, I'd call the police to report them."

"You tried to run away," he reminded me. "That's why they took your shoes away."

"I ran away because they're abusing me. I hate you for making me be here," I told him. "And if Mom were alive, she'd hate you for it too."

He closed his eyes, wincing, before opening them back up to look right at me. "ED is trying to push me away from you, but you're not his daughter. You're mine. And he's not going to succeed."

*   *   *

Later that evening, while I was in the shower, I was in a rage, thinking about the card Dad had brought from my former teammates. I grew angrier and angrier thinking about how they all got to play soccer while I had to eat to earn the right to see my dog.

I also had ED in my ear, beating me up, telling me I was a failure because of the hamburger and fries I'd eaten the night before so I could see Rascal. I had infinite calories to burn and no way how. I wasn't allowed to exercise. I didn't even have my gym shoes.

As I lathered shampoo in my hair, a thought popped into my mind: Why not exercise while in the shower? Even though the bathroom door had to remain slightly open while we bathed, there was a curtain that could conceal any activity I did behind it.

I quickly dropped down into the tub and started doing push-ups. Before I knew it, I was jogging in place. The shampoo was getting in my eyes, making them tear, but I didn't care. I was burning calories, and ED was back to being proud of me.

I started brainstorming about where else I might be able to sneak in exercise—the ranch had two floors, so during the day, I could make excuses about why I had to go upstairs to my bedroom, giving me a reason to run up and down the stairs. I could also exercise in bed underneath my comforter during the night between staff check-ins.

"Beatrice?" Dr. Larsen said, knocking on the bathroom door. "You've been in the shower for a while. Are you okay?"

"I'm fine, just finishing up," I said.

Late that night, I started my covert exercise operation. Between the hourly staff check-ins, all through the night, I did hundreds of sit-ups and butt-tightening exercises beneath my blanket.

Over the following week, my evening showers grew longer and longer as I transformed the bathtub into my own personal gym. Any exercise I could do in a sixty-inch space—lunges, squats, calf raises, push-ups—I did.

During the day, I made up all kinds of excuses for why I had to go upstairs—I forgot my sweater in the bedroom, I needed to brush my hair—whatever I could come up with that allowed me to run up and down the stairs.

Staff members occasionally asked us to do errands for them, requests that I had always turned down since I was so bitter about being there, but now I was the first to raise my hand, eager to help. I turned the most mundane errand, like mailing letters in the mailbox in front of the ranch, into an Olympic sporting event, moving my arms up and down as if I was lifting a two-handed barbell in the air.

I began eschewing sitting down when we wrote in our journals in the living room. Instead, I wrote while standing up in the corner. Eventually, I could no longer stay seated during mealtime, claiming my back hurt and that I needed to stand up. I was tempted to jog around the dining room table, but I knew that would draw too much attention and risk exposing my covert exercise operation, which had rapidly become a compulsion.

Whatever exercise I did on one day, I not only felt compelled to do the next, but ED kept telling me I needed to raise the ante and do more and more.

I even partook in an equestrian therapy session, riding a horse, despite hating its smell. Any movement was better than none. It was exercise, after all.

I was in the grips of a severe exercise compulsion, an extension of my eating disorder, until Dr. Larsen appeared at our bedroom door one morning. Emily was at the nurses' station having her feeding tube cleaned out, so I was alone.

"Good morning, Beatrice," she said, stepping inside the room.

"What do you want?" I said.

She didn't respond and walked toward my bed.

"Why are you in here?" I asked.

She pulled back the blanket from my bed, revealing a large egg-shaped circle of sweat on the bottom sheet.

"Your bedsheet is wet," she said.

"So?" I said. "I sweat during the night when I sleep. Some people do."

"That's not why you sweat," she said. "You're exercising through the night. You're also running up and down stairs all day. Your showering time has increased to the point that the skin on your elbows is cracking." She pointed to two small ulcers, on each of my elbows. "Beginning tonight, a staff member will be seated by your bedroom door to ensure you don't exercise at night. You'll only have a bedsheet, no comforter. Showers will take place on alternate days, timed to three minutes. The staff has been instructed that you're barred from doing any errands for them moving forward."

"What is wrong with you, you fucking Nazi!?" I screamed at her. This was something, coming from a Jewish girl like me whose own grandmother had fled the Holocaust. "You micromanage every part of my life. You don't even let me wear shoes. And now, you won't even let me sleep with a blanket!"

"That's right," she calmly said. "For now."

She was doing what was needed to corner ED. Going up against him meant playing a never-ending game of whack-a-mole. He'd always come up with new ways to restrict calories or expend energy. Someone had to be there constantly, boxing him into new corners in a sustained effort to extinguish him. At the time, I was unaware of this and was terrified that Dr. Larsen threatened my ability to burn calories.

"You're just a narcissist that wants everyone to be like her, so they'll be miserable too," I told her.

"This isn't you talking now," she told me. "It's ED. He's pretending to be a comforting friend when he's really a monster trying to destroy you. I'm here to tell him to take a hike until you're strong enough to do it yourself. You may not believe me yet, but one day you'll not only be strong enough, you'll *want* to."

As if, ED told me.

CHAPTER

20

As A PSYCHOLOGIST, I'm trained to observe what isn't said—the unspoken. Because, often, the most important part of a patient's story is what they deliberately or subconsciously leave out.

And there's something I didn't tell Eddie when he asked me to make a list—what Pearl told me this morning. When Mom first arrived in LA, she was relieved to have put New York behind her, but she wouldn't tell Pearl why, not even when Pearl asked her, which was why Pearl was surprised when, years later, Mom decided to return to New York for her college reunion.

Why would Mom have gone to the reunion if she was happy to put New York behind her? I guess, maybe, if enough time had passed, she might've had a change of heart.

But she also told me she was *nervous* before the trip. She said it was because some of her former classmates had gone on to have big theater careers, and she wondered if they'd still have anything in common. But maybe that wasn't the reason. Maybe something happened to her in college that she was worried about revisiting.

When she returned from that trip, I saw her bruised body up close, which she said happened when she was mugged. After that incident, she warned me to stay away from New

York. And I always did because Dad never seemed keen on me going there, either.

After he died, I was supposed to visit for a bachelorette weekend. But when my girlfriend called off her engagement, the weekend was called off too.

What was it about New York that made Mom so nervous about me going there? Did the Cadells try to go after her during the reunion weekend, and she worried they'd target me there if I went to college in the city or ever visited?

That doesn't make sense, though, because if she's still alive, it was her life in LA that she ultimately abandoned. And if she feared the Cadells might come after me, she would've been just as worried about it happening in LA.

Maybe she wasn't worried about something *happening* to me in New York. Maybe she was nervous I'd *discover* something there. Something about her. Something that might end up compromising me . . .

I call several hospitals near NYU to see if they have any medical records of Mom being admitted as a patient after the mugging in 1997. A hospital record might provide more information about what really happened if what she told me wasn't true.

I know it's more than a long shot because of HIPAA laws, which I'm well versed in, but I'm desperate, so I still try. Every hospital employee I speak with tells me that I need to email them her death certificate and my identification as her daughter before they can look into it. Nobody can tell me when or if anyone from the records department will get back to me. Only one young woman even asks for my name and phone number to get back to me.

I know I'd have a better chance of getting answers in person. It's harder to turn people away when they're standing in front of you.

This is why I didn't ask Eddie to put on the list what Pearl told me, because I would've come to the conclusion that

I've reached now: I need to go to the one place Mom warned me to stay away from—New York City.

I book a red-eye flight for tonight and text Eddie to let him know. I also apologize because we were supposed to go to the Four Seasons in Santa Barbara this weekend to celebrate our second anniversary, where we celebrated our first last year. He immediately texts me back not to worry, that we can reschedule our trip, and that he's contacting Paul to see if I can stay with him and Anthony at their apartment in New York.

After a couple of minutes, Eddie calls me.

"I just spoke with Paul. His dad had emergency heart surgery last night in North Carolina, where his parents live. He and Anthony are leaving soon. They've offered to let you stay at their place and can leave you a key with one of their neighbors."

"I think I'll feel more comfortable staying at a hotel," I say. I don't tell him the reason why—that I'll feel safer being around people than in an apartment alone.

"Okay," Eddie says.

"Thanks for asking him," I say, and we hang up.

Since yesterday morning I've gone from sadness to anger to sadness for being put in this situation. Now I'm back to anger again.

If Mom's still alive, finding her is no longer just about warning her that she's in danger. It's about me being able to safely return to my life, which it doesn't seem I'll be able to do until I figure out what's going on. People are following me. I don't even feel safe being in my own home now.

I went through hell after her death and have worked hard to move past it and build a life for myself. And now, because of whatever web she got herself entangled in decades ago, that life is at risk.

I start packing.

CHAPTER

21

B Y THE TIME girls arrived at Better Horizons, their entire lives revolved around their eating disorders. Their days were spent counting calories, obsessively focusing on their weight, measuring every inch of their bodies to see if they had lost or gained weight (at first, they always thought they had gained).

Doing chores allowed them to get back in touch with daily tasks that didn't revolve around ED. The staff was mindful of assigning ones that weren't physically strenuous, like folding laundry, dusting, or throwing out the trash.

Given my recent exercise compulsion, I was assigned the least strenuous task—folding brochures for the treatment center and inserting them into envelopes to be mailed to hospitals and doctors' offices.

Emily was assigned the same chore because she had a feeding tube and needed to exert herself as little as possible. It was bad enough that I had to room with her after she had lied about ratting me out when I tried to run away, not to mention all of her constant digs that I had to suffer through about how she was more committed to ED than me. Now I was forced to sit next to her at the dining room table doing our chores.

While waiting for Dr. Larsen to bring the brochures, Emily was busy doing her daily compulsive body-checking ritual, seeking information or rather confirmation about her slight weight and size. Sometimes she'd feel her collarbones. Other times she'd measure her thighs with the palms of her hands. On this particular day, she placed her fingers around each of her wrists, meticulously checking their circumference to see if her fingers still fit around them with ample room to give.

Dr. Larsen stepped into the dining room with a stack of brochures. "Emily, please take your fingers off your wrists," she told her. Emily dropped her hands to her side.

Dr. Larsen placed the brochures in front of us, took the top sheet off the pile, and laid it flat on the table to show us how she wanted it folded.

"The letterhead is at the top," she said. "Visualize each sheet in thirds, one-third on top, one-third in the middle, and one-third on the bottom. First, you take the bottom third and fold it toward the top—"

"We know how to fold a piece of paper," I cut her off. "My God, it's not that hard." I shook my head angrily. But what I was really enraged about was that she had put a stop to my exercising.

"Okay," she said. "I'll be back in a bit to see how you two are doing."

I rolled my eyes at her as she walked out of the room.

I wanted this over with as quickly as possible to get away from Emily, so I began attacking the pile of papers, folding one sheet after another without stopping while Emily was going at a snail's pace.

"If you don't start helping me, I'm telling Dr. Larsen," I said.

Emily continued moving like a turtle.

"Did you know that folding paper burns calories?" I asked her.

She didn't respond.

"Never mind, don't help me," I told her. "I'll just burn more calories than you."

She looked down, ashamed, realizing I was right, but she was still moving very slowly.

I folded sheet after sheet and was halfway done when I looked over at her. She was still on her first one. Even though I was burning more calories than her, my pent-up resentment boiled over.

"That's it," I said. "I'm getting Dr. Larsen and telling her you're not doing your chore."

"I am . . ." Emily said when her head suddenly thumped down on the table, loudly.

"Jesus Christ," I said. "Now you're pretending to be too tired to fold?"

She didn't respond.

"Emily?"

She still didn't respond.

I tapped her shoulder, but she was unresponsive. I shook her, but still no response. Her eyes were half-closed, and her pupils looked like they had rolled to the back of her head.

"Emily!" I screamed, before running to the nurses' station where Dr. Larsen was.

"Emily passed out," I told her and the nurse.

They both jumped up and ran out as I followed them. The nurse took Emily's vitals.

"Her heart rate is too low. Call an ambulance," she told Dr. Larsen.

When the ambulance arrived, I watched the paramedics lift Emily's body onto a stretcher before whisking her away. The sirens roared down the street until they turned into a faint whisper.

Afterward, I sat back at the dining room table to finish our chore.

Dr. Larsen reappeared. "Are you okay?" she asked me.

"I'm not the one who passed out," I snapped back.

"It must've been scary to see Emily like that."

"Not really," I said. "I'm sure she'll be fine."

"How can you be sure of that?" Dr. Larsen asked.

"Because she's made it this long," I responded.

"It's not a given. I'm not speaking out of turn because Emily already knows this, but she's suffering from heart failure. Her heart no longer pumps blood properly because its walls have thinned and weakened due to long-term anorexia."

"So, what do you want me to do about it?" I asked.

"There's nothing you can do for Emily. But you might want to consider if her path is what you want for your future."

She left the room, and I continued silently folding the brochures. It almost felt like she had disparaged Emily by asking me if I wanted to follow in her footsteps, insinuating her path wasn't one to emulate.

Later that night, I was lying alone in our bedroom. Emily was still at the hospital. A thin sheet covered my body since my comforter had been taken away. Kyle was stationed by the door to ensure I didn't exercise through the night.

I thought again about what Dr. Larsen had asked me, whether I wanted to follow in Emily's footsteps. I hadn't thought about my future since before Mom died, when we'd talked about where I might want to go to college and what I might want to do with my life.

I wondered whether I'd spend the next five years as Emily had. In and out of hospitals and treatment centers. Not allowed to wear shoes or to use a blanket. Not allowed to see my dog or friends. Sleeping and bathing while a guard watched over me.

Before Mom died, I had experienced enough of life to remember being happy and enjoying time with people who loved me. The problem was that life felt so out of reach for someone as broken as me, even though I knew there was another way to exist.

Maybe what Dr. Larsen had said about Emily wasn't disparaging. Maybe she *was* trying to help me.

Maybe she thought I was still worth saving.

CHAPTER

22

THERE'S A RUNNING joke in my eating disorder recovery group that if the apocalypse happened and any one of us was left standing, we'd still find our way back to our weekly meeting—even if we were in tethers, the building was gone, and we had to do it alongside a few zombies.

So I'm here today despite everything that's happened since yesterday morning.

The women in my support group have seen and endured unimaginable things during their recoveries.

After starving herself for five months, Linda was pronounced dead twice when her heart stopped before successfully being resuscitated.

After years of battling ED, Tonya had had enough and was about to kill herself with poison she'd purchased off the dark web when an earthquake struck. But the vial fell, crashing on the ground, convincing her that God didn't want her to die.

After a decade of binging and purging, Jill's parents, who'd always been there for her, finally kicked her out of their house. They changed their locks and called the police to arrest her for trespassing when she tried to return. Left on the streets, without anyone or anything besides ED, she hit rock bottom and turned her life around.

Given their checkered pasts, these women have always remained nonplussed, regardless of any member's revelation, so when I tell them what's happened to me since yesterday morning, what comes out of their mouths is the last thing I expect.

"Holy crap," Linda says.

"That's fucked up," Tonya says.

"It sounds like a movie plot," Jill says.

Their reactions don't make me feel better because this isn't a movie—it's my life.

"Sorry," Linda says, catching herself. "How can we help?"

"I'm leaving for a while until everything gets sorted out," I say.

"Where to?" she asks.

"New York," I say. "A friend invited me to stay with her."

The lie surprises me because it's the first one I've ever told here, but given their reactions to what I just shared, I don't want to tell them that I'm going to New York to chase leads. They'd probably raise concerns for my safety or cast doubts about my plans, and I don't want to hear either.

If Mom is still alive, the only way I see out of this is to find her, warn her that she's in danger, and tell her she needs to disappear again. That way, the people after her won't follow me anymore, and I'll be able to return to my life safely.

"Are you worried about relapsing?" Tonya asks me. "Seems like now's a high-risk time since ED first surfaced after your mom died."

I shake my head. "I don't want to go down that path again."

This is my second lie of the day, or rather not a lie, but I'm withholding something from them, which is its own kind of lie.

I don't mention that yesterday I had trouble eating the mac and cheese at my office or how last night I only ate half of my spaghetti dinner with Eddie and Sarah, or that this morning I skipped breakfast with them and, instead, rushed out to meet Pearl.

Because if I tell them the truth, I know they'll tell me I shouldn't leave, that I need to stay here until I'm more stable. And I have to go.

As I withhold this information from them, I feel ED, a cunning, sleeping giant, begin to awaken, stretching out his elongated tentacles in the air.

In recovery, it's said that we have the *clock*, proudly counting and tracking the days, months, and years since we last restricted—while ED has the *time*. All the time in the world to wait for a crack, an opening, however long it might take, and to pounce again.

23

February 1998

S EVERAL DAYS HAD passed since Emily had been whisked away in an ambulance from Better Horizons to the hospital. The days blended, and I didn't notice her absence until the nights when I was lying alone in my bed in our room.

This particular day began like all the others. It was morning, and the girls lined up at the nurses' station for their daily blind weigh-ins, meaning we got on the scale and turned around so our backs faced it, and we couldn't see the number.

One of the diagnostic criteria for anorexia is fear of gaining weight. Seeing the number on the scale go up can cause enormous distress and subsequent resistance to eating.

After the nurse weighed us, she administered medication to the girls who required it—mood stabilizers, vitamins, bone density meds for girls like Emily who suffered from osteoporosis. She always checked the inside of their mouths to ensure they hadn't secretly hidden any pills underneath their tongues to spit out later.

Then we headed to the dining room for breakfast, where Dr. Larsen was already seated. "Today is cooking day," she announced.

We all groaned. Cooking is a minefield for those recovering from an eating disorder. ED's rules stop sufferers from cooking and eating what they want. Instead, they focus on how to get away with eating as little as possible and, ideally, staying away from food altogether.

"Iris will lead our cooking session today," Dr. Larsen told us. "After you finish breakfast, please go to the kitchen. She's waiting for all of you there."

"Since I'm not eating, I don't have to cook," I announced, lifting the Ensure bottle in my hand.

"Everyone has to cook, whether you're eating food or not," Dr. Larsen told me.

I rolled my eyes at her and took another sip of my chocolate cardboard-tasting shake.

After breakfast, we filed into the kitchen. Every cupboard was locked and childproofed to prevent girls from hiding pieces of food. I had a flashback to home when I hid snacks Dad gave me inside the piano bench. I wondered if he'd ever found them or if they were still there.

"Today, we're making chili for lunch," Iris told us. It was a smart choice because liquid food, like soups and smoothies, is hard to hide. She had all the ingredients laid out on a giant island in the middle of the kitchen.

"Before we brown the meat inside the pots, we need to add things to it," she said, motioning to the ingredients. She pointed to one of the girls. "Please add the olive oil."

She handed her a measuring cup filled with oil to add to the pot. The girl took it, terrified, as if the calories inside were contagious. She quickly tossed the oil inside and handed the measuring cup back to Iris.

As more girls tossed more ingredients inside, my anxiety rose because the ingredients were rapidly running out. I was most worried about being asked to stir the meat, worried about the steam hitting my face, worried about its calories.

"Beatrice," Iris said.

"What?" I asked.

"Time to stir the meat."

Fuck, fuck, fuck.

She turned on the burner. I watched the orange-blue flame ignite below the pot.

"I'm not comfortable doing that," I said.

"Why not?" she asked.

"I'm scared of getting burned," I told her.

"I'll lower the heat, and you can stand a foot away. There's no risk at all," she said.

"I don't want to do it."

"It's not a choice," she reminded me, knowing the real reason why I didn't want to stir the meat. "You don't overcome your fear of being inside an elevator by avoiding riding it. You get over it by riding the elevator over and over again." She handed me the spatula and stepped away.

ED was all over me as I moved closer to the stove with the spatula.

"You didn't have to take it from her, you stupid, worthless cow. You say you're devoted to me, but you ate a hamburger and fries just to see your dumb dog. And now you're cooking! I'm done with you, and once I'm gone, you'll have NOBODY!" he screamed.

With my back facing Iris, I covertly placed the palm of my right hand on the side of the burner until I heard my skin sizzle and crackle.

"AHHH!" I screamed.

"What's wrong?" Iris asked, walking up to me.

I removed my palm from the burner. A large throbbing white blister had already formed on the top layer of my seared skin. As painful as it was, I felt relief too, knowing I wouldn't have to stir the meat.

Iris stood there, horrified, fully aware this was no accident.

"I need to go to the nurses' station," I told her.

As the nurse bandaged my palm, Dr. Larsen appeared by the door. "When you finish here, please come to my office," she said.

"You won't be able to use this hand for at least a week," the nurse instructed me.

Good, I thought. *That means I won't have to do Dr. Larsen's stupid journal writing assignments.*

When I was done being bandaged up, I dutifully walked to Dr. Larsen's office next door, where she was seated at her desk.

"Please take a seat," she told me. "And close the door behind you."

I did as she asked and sat on a chair across from her.

"Emily is supposed to return tonight," she said.

"I told you she'd be fine," I muttered.

"We're thinking of moving you to another room and having you share one with a staff member instead," she said.

"Why?" I asked.

"You just engaged in an act of self-harm. That requires a higher level of care."

"But that's not fair! I only did it because I didn't want to stir the meat. I *told* Iris I didn't want to. The smell was making me nauseous. But she didn't listen to me and made me do it anyway," I said.

"I think you were worried it would make you gain weight," Dr. Larsen said.

I didn't say anything for a long while. "I don't like being here," I finally said. "I want to go home."

"You may not believe me, but I want that for you too, Beatrice," she said.

It was bad enough having someone guarding the door while I slept, and it's not that I even liked Emily, who was always in my grill about being more committed to ED than I was, but the idea of sharing a room with a staffer sounded

awful. My every move would be scrutinized even more than
it already was.

"Will you give me another chance to room with Emily?"
I asked Dr. Larsen.

"You'll need to sign a no-harm contract," she said.

"Fine."

"But if you engage in another act of self-harm, you won't
get another chance, and you'll be placed with a staffer."

"Anything else?" I asked.

"Yes, you're also going to have to eat one meal of food a
day, no liquid supplementation, starting today," she said.

Fuck. How was I going to get out of this?

Kick the can down the road, ED told me.

"It's been a rough day. How about tomorrow?" I asked.

"Today," she said.

Bitch, I thought. But I was cornered and had no other
choice.

"Fine," I said.

That night at dinner, Emily returned from the hospital.
A kitchen staffer brought out my dinner—meatloaf, mashed
potatoes, vegetables, and a chocolate chip cookie for dessert.
I stared at the food, ED screaming at me not to eat it, but I
had to if I wanted to avoid rooming with a staffer.

I looked up from my plate and saw Emily with her feeding tube staring at me, wondering if I was going to eat. She
probably wondered if I'd been eating the entire time she was
gone.

I picked up my fork with my right hand, forgetting the
burn. "Ow," I said. My palm immediately started to throb
again. I just wanted this over with, so I could leave. I moved
the fork to my left hand and started eating. After I finished, I
left one tiny bite on my plate to let ED know I had tried not
to eat it all.

"There's still food left on your plate," Dr. Larsen said.

"It's normal not to finish every bite," I said.

"Not when ED is telling you not to finish it," she responded.

"I'm full and listening to my hunger cues. Ever thought of that?" I asked.

"But it isn't that," she dug in.

"It's one fucking bite!" I shouted.

"If I were an oncologist, I wouldn't let one bite of cancer remain," she said, sounding more like she was trying to convince herself why she needed to follow through with me. It was an unenviable, arduous task to be a shock absorber for all of ED's venom.

A civil war was brewing inside of me. If I didn't eat the last bite, I'd be forced to share a room with a staffer, which would be hell. If I ate it, ED would never let me live it down.

I looked up from the plate and stared out the large bay window behind Dr. Larsen. The sun was setting behind the Santa Monica mountains, turning the vast skies orange and pink.

I looked back down at the last tiny bite of food on my plate. The open skies lied. My world had slowly and all at once shrunk into a crumb. I quickly shoved it into my mouth and got up from the table.

Later that night, Emily and I were in our beds as Kyle sat stationed at our door. She turned to me. "So you're back on food?"

It was another dig to let me know I was lesser than her because she was still fiercely committed to only getting food through a feeding tube.

"I have to eat one meal a day, or they threatened to make me share a room with a staffer," I explained.

"Oh," she said, considering what this might mean for her. She quickly changed the subject. "It went well at the hospital. I know I lost weight because I heard the doctor and nurses talking about it."

I ignored her, turning away, lifting the thin bed sheet over my body, wishing I had a comforter I could hide underneath, not to exercise, but just to get away from her.

"Well?" she pressed.

I sat up and faced her. "What do you want?" I asked. "A prize?

She didn't respond.

I turned away from her again, facing the window next to my bed, hoping she'd finally leave me alone.

"You don't have to be such a bitch," she said.

Those were her last words to me.

They were her last words at all.

The following morning, she didn't wake up.

First the nurse tried to resuscitate her, then various staff members and an EMT. When the police finally arrived at the scene, they called in a 10-45D code—the patient was deceased.

As I watched the officers lift her lifeless body onto a gurney, I was in shock. Despite her deteriorated physical condition and Dr. Larsen's warning, I hadn't thought she'd really die.

As they covered her body with a white sheet, I thought about my mom. All the times I had imagined her dead body being lifted off the concrete after the car hit her, desperately wishing I had been there to say one final goodbye.

I started to cry.

Dr. Larsen and the nurse were standing nearby with tears in their eyes. They tried to comfort me but had to turn their attention to the officers. Instructions were given about getting Emily's body downstairs so it could be transported to the local coroner's office for an autopsy and who would call Emily's parents to deliver the devastating news.

After everyone left the room, I sat alone on Emily's bed and picked up her feeding tube that had been removed during the unsuccessful attempts to resuscitate her.

I wondered what she would've thought about what had happened. And I realized she would've been proud. It would've been the ultimate confirmation that she had won her coveted title. It turned out the best anorexic was the dead one.

CHAPTER

24

I HAVEN'T BEEN BACK to my old house in the Fairfax district of Los Angeles since I moved out ten years ago. When we divorced, Jay bought me out. His parents helped him because he loved this place and didn't want to leave. I, on the other hand, couldn't wait to take my money and run from my painful memories here.

We haven't been in touch since, but a few years ago, I heard through a mutual colleague that he had remarried and has a couple of kids. At the time, I was heartbroken, thinking how I'd been too sick to go on that journey with him.

When I ring the doorbell, I hear a child crying inside. Despite knowing he has kids now, I somehow hadn't expected this and am tempted to run away. But I wouldn't be here unless I had no other choice.

Jay, as my mother did, specializes in treating addiction. When we were in graduate school together, he did a deep-dive research report in his psychopharmacology class about the opiate overdose crisis. He knows more than anyone about TriCPharma and the Cadell family. And before I leave for New York, I want to be as clear-eyed as possible about what I'm up against.

He opens the door with a crying toddler boy in his arms and a girl who looks around five years old wrapped around his left leg.

"Uh . . . hi," he says. His face is whatever's after shocked to see me.

"I'm sorry for showing up unannounced," I say. "It's an emergency."

The little boy in his arms wails louder.

"Can you give me a second? Barbara is out of town—" He catches himself, realizing I don't know who Barbara is. "I'm alone with the kids."

I don't know how to respond other than to ask, "Can I help?"

"It's okay, just give me a sec."

He carts the crying boy away and drags the girl, who still won't let go of his leg, into our former living room. He turns on *Peppa Pig* on a mounted television screen that didn't exist when I lived here. Peppa seems to do her magic because the kids are quickly and quietly transfixed.

He returns to the front door. "What's going on?" he asks me.

I tell him everything. He's the first person I've told, including Eddie, Pearl, and my recovery group, that doesn't look shocked—not even at the prospect that my mom might still be alive.

"You don't look surprised," I say.

"TriCPharma is a crime syndicate operation, so no. If your mom somehow got caught up in the Cadells' crosshairs, I get why she would've had to disappear. You and your dad would've been in danger too. Faking a death is a bit . . . extreme, but it's not unheard of."

This was Pearl's hunch too—that if Mom left, she had to do it for us.

"But was this an issue in the nineties?" I ask him.

"The Cadells started working on perfecting their drugs in the seventies, but it took them a couple of decades to carry enough weight at the FDA to pay off officials there to get their drugs to the masses. The first wave of prescription overdoses didn't begin until the nineties," he says.

I nod, taking in the information.

"Their only goal was to make money. Anyone who got in their way wasn't safe. And they've only become more ruthless and dangerous through the years, infiltrating the government at the highest levels, paying off senators and governors to look away."

Oh my God. How is this even possible?

"How?" I ask.

"Through campaign contributions. They also use witness intimidation to prevent people from testifying against them in Congress. A colleague of mine testified in DC a couple of months ago before the Feds filed their current charges against the Cadell brothers, William Jr. and his younger brother, Quentin. He now has to wear an armored vest to work and change his route to his office daily to avoid being followed by them."

This must be why Cristina told me to stay away from the FBI and the police. If the Cadells have figured out how to infiltrate the US government, they've probably gotten to law enforcement too. For all I know, the detective that showed up at my office yesterday trying to find out information about her is working for them too. My stomach turns.

I think about Cristina's text, how she said she's being framed for her mother's death, and how Eddie said that Paul mentioned her mom was a pharmaceutical rep for TriCPharma long before marrying her father, William Cadell Jr.

"Do you know anything about the TriCPharma sales reps?" I ask Jay.

He nods. "The Cadells lied to them, telling them they were selling drugs that could give people in chronic pain their lives back, failing to mention patients could become easily addicted. They also lured reps in with parties and money. Reps who sold higher doses of their drugs got bigger bonuses."

Maybe Cristina's mom learned about this after she married William Cadell Jr., and they were worried about her speaking out?

"They got some doctors on board with monetary bribes and lies too," Jay continues. "When these doctors' patients became addicted to TriCPharma drugs and begged for more prescriptions, some doctors behaved unethically—some even traded sex with patients in exchange for more pills. And the good doctors who tried to speak out against the dangers of TriCPharma drugs were threatened, and their families were harassed, so they stopped."

My mouth goes dry. My palms feel sweaty. It may be too dangerous for me to pursue this. Maybe I should let the criminal justice system try to work. There are charges against the Cadell brothers now. Maybe, for once, justice will prevail against this family. But I also know that courts move slowly—not quickly enough to help save Mom if she's still alive and the Cadells are after her.

"Do you know what's happening with the current charges?" I ask Jay.

"My buddy that testified told me that for the first time, the Feds have incriminating emails acknowledging that the family knew their drugs were addictive, which in theory should be a big deal. But, sadly, I don't have a lot of hope."

"Why not?"

"Historically, the government has squashed prosecutors who try to go up against TriCPharma. They've always allowed the Cadells, both the brothers and their father, when he was still alive, to settle by making them pay small fines, giving the false illusion of justice when it's less than a slap on the hand for these guys."

As he's speaking, I realize something isn't adding up. If the Cadells have influence over officials at the highest levels of government and have been able to get every lawsuit ever brought against them effectively tossed, why would they care about my mother, a random woman who supposedly died decades ago?

"If the Feds have concrete evidence that TriCPharma knew its drugs were addictive, why would the Cadell brothers care about my mom?" I ask Jay. "Even if she's still alive, what could she possibly know that would top that?"

"Maybe it isn't something she knows," he says. "Maybe it's something she *did*. She might've crossed someone in that family, and they're out for retribution."

"But in college?" I ask. "She was a theater major in the Village. What kind of trouble could she have possibly gotten into involving TriCPharma back then?"

"Maybe it wasn't during college. Maybe it was after, like you said, with her patient Margot Cadell. It doesn't matter when it happened. If your mom did something to piss them off, they won't stop until they find her. She's a loose end that needs to be tied up. And just because she got away before doesn't mean she'll be able to this time."

He bites his lip awkwardly, like he wants to say something but isn't sure how.

"What is it?" I ask.

"I'm not sure what your situation is . . . your personal situation."

He's referring to whether I'm with anyone, like he is, married with kids.

"If you have anyone special in your life you care about, and you pursue trying to find your mom, you won't be the only one at risk. They'll be too."

I feel my face go white. "But . . . not if I keep my distance from them, right? I've already planned to stay away until all this is over."

Jay shakes his head. "The Cadells have a history of going after families, Beans. They'll stop at nothing to get what they want."

25

February 1998

T HE NIGHT EMILY died, I tossed and turned in my bed, unable to sleep. Something was stirring inside me, a sense of unease that I couldn't pinpoint.

Kyle was still stationed at our bedroom door to ensure I didn't exercise through the night. I finally sat up in bed and asked him, "Can I call my dad?"

When Dr. Larsen asked me earlier in the day if I wanted to call Dad with the news of Emily's passing, I'd said no, because I wasn't sure how he would react. A part of me worried that if he found out, he might use her death against me in the future to remind me that if I didn't eat, I could end up like her.

But now, something was beginning to bubble up inside me, and I felt the need to call him.

"It's after hours," Kyle said. "But you've been through a lot today. Come with me."

I got out of bed and followed him into the nurses' station in my pajamas. He picked up the receiver from the phone on the wall and handed it to me. I dialed Dad.

"Hel-lo," Dad answered, clearing his voice. My call had woken him.

"Daddy?" I said.

"Beans? Are you okay?" he asked, now sounding very alert and worried.

"My roommate died." I sounded more like a scared little girl than a defiant ED patient.

"Oh . . . I'm so sorry." His voice wobbled and he coughed, clearly trying to cover his fear.

"Thanks," I said, my voice cracking.

"You've had to deal with so much loss," he said.

He was right about that.

"Are you okay, Beans?" he asked.

"I'm not sure," I said, honestly, for once.

Since ED had gotten a hold of me, he had done an excellent job of repeatedly reminding me how worthless and horrible I was, so much so that I'd begun to believe that's why Mom had been taken away from me. I'd also started to think nobody would care if I vanished into thin air, that it didn't matter if I died.

But Emily's death struck something deep inside me, igniting a life force that had been dormant for many months. A reminder that maybe I didn't want to die.

ED could threaten to abandon me and tell me I would have nobody if I didn't listen to him. But what he couldn't do was guarantee that I wouldn't die if I continued following his orders because, now, I had concrete proof that I could. My roommate had died. She was gone forever and never coming back, just like my mom.

"The thing is . . . I'm scared of dying," I told Dad.

"I'm scared of that too," he said, trying to muffle his cries. "I love you so much."

"I love you too." This time, I meant it. It wasn't a manipulation ED had masterminded to help get me out of Better Horizons. It had just slipped out, unconsciously, like old times.

Dr. Larsen appeared at the door of the nurses' station. "Are you okay, Beatrice?" she asked me.

"I'm talking to my dad," I said.

"I'm glad," she said. "I'll be waiting in your bedroom after you finish."

After I hung up with Dad, I walked back to the room. She was there, sitting on Emily's bed.

"How was your call?" she asked.

"Okay, I guess," I said.

"I want you to know that I'm really glad you're here," she told me.

It was an incredibly generous thing to say, given how abysmal my behavior toward her had been, and I didn't understand why she had said it.

"Why?" I asked her. "I'm not a particularly nice or good person, especially to you."

"I think you're a good person who's been through a lot," she said.

"Thanks," I said, unconvinced.

"I also think the world is better with you in it. You may not believe it because of all the lies ED has told you, but I know one day you will."

I slid into my bed and lifted the thin sheet over my body. "Can I have my blanket back?" I asked her.

"Not yet," she said. "It's not because I don't trust you. It's ED I don't trust. For now, I need to keep you safe from him."

"Okay."

Unlike before, I wasn't angry with her. Something had shifted. If I wanted to live, I would need her help. For the first time since I'd arrived at Better Horizons, her intervening felt like a relief.

CHAPTER

26

I CALLED EDDIE BEFORE going to his place tonight to say
goodbye to Sarah and him, wondering if it was safe for me
to do. He let me know Paul had a colleague from the Bureau
dispatched to his house for protection.

As I pass the agent dressed in uniform, I weakly smile at
him before knocking on Eddie's door. Even though none of
this is my fault, I can't help but feel guilty that I've unwittingly dragged Sarah and him into this mess. At least they
have someone watching over them now.

"Hi," Eddie says, opening the door. "I saved you salmon
and rice for dinner."

"I already ate," I lie.

For most people, it doesn't feel good when they're hungry
and haven't eaten for an extended period. But for someone like
me, who's suffered or is suffering from anorexia, it does. That's
the rub of it all and one of the many dangers of the disease.

It finally made sense to me when researchers discovered
genetic markers associated with anorexia a few years ago,
including one that has to do with how a person's body metab-
olizes fat. It turns out that those of us who are prone to this
disease metabolize fats differently. For this reason, it's now
considered a metabolic psychiatric disorder.

Despite how hard it was seeing Jay with his two small children in our old home, and getting confirmation that by being around Eddie and Sarah, I could be putting them in danger, the warm buzz I felt when I left his house—the one that comes from not having eaten all day, the one I haven't felt in nearly a decade, since I was pregnant—helped blunt my sadness.

"Do you think it's safe for you to go to New York?" Eddie asks me now. He looks worried.

"I'll be in a city with nine million people and cameras on every street corner," I say, trying to reassure him.

We're not having the real conversation, which involves acknowledging I'm out of good options. If I stay here, it's not safe for any of us. And if I go to New York, I'll likely be at risk there too. And there's a larger issue—when, if ever, will any of this be resolved, and what does that mean for the three of us?

Instead, we're dancing around it, the way human beings do when they're trying to run away from a difficult truth.

Sarah appears in the living room dressed in her pajamas. "I brushed my teeth," she says. "I'm ready for bed. Will you tuck me in?"

"Sure," Eddie says.

"No, I meant Beans," she says.

Usually, anytime Sarah brings me into the fold, Eddie lights up, but tonight he doesn't. His face is only worry.

"Why don't we both tuck you in?" I say.

She nods. "Okay."

We follow her through the hallway to her room. She gets in bed, and we sit next to her. She asks me to read from Shel Silverstein's *Where the Sidewalk Ends*. Eddie's been reading her a poem a night from the collection.

I open the book to where they last left off and read *Smart*, a poem about a boy whose father gives him a one-dollar bill that he keeps trading for coins until he proudly ends up with five pennies, thinking they're worth more than the single dollar his dad had first given him.

"But five cents is less than a dollar," Sarah says, turning to Eddie. "Why's his dad proud of him?"

"Because he's his child," Eddie explains, and kisses Sarah on her forehead.

"Love you," she says.

"Love you more," he says.

"Love you too," I blurt out.

Eddie looks at me, surprised. It's the first time I've ever said it to Sarah, even though it's what I've long felt deep inside me. I say it now because I don't know what tomorrow will bring, but what I do know is what I think my mom knew too—she never wanted to leave any doubt in my mind about how much she loved me.

The last time she told me she loved me, it was a regular school day morning. But when I went into the kitchen for breakfast, she wasn't there to greet me with her cup of coffee in hand like she usually did. Dad was there instead.

"Where's Mom?" I asked.

"She's not feeling well," he told me. "I'm taking you to school today." Mom was the one who usually dropped me off at school on her way to work.

"What's wrong?"

"She has a stomachache."

After eating, I went to their bedroom to say goodbye to her and heard her throwing up in the bathroom.

"Are you okay, Mom?" I asked, standing in front of the bathroom door.

"I'm fine," she said. "Just have an upset stomach."

"I wanted to say goodbye before Dad takes me to school."

"One minute," she said.

I sat on their bed, waiting. She took a long time, and I started to worry she might be sicker than Dad had let on. When she finally appeared, she looked like a shell of herself.

Her face was ashen, and she was clutching her stomach in distress.

"Maybe I shouldn't go to school today," I said. "I think someone should stay here to be with you in case you need anything."

"I'll be fine," she told me. "It's important for you to go to school . . . and live your life." She struggled to get the words out.

When she hugged me, I saw the tears in her eyes.

"Were you crying?" I asked.

She shook her head. "No, I just don't feel well."

"I'm sorry."

She hugged me tightly. "You know how much I love you, right?"

"Yes."

When I pulled out of the embrace, I could tell she was having trouble letting go. I wondered if I should stay and be with her despite her telling me not to.

"Good luck with your test today. You'll do great," she said. "Remember, I love you."

"I know," I said. "I love you too."

Now, Sarah hugs me, pulling me out of my memory.

"Love you too, Beans," she says.

Eddie looks at us both with a pained smile.

And, like that, we all say goodbye.

PART II
Case History

The art of clinical diagnosis lies in the ability to ask the right questions.

—Harriet B. Braiker

27

T HE SKY IS painted black and sprinkled with white stars.
With Mom's death certificate tucked into my purse and her lima bean charm bracelet dangling on my wrist, I roll my carry-on suitcase out of my house.

When I lock the door and turn around, I find Detective Thompson standing on the street next to my car.

"Going somewhere?" he asks me.

I stare at him, unsure of how to respond.

"What do you want?" I ask levelly.

"I think you already know," he says.

We both stay silent. I consider telling him that Cristina texted me that she's being framed for her mom's murder. If he's working for the Cadells, it won't be anything he doesn't already know. And if he isn't, maybe it'll send him on a path to finding her mother's real killers, who also may be after Mom.

"Cristina told me she's innocent," I finally say.

He looks surprised. I'm unsure if it's because yesterday morning I refused to speak with him about her, citing patient confidentiality, or if it's because of what I've just told him.

"She says she's being framed. So if nobody's bought you out yet, you're being played," I tell him.

"Bought me out?" He looks confused. It might be an act, but it seems genuine.

"I think her mother knew something that the Cadells didn't want to get out, so they made her disappear. If they haven't gotten to you yet, they're using you to frame Cristina," I say.

He bristles. He seems like the kind of guy that doesn't take well to the idea of being used.

"Careful, doc," he says. "Stay in your lane."

"I'm leaving," I say, tossing my suitcase in the trunk of my car.

"Where to?" he asks.

"If you need to reach me, I'm sure you'll figure out a way to find me again."

I turn on the engine and drive to the airport.

* * *

I'm seated by the window and look out of the airplane window. I pull my phone out of my bag to let Eddie know we're about to take off—and discover two new texts from a number I don't recognize:

She isn't who you think she is.

Get off the plane . . . or you'll regret it.

My cheeks flush as adrenaline courses through my veins.

Cristina? Is this you? I quickly text back.

Message undeliverable.

Cristina has never used a threatening tone with me before. Not to mention she's been telling me to do the opposite— find my mother as quickly as possible—because she's running out of time. This text doesn't sound like Cristina.

Did the detective send this? I knew it was a risk disclosing what Cristina told me about her mother, especially if he's working for the Cadells. But he didn't seem like he was, which means whoever sent this is someone else. Someone working for the Cadells. Maybe the people who went after

Cristina's mom. Maybe the same people who broke into my car last week when I was with Sarah. They want me to disembark from the plane.

I look around, trying to figure out whether whoever's following me is a fellow passenger, but I can only see a few rows of seats in front of me and a couple of rows behind me. And no one is looking up. Everyone's glued to their phones, except for a man that's already passed out with a dark blue eye mask on, an older woman who appears to be having a panic attack that a flight attendant is trying to talk her through, and a three-year-old boy having a tantrum whose young mom is desperately trying to get him to stay in his seat.

I want to call Eddie and tell him about the text. But I know how worried he was about me leaving for New York, and this will only worry him more. At least I can take some comfort knowing he and Sarah are safe with Paul's colleague from the Bureau posted at their front door.

I take out my phone, staring at the text again:

She isn't who you think she is.

Get off the plane . . . or you'll regret it.

Someone's nervous about me going to New York and discovering something—something they don't want me to know.

"Flight attendants, please prepare for takeoff," the captain's voice thunders from the airplane's speakers as the plane begins to glide. Guess I'm not going anywhere.

As we coast down the runway and climb up into the night sky, I look down at the City of Angels, a web of flickering lights connecting freeways and dreams, wondering when—or if—I'll be able to return home again.

28

March 1998

THREE DAYS AFTER Emily died, my new roommate arrived. Given what I had gone through, Dr. Larsen asked me if I wanted to change rooms, which would have meant sharing a room with a staff member since there were no beds available in any of the other girls' rooms. While I was no longer opposed to the idea for fear of being micromanaged, I didn't want to change rooms, which meant I was getting a new roommate.

It was early in the morning when the new girl arrived, carrying a small dark green duffel bag into our room. She was fourteen years old and wasn't underweight. She had previously been considered "overweight" by medical professionals who used the BMI calculator to assess her, and she had lost thirty pounds in the four months before her admittance.

Because of this, she was diagnosed with "atypical" anorexia. Atypical anorexia is, in fact, not atypical at all. In the nineties, there was even less awareness than there is now that eating disorders affect people of all shapes and sizes, all genders, all races, and from all socioeconomic backgrounds.

"Hi, I'm Beans," I told her.

"Amanda," she said, plopping down on her new bed. Emily's old one.

"We need to go downstairs for breakfast," I said.

"Oh, I'm not eating," she said.

"You still have to go. They'll give you Ensure," I explained.

"What if I refuse that?" she asked me.

"Then you'll end up with a feeding tube," I said.

Her eyes briefly lit up, excited about the prospect.

"The girl here before you also had a feeding tube," I said.

"Why did she leave?" she asked.

"She died of heart failure," I said.

She looked at me, uneasy, as Dr. Larsen appeared at our door. "Have you two had a chance to meet each other?" she asked.

"Yes," I said.

Amanda quietly nodded, still taking in what I had just told her.

"Please come down for breakfast," Dr. Larsen said.

I left the room, and Amanda followed, her footsteps behind me, walking down the stairs. We got to the dining room and took our seats.

The staff started carrying our breakfasts from the kitchen. Iris brought Amanda a plate of waffles with syrup and berries. Amanda opened her mouth, about to say something. I thought she would ask for Ensure, but she stopped herself.

As the meal progressed, I could tell she was struggling to eat breakfast. I recognized her discomfort as my own, wincing each time she swallowed. But she ate the food.

That night when we were getting ready for bed, she turned to me.

"Did the last girl really die, or did you make it up so that I would eat today?"

"What?" I ask, confused, taken aback that she thought I'd made up Emily's death.

"Are you happy because I'm bigger than you, and you want to make sure it stays that way?" Amanda asked me.

"No," I said.

"Everyone at school used to call me A-minivan-da. Not anymore," she said, determined never to let a hurt like that come her way again. A hurt that had given ED the chance to infiltrate her body and soul.

"The girl's name was Emily, and she died while sleeping in that bed," I said, pointing to Amanda's new bed.

Amanda quietly took it in. "That's fucked up," she finally said.

I nodded in agreement.

During the rest of her stay, Amanda never refused any meals she was given, never asked for liquid supplementation, and never ended up on a feeding tube. She also never asked to be switched out of our room, despite learning that Emily had died in her bed. Maybe the healthy voice inside of her knew she needed to stay there as a reminder of her fate if she didn't put up a fight against ED.

Emily's legacy turned out to be not the one ED had envisioned. Her premature death had lessened his grip over another one of his victims. Not just Amanda's, but mine too.

Emily had saved me once when she told on me after I ran away. Now she had saved me again.

29

Day Three

I'VE SPENT THE last five hours in my airplane seat, hyper-alert, with my overhead light turned on. But nothing's happened, and no additional texts have come through.

Staring out the window, I watch the sun rise on a blanket of white clouds. Night turning into day. Every time I think about who or what awaits me in the Big Apple, my stomach turns.

I pull out my phone to text Eddie to let him know I'll be landing soon, but he's beaten me to the punch.

Paul just texted me. Change of plans.

His mom asked them to visit this weekend instead after his dad is out of the hospital.

He'll pick you up curbside. Stay with him and Anthony.

Blue Prius, plate #: ZB31256.

I breathe a sigh of relief. I won't be alone in New York after all.

I start texting Eddie back to thank him when a flight attendant loudly wheels a cart filled with food down the aisle.

"Pancakes or omelet?" she asks the passenger seated next to me.

"Pancakes," he says.

She removes a sheet of tin foil from a tray, letting out a small cloud of steam, and hands the food to the man who rips open a white plastic package of syrup that he uses to douse three mini pancakes and an overcooked sausage link.

She turns to me, "What'll it be, pancakes or omelet?"

Since Cristina Cadell blew into my office forty-six hours ago, I've eaten a frozen Amy's Mac & Cheese meal, half a plate of spaghetti and meatballs with Eddie and Sarah, and one protein bar. I've also drunk one Diet Coke and several cups of black coffee.

When I first started restricting as a fifteen-year-old, I drank *a lot* of coffee—black coffee. It made my stomach feel fuller, helped suppress my hunger pains, and the caffeine kept my body functioning without food. Among anorexics, coffee is considered a "free" food because as long as you don't add sugar or milk, it has little to no calories.

Over the last couple of days, whenever the healthy voice in my head has been there, reminding me that I can't solely subside on black coffee and that I have to eat real food, ED has also been there quick to rationalize why I can't: *You're too busy. Things are so chaotic now. How could you possibly eat with the stress you're under?*

"So what'll it be?" the flight attendant asks me again.

"Coffee, black," I say.

"The drink cart's separate," she says. "You'll have to wait."

Even better, ED tells me.

30

March 1998

WE WERE ALL seated outside on the deck at Better Horizons. Girls who had eaten real food were allowed to take timed walks around the ranch. Even though I had started eating food, I still wasn't allowed to walk because of my previous exercise compulsion.

I was seated on a bench next to Dr. Larsen. In an unexpected turn, ever since Emily's death, she had become a touchstone of comfort for me.

"I wanted to let you know that we're going out to eat tonight," she told me.

I immediately felt anxiety starting to rise in my body. It had been hard enough to eat real food consistently, even though I knew I needed to if I wanted to avoid Emily's fate, but the prospect of going to a restaurant felt like a bridge too far.

A bunch of ED thoughts began flooding my mind— the main one was that I needed to quickly come up with an excuse for why I couldn't go. Maybe I was feeling sick or still struggling because of Emily's death.

It was so exhausting living with ED's voice in my head, which at times seemed to merge with mine, a voice I worried would one day completely take over, from which I might no longer be able to discern my own. Sometimes I even put my hands over my ears, trying to shut him out.

The anxiety kept rising. I felt like I couldn't breathe. Air was difficult to get into my lungs. I was having a panic attack when Dr. Larsen put her hand on my shoulder.

"Are you okay?" she asked me.

I nodded, even though I wasn't.

"If it's too difficult for you to eat at the restaurant tonight, just come with us and sit at the table," she said. "That in itself will be a success."

"I don't think I can go," I told her.

"I understand," she said. "But remember, you won't be alone."

Her words gave me enough courage to go. But as soon as I got to the restaurant and the smells of pizza dough, fries, and burgers hit me, ED began his usual lies, telling me I was breathing in the calories and what a gigantic failure I was for even agreeing to go.

"What'll it be?" a young waitress with two brown pigtails asked me.

"A slice of pepperoni pizza and a brownie," I said.

"We don't have brownies, but we've got chocolate lava cake," she said.

"Okay," I said.

After all the girls had ordered, I began a countdown, waiting for the food to arrive, both exhilarated and terrified.

But when the slice of pizza finally arrived, I sat there paralyzed in fear, unable to eat it.

"I feel like such a failure," I told Dr. Larsen, staring at the slice.

"You're not a failure. You're sitting in a *restaurant*, which is a major accomplishment. I'm proud of you," she said, taking my hand.

With this small act of love and grace, I felt ED's power over me loosen a bit in real time.

"Maybe try taking one bite instead of focusing on eating the entire thing," she suggested.

I took a deep breath, picked up the slice, and took a small bite off its triangular end.

"I just imagined ED melting into a puddle of water," Dr. Larsen said, smiling.

I smiled back.

Even though I didn't finish the whole slice that night, and I didn't eat any of the lava cake, it was the first time I had consciously stood up to ED during my stay at Better Horizons. I didn't yet know that the more I did it, the less difficult it would become.

31

THE PLANE SPEEDS down the runway as if it might never stop and then screeches to an abrupt halt. We taxi for a bit before parking at the gate. When the lights turn on, passengers begin to remove their luggage from overhead bins and line up in the aisle to disembark.

I drank two cups of black coffee during the flight and desperately need to use the restroom. An image suddenly flashes through my mind of being pinned inside an airport bathroom stall by whoever sent me the threatening text.

I still don't know whether they're on the plane or not. If they are, they will undoubtedly follow me off. And I only have one goal now—to make it to Paul's car safely.

I look around, calculating what to do. I decide to follow the mother of the unruly toddler a few rows behind me. I bet she'll need to make a pit stop with him, and if someone's following me it'll be more challenging for them to be inconspicuous around a three-year-old and a young mom.

I remain seated until she and her son make their way into the aisle and then get up and follow them off the plane. Sure enough, she ducks into the first bathroom she passes, pulling the little boy by his hand, who doesn't want to go inside but relents.

I follow them in and use the stall right next to them. When I finish, I look underneath the divider and see their feet. The boy is whining and protesting using the toilet, until he finally does, and they exit.

We stand side-by-side at a row of sinks. The boy doesn't want his hands washed and throws another fit, legs and arms everywhere like a belligerent octopus. The mother looks at me apologetically.

"It was a long flight," she says.

"It was," I agree.

He won't comply, so she takes out a small bottle of anti-bacterial hand sanitizer and squirts a dab of the liquid onto the top of his pointer finger. He starts dabbing the gel on the side of the sink like it's finger paint until she takes his hand and walks him out of the bathroom.

I follow them to an escalator and stand on the step right behind them as it leads us to the baggage claim area. I don't have any luggage other than my carry-on, so once I'm downstairs, I scan for the exit and run outside the terminal, searching for Paul's blue Prius with the license plate number Eddie gave me.

He immediately pulls up, and I breathe a sigh of relief for the first time since I got the threatening text on the plane.

"Beatrice," he says, rolling down his window.

"That's me," I say, quickly jumping into the passenger side.

"It's so nice to meet you finally," he says.

He has a clean-cut haircut and a warm smile. I couldn't be happier to see him. "Same," I say. "Thanks so much for picking me up."

"Of course," he says. "How was your flight?"

I debate whether to tell him about the text and opt not to because there's no doubt in my mind that if I tell him, he'll tell Eddie, and the two of them would put the kibosh on what I need to do now that I'm finally in New York.

"It was fine," I say. "I should text Eddie that you picked me up."

"Good idea," he says.

I take out my phone:

I'm with Paul heading back to his place.

Thank you for arranging this. Love you.

He immediately texts me back:

Tell him I say hi.

Be in touch soon, and stay safe.

Love you.

"Eddie says hi," I tell Paul.

He nods. "When was the last time you were in New York?"

"Eddie didn't tell you?" I say.

He shakes his head.

"I've never been."

"Really?" he says, genuinely surprised.

It is surprising, at forty-one years old, having been born and raised in Los Angeles, to have never visited New York City.

"I'm not sure how much Eddie has told you about my background beyond what's recently happened with my mom," I say. I tell him how Mom went to NYU and how, decades later, she was mugged at the reunion and told me to stay away from NYC. I explain that now I'm here to search for her medical records from that incident to see if there's any information that might connect me to her if she's still alive.

"And I thought *my* background was out there," Paul says. He tells me about being a closeted gay boy growing up in North Carolina who was bullied in high school and nervous about going to college.

"I remember how scared I was when I first got to the University of Michigan and met Eddie. I was worried about having a straight male roommate who might bully me if he found out I was gay. But I hit the jackpot. He didn't care. He accepted me for who I was. Do you know that he invited me to go home with him to LA during the holiday breaks, so I wouldn't have to return to North Carolina and possibly run into the kids I grew up with who tortured me?"

Eddie never told me this, which is consistent with who he is, because doing good by others isn't something he talks about. It's just something he does.

"No, I didn't," I say.

"I'm not sure if I'll ever be able to repay him," he says.

This is why I'm sitting in this car, why Paul and his husband are opening their home to me, despite the precarious place I find myself in.

We drive over a large bridge. "This is the Triborough Bridge," Paul tells me.

"What part of the city do you live in?" I ask.

"NYU faculty housing in the Village through Anthony's job."

"How's he been?" I ask.

"Thankfully, better," he says.

"How's your dad doing?" I say.

"He made it through surgery with flying colors. I'm so relieved. I can't wait to see him this weekend," he says.

We continue driving. When we reach the iconic arch in Washington Square Park, I know we're in the Village. The only picture mom ever showed me of her time in New York City was the one of her graduating from NYU, clad in a purple cap and gown, standing in front of that arch.

I look out the car window and see young students zigzagging through the park with backpacks on their shoulders and books in their hands. Their faces are bright and round with hopes about the marks they want to make on the world.

I think about how Mom was once one of them, arriving here as an eighteen-year-old with big dreams, until something bad happened—the something that Pearl said she was relieved to leave behind.

Paul parks his car on a tree-lined street. He gets out and walks toward a small reddish brownstone. It's autumn in New York. I follow him, stepping and crunching on small mounds of dry red, orange, and brown leaves that have fallen on the ground.

We reach the brownstone, walk up to the second floor and enter a stylish modern apartment with views of adjacent rooftop gardens. The place is decorated with artwork and several framed pictures of an adorable Labradoodle dog.

"You guys have a dog?" I ask.

"Had," he says.

"I'm sorry," I say.

He leads me to a second bedroom.

"This is our guest bedroom and my office. You can sleep here," he says.

"Thank you," I say. "I'm leaving now, so I'll be out of your hair."

"I wish I could go with you, but I've got a Zoom work call in about fifteen minutes that I can't miss, and Anthony is at work already."

"No worries. You guys are doing more than enough by welcoming me into your home. I'm very grateful," I say.

"I'm glad I can help Eddie out. He asked me to put this tracker on your phone, so I know where you are at all times." He holds up a square-looking tile. "You should also program my phone number in your phone, so you can reach me anytime if you need to."

"Eddie and I use the Life360 app to track each other, if that's easier," I say.

"This is better," he says, holding up the tile. "It'll work even if you lose your signal."

"Okay," I say, handing him my phone.

He attaches the tracker, hands me my phone, and I program his number into it.

I suddenly feel scared about heading into the city alone, and once again, I'm tempted to tell him about the threatening text I received on the plane.

She's running out of time.

If I tell him, he won't want me to go anywhere, and I need to go. At least he'll know where I am at all times.

"Eddie also wanted me to make sure to give you breakfast before you left," he says. "I already ate on the plane," I lie. "But I'll come back for lunch if you're free."

"Sounds great," he says.

My phone vibrates—a text from Eddie. Actually, from Sarah on Eddie's phone.

It's Sarah. I'm going to school. I miss you Beans.

I miss you too, I text her back.

More than she knows.

CHAPTER

32

March 1998

THE WEEKS AFTER Emily died marked a shift in my stay at Better Horizons. The staff knew her death had deeply impacted me, and that I was in a place where I wanted to recover and recognized that I needed their help to fight ED.

They began focusing on increasing the variety of foods in my meals to help me become more flexible after I left the treatment center. As long as there are rules about food— "This serving is too big," "This food is too fattening," or "If I eat this food, I'll gain weight"—relapsing is much more likely to happen.

Making myself eat pasta, cake, chips, and everything else under the sun was excruciating. But I persisted because I knew what awaited me if I didn't—Emily's fate.

I also knew I was gaining weight. The clothes I'd arrived in felt tighter. When I first got sick, I would only wear over-sized clothing—sweatpants, hoodies, refusing to allow the world to see how horrible I thought I looked due to the body dysmorphia that had overwhelmed my starved brain. Now I had to learn to live with the discomfort of my growing body, and I hated it.

One morning, when I went for my daily weigh-in at the nurses' station, Dr. Larsen was there.

"Good morning," she said.

"Hi," I said.

I stood on the scale, my back facing it.

"Today, we want you to turn around," Dr. Larsen told me.

"And see the number?" I asked, terrified.

"Yes," she said.

My heart started pounding. I was beyond petrified to see it.

Nowadays, weighing oneself and seeing one's weight is mainly contraindicated for those in recovery, but back in the nineties, this wasn't the norm. And the team wanted to prepare us for when doctors would inevitably weigh us without caring whether we saw the number on the scale.

"It's just a number," Dr. Larsen reminded me.

I took a deep breath in before slowly turning around. I was almost twenty pounds heavier than the last time I had weighed myself at home before Dad had confiscated our scale.

"I know you may be tempted to fixate on it," Dr. Larsen said. "But instead, try focusing on the fact that your body is working again, which will allow you to grow and thrive and have a full life after you leave here."

I nodded, trying to block out ED's roaring voice screaming at me about what a colossal failure I was to allow myself to get to this point. Thankfully Dr. Larsen was there to beat him back.

"Is he giving you a hard time now?" she asked me.

"Yes," I admitted.

"We're going to do something," she said.

"What?" I asked.

"Come with me." She led me outside to the ranch's deck, where we stood facing the Santa Monica mountains. "On the count of three, let's shout at him, 'You're dumb!'" she said.

"Shout at him?" I asked.

She nodded. "One, two, three . . ."

"YOU'RE DUMB!" we screamed together.

It was so simple, but it felt good, really good, to scream at him. I kept shouting "You're dumb!" over and over again, and for those brief moments, my voice drowned his out.

I finally stopped when my throat felt sore from screaming.

Dr. Larsen put her hand on my shoulder and told me, "I'm proud of you, and I know your mom is too, wherever she is."

As soon as she brought up my mom, my mind immediately returned to familiar, restricting thoughts. After Mom died, all of my focus and energy had been on ED, so I didn't have to deal with the pain of losing her. But I couldn't run away from that pain anymore.

Well, I *could*. I could return to restricting my food to avoid the unbearable thought of living in a world without her, but I also knew that I didn't want to end up like Emily—a life of hospital stays and treatment centers that ended in death.

Dad started visiting me twice a week, sometimes alone, sometimes with Rascal. We talked about Mom, about how much we missed her. He also reminded me of how much she loved me and how proud she would've been of the hard work I was doing.

After a while, I was able to remind myself on my own. When our visits ended, I always told him I loved and thanked him for visiting me, and he always hugged me and told me he loved me too.

Every bit of love, grace, and care people showed me over the subsequent weeks allowed my voice to grow louder whenever ED tried to harass me. Saying no to him became easier. It was a slow process, but I was beginning to learn how to fight ED on my own. Every time I told him to take a hike or let him know how dumb he was, I grew taller. I was starting to see the light at the end of the tunnel, and that light was my life.

CHAPTER

33

I HATE HOSPITALS. THE antiseptic smell mixed with air freshener trying to cover it up. The cries and moans that come from the rooms. The loud machines rolling down the corridors. The hollowed-out look in the eyes of patients and visitors who roam the hallway.

I've been to the hospital three times in my life. The first time in high school, when I fainted and had a feeding tube inserted. The second time when Dad was dying of cancer, and a doctor told us we should prepare for hospice care at home. And the third time, after I miscarried and was admitted for a D&C when they scraped my uterine wall, leaving it an empty cavern.

I once shared my aversion to hospitals with a therapist due to my history. She pointed out that hospitals can also be places where people get help, begin to heal, and even get a second chance at life.

Her words didn't land because, in my experience, they had been places where a person went to try to fix irreparable parts of themselves.

I step inside the first hospital on my list and immediately tense up, so I'm relieved when the man at the information desk lets me know that the records department is in an office building across the street on the sixth floor.

I quickly exit and walk there as a brisk autumn wind hits my cheeks. I step inside the building and take an elevator upstairs. When it opens, I spot a receptionist with a buzzed, military-style haircut sitting behind a desk.

"Good morning," he says. "How can I help you?"

"Hi," I say. "I'm trying to find out whether my late mother was admitted here as a patient in 1997."

"That kind of request takes at least two weeks to process," he tells me.

"Oh," I say.

"But I can make copies of your paperwork, and someone will get back to you if the records department has anything on file for her," he says.

"Okay," I say, pulling out my mom's death certificate and my own driver's license from my purse. I hand both to him, he makes copies, and I take down his name and phone number to follow up.

I repeat this process three more times at three additional hospitals. As I make my way around the city, I take precautions not to bring any attention to myself by walking in the middle of packed sidewalks, aware that whoever sent me the text on the plane might be following me.

After leaving the fourth hospital on Second Avenue empty-handed, I feel dizzy. And not just because I haven't eaten anything real in the last couple of days. It's the desperation that's setting in.

There's no plan B. Either I find something here that leads me to my mom, if she's still alive, or she and I, and possibly Eddie and Sarah, will be in danger because of the Cadells and whoever they have following me.

I feel like I might faint. I spot a diner up the block and race toward it. I duck inside, opting for a booth in the back of the restaurant instead of a fishbowl one near the front window, where I'd be on display for anyone passing by.

A waitress in her sixties, dressed in an old-fashioned pink apron with a name tag written in faded black cursive—*Mabel*—approaches me.

"What'll it be?" she asks.

"Coffee, black," I say.

"That's it?" she says.

I nod.

She gives me a once-over. "No offense, hon, but you don't look so good. A little pale. How about a bagel? You could use it."

The truth is I've reached the point where I wonder if I'll have enough strength to keep going without any food. I don't feel well at all.

"Okay," I cave.

When she returns with the bagel, I smear one side with cream cheese. As soon as I take a bite, ED immediately starts making me feel like shit for it.

No wonder your life is so fucked up. You can't even say no to an itty-bitty bagel. You're pathetic, weak—

I drop the bagel on the plate and smack down a twenty-dollar bill on the table, Mom's charm bracelet hitting it.

I stand up, about to walk out, when my phone starts to ring—a New York City number—but it isn't Paul's number. Maybe he's calling me from another line. I pick up.

"Hello?" I say.

"Hi, is this Beatrice Bennett?" a woman asks me.

"Yes . . ."

"This is Ramona Marino," she says.

Ramona . . . Marino . . . My foggy, starved brain can't place her.

"From Bell Hospital," she says. "You contacted me yesterday about your late mother's medical records."

I now remember that she was the only hospital employee I spoke with who took down my information.

"Hi," I say.

"It turns out we do have records for your mother," she lets me know.

"You do?" I say.

"Yes, but the hospital won't let me release them unless you come in person with her death certificate and your identification. They won't accept emailed copies. You mentioned you're in LA, so I'm not sure how that could work—"

"I'm actually in New York now," I interrupt.

"Oh, great," she says. "I'm not at the hospital. I'm at the office building next door on the fourth floor."

She gives me the address. I jot it down on a napkin, about to leave, when Mabel walks back to me with her pink apron.

"You barely ate," she says, pointing to the bagel that's only missing one bite.

"I'm in a rush," I say.

"Let me get you some foil so you can take it to go," she says.

"It's fine," I say, picking up the twenty I dropped on the table, handing it to her. "Keep the change."

"Thank you," she says, putting her hand on my shoulder. "Remember, take care of yourself."

I nod my head and leave.

CHAPTER

34

April 1998

"WE'RE PREPARING FOR your discharge," Dr. Larsen told me during our daily therapy session.

"Discharge?" I said. The word stuck in my throat.

"Yes."

"Why?"

"Because it's time. You're ready," she told me.

I sure didn't feel ready. Even though there were concrete goalposts I could point to that marked progress in my recovery, like how my shoes and comforter were returned to me, and the fact I was eating a variety of foods with more ease, I was still terrified. Change is hard for those used to the rigid tendencies of eating disorders, and I was no exception.

It had been three and a half months since I had first arrived at Better Horizons, and Dr. Larsen, the nurse, Iris, Kyle, and the entire staff had grown to feel like family. Contemplating leaving them and returning to a house without Mom was too overwhelming.

"I don't want to go," I told Dr. Larsen.

"That's understandable," she said.

"What if I relapse?" I asked her.

"I'll still be here," she told me. "But keep in mind, you're not the girl who arrived here in January."

"How do you know?" I asked.

"You just told me you don't want to leave and are scared to go."

I thought about that. When I first arrived, all I wanted to do was leave.

"I'm also nervous about school and if I'll be able to maintain my recovery there," I told Dr. Larsen.

"You'll attend an outpatient program a few nights a week near your home and build a recovery community. You won't be alone. And your teachers will help you make up the work you've missed. You'll have the summer to do that as well."

I could feel the tears bubbling in my eyes.

"I don't think I can do this without you," I finally admitted. I realized she was the closest thing to a mother figure I had had since Mom. The prospect of letting her go had echoes of losing Mom.

"I believe that you can. You've learned how to fight ED, the most ferocious foe, which means you can do anything with your life. You have so much to be proud of. I'll still be here, rooting for you on the sidelines. Someone you can always turn to."

"When am I leaving?" I asked, blinking away tears.

"In a couple of days," she said.

Two days later, I walked down the same stairs I had tiptoed down a few months before when I had tried running away. But this time, I had my luggage in my hands, and I was going home. The entire staff was waiting for me in the living room and started clapping.

Dr. Larsen handed me a goodbye book that they had all signed. She hugged me and whispered in my ear, "This isn't the end. It's the beginning of your life."

At the time, I had no idea that over a decade later, under very different circumstances, she'd make a reappearance in my life.

CHAPTER

35

RAMONA MAKES COPIES of Mom's death certificate and my driver's license. She's in her early thirties and has long, wavy dirty blond hair pulled back by a thin silver headband with rhinestones.

"Thank you for following up," I tell her.

"My mom died when I was ten," she says. "I know what it's like to try to piece their lives together after they're gone."

"I'm sorry," I say.

"There are so many things I wish I could ask her—some important, some silly. Know what I mean?" she asks.

I nod.

"How will I know if I've found the one? Am I allergic to bees? Is it normal to wonder if you're fulfilling your life's purpose? Sorry," she says, blushing. "This isn't very professional."

"You don't have to apologize," I say.

"I'll be back with your mom's records." She stands up and leaves the room with the photocopies.

ED is still hustling me about eating the bite of bagel. I cover my ears like old times, trying to tune him out, when Ramona returns.

"You okay?" she asks.

I quickly drop my hands from my ears back to my sides. "My ears are still popping from the plane," I lie.

"I hate when that happens," she says.

I notice the single sheet of paper she's holding. And my heart starts to flutter like my entire future hinges on this one thin slice of tree.

"I forgot to mention on the phone that the year your mom was admitted to the hospital is different from the one you asked about," she says.

"It wasn't 1997?" I ask.

She shakes her head. "It was 1974."

1974? I quickly do the math in my head. Mom was a college student then.

"She spent a month at the hospital," Ramona adds.

"A month?" I repeat, stunned.

Ramona pushes the paper toward me.

Irene Mayer, DOB: 01-02-1955
Admitted: March 23, 1974.
Discharged: April 27, 1974.

Mom never told me she was hospitalized during college, let alone for a month.

"This record doesn't explain why she was admitted," I say.

"The hospital's gone through several system upgrades since the seventies. They stopped keeping track of admittance reasons after 1990," Ramona explains. "You could try NYU. They might have it in their records."

"Okay," I say.

I thank her again for following up with me before leaving.

When I step outside, I stare at Bell Hospital next door, feeling more confused than when I arrived. Mom spent a month here in college, and I have no idea why.

My phone starts ringing. It's Eddie, and I quickly pick up.

"Hi," he says. "Just checking in. Everything okay?"

"Yes," I say.

"When are you going back to Paul's for lunch?" he asks.

"After I go to the NYU registrar's office. I just found out my mom was hospitalized for a month during college, and I'm trying to find out why."

"Okay," he says. I can tell he's trying to cover his worry. "Please call me when you're back at his place."

"I promise I will."

"And Beans . . ." He stops himself.

"What is it?" I ask.

"Sarah misses you," he says.

"She texted me earlier," I let him know.

"She did?" he asks.

"I guess she got a hold of your phone," I say.

He lets out a small chuckle that briefly cuts through his worry. "That's a first. I had no idea she knew my passcode."

"An early adopter," I say. "And I miss you both."

* * *

The line at the NYU registrar's office is endless. Purple and white signs line the wall with instructions for registering online. A female student in front of me with a dyed blue bob is tapping her foot while listening to headphones.

When it's finally my turn, I walk up to a thin man in his forties with a long, pointed nose and one deep crow line between his brows. He waits for me to speak first.

"Hi," I say. "I recently learned that my mother was hospitalized for a month while she was a student at the Tisch School of Arts, and I'm trying to find out why for my own medical reasons. Is this something that would be in your records?"

"What was her name?" he asks.

"Irene Mayer."

He types on his keyboard. I notice the name tag pinned to his brown shirt pocket: *Neil*.

"Thank you for helping me, Neil," I say.

"I can't find her," he says. "When was she hospitalized?"

"March to April of 1974," I say.

"She wouldn't be in this database," he explains. "That was too long ago."

"Do you know who I might be able to speak with that has access to older records?" I ask.

"Technically, I'm not supposed to access them, but since you thanked me . . ." He types some more.

"Thank you," I make sure to say again.

He stares intently at his computer screen, searching and searching.

"I found her," he finally says.

"You did?" I say more excitedly than I meant to.

"She was enrolled as a freshman in the Tisch School of Arts in the fall of 1973. It looks like she went on leave in spring semester of 1974."

"On leave?" I say.

"She took a semester off," he says.

A semester? According to the Bell hospital record, she was only hospitalized for a month between March and April of 1974. Why would she have taken an entire semester off?

"After she returned to the university, she transferred out of the Tisch School of Arts and into the College of Arts and Science," Neil continues.

"Really?" I say. I thought she'd graduated from Tisch. She always made it sound that way.

"Is there any mention of why she took a semester off?" I ask.

"No," he says. "But I see that she still graduated on time. Must've been a smart cookie to make up an entire semester."

I wonder if I can contact someone who was with her at Tisch to see if they know why she took a semester off and transferred colleges within the university. The problem is she didn't keep in touch with any friends from NYU, at least none that I know of. Maybe that was by design, related to what Pearl said, how Mom told her she was relieved to put New York behind her.

"Are you done yet?" a male student behind me in vintage Levi's calls out.

Neil shakes his head behind the Plexiglas, displeased with the display of rudeness. "No, she's not," Neil tells him. The student rolls his eyes.

"Do you by any chance have a list of Tisch alumni that were freshmen in the fall of 1973?" I ask.

"The university doesn't give out personal alumni information. Maybe try LinkedIn? You could do a search for NYU alumni that graduated the same year as your mom."

The hope I felt a few minutes ago when Neil found Mom's name in the database vanishes, and the desperation settles back in. He clocks my disappointment.

"Do you live in New York?" he asks me.

I shake my head.

"I can give you a pass for the university library if you want to search on one of their computers," he says.

"Thank you," I say. "I'd appreciate that."

He hands me a pass. I thank him again and leave my business card for him to contact me if he comes across anything else.

I turn around to leave, passing the guy in Levi's, who groans, "Finally."

When I open the door to exit the registrar's office, I almost bump into a man entering who puts up his right hand to stop me from crashing into him. I notice a small heart-shaped birthmark that almost looks like a tattoo on the top of his hand.

"Watch it," he says.

36

April 1998

Returning home after Better Horizons was hard. Mom's absence in our home was profound. Unlike before, when ED had given me a way out of feeling my grief by obsessing over my weight and food, I wasn't running away from my sadness anymore.

Returning to restricting my food was tempting, but I knew the path it would lead me down—Emily's. Still, eating was difficult at home.

Rascal was a marvel to me, how he ate with so much ease. How he'd lick the inside of his bowl dry and the outside too, making sure he hadn't left a morsel of dog food behind.

Every time Dad and I were in the kitchen, he'd run up to us, bending his head sideways, lifting one of his paws, trying to look as cute as possible, hoping to score another crumb.

Sometimes when I struggled to eat, I tried channeling him, imagining him licking every last bite without a care in the world.

Dad did his best to serve me different kinds of food. I no longer screamed, hit him, or threw plates on the ground. Instead, I shared with him how I felt.

"I'm scared I'm going to gain weight from this pasta," I told him one night.

"It's okay to be scared," he said. "But you need to eat it so you can grow."

The week I returned home, I began an outpatient program. It was at a recovery center in West Hollywood perched above the Sunset Strip and its legendary landmarks, including Whisky a Go Go, the Viper Room, and The Comedy Store. It was the one closest to where we lived, and Dad drove me there.

In a no-frills, cramped office with one tiny window, I ate dinner with a group of fellow ED patients three times a week. The main difference from Better Horizons, apart from it not being inpatient, was that the group didn't include any girls my age. The youngest woman was nineteen years old, and the rest were well into their twenties.

Because they were older than me, the magnitude of what ED had stolen from them—college degrees, jobs, marriages— was beyond anything I could have imagined as a teenager in high school. What these women had lost due to this disease was even more pronounced in the backdrop of their contemporaries flourishing in their careers and relationships.

Ginny, a twenty-six-year-old woman, was crying as she spoke about her fiancé, who had just broken up with her because of ED. "He said I keep choosing the eating disorder over our life together, and he's lost hope that I'll ever make a different choice. I don't blame him," she said. "I'm losing hope too."

Another woman, Carmen, had just been put on leave from her law firm after passing out at a meeting with opposing counsel. "The partners told me that I can't return until I have medical clearance from my doctor. But my rent doesn't stop. My bills don't either. And unemployment doesn't cover everything. If they don't take me back, I'm worried they won't give me a reference to get a job somewhere else." She shakes her head. "The saddest thing is when they first hired me, they told me I was partner material."

Susie, a twenty-two-year-old graphic designer, was also on the cusp of losing her job due to exercise addiction. "I was going to the gym across from our office building during lunch. Every ten-minute break, I'd go there to run a mile on the treadmill. My boss started to notice. I could tell he thought it was weird. Last week the gym deactivated my membership and barred me from entering because they were scared I might die on one of their treadmills. So I bought my own and had it delivered to my apartment. I've been late to work every day this week because I can't pull myself away from the treadmill. Yesterday, my boss gave me a final warning."

I remember feeling out of place with these women and wishing there were girls my age, but being around them served a purpose. Listening to them made me realize death wasn't the only possible endgame with ED. A hollowed-out life and living on the fringes were possibilities too.

Their stories shook me. I wanted a full life, the kind I knew my mom had imagined for me when she had me, but I still had my recovery floaties on, swimming in the shallow end of the recovery pool. I kept reminding myself what Dr. Larsen had told me—that she believed in me. Her words helped buoy me, especially knowing school was about to start, where I'd soon have to navigate much deeper waters.

37

I'M SEATED AT a desk in front of a computer inside the NYU library off of Washington Square Park, searching for alums on LinkedIn. Thousands of names come up. I don't have the time to go through every single one to see if they attended Tisch in the fall semester of 1973 with Mom.

I stop typing, close my eyes, and try reaching back into the crevices of my brain to see if I can remember any time Mom spoke of anyone she went to NYU with . . . but nothing comes up.

I stand up, leave my stuff on the library desk, and walk outside to call Pearl, who thankfully picks up.

"Hi, it's Beatrice," I say.

"Are you okay?" she asks me.

"I'm fine, just had a question for you. Did my mom ever mention any friends of hers from NYU?"

She pauses before responding. "Are you trying to track down that other guy?"

"No, I'm trying to understand what happened to my mom when she was in New York and why she was glad to leave it like you told me."

"She had a friend from NYU that once stayed with us," she says.

"She did?"

"Yeah, she was a Broadway actress and came to LA one pilot season to see if she could book any TV roles. I don't think anything came of it because she never ended up moving here."

"Do you remember her name?" I ask.

"Liz, maybe? Or was it Polly? I'm not sure. It was over forty years ago. But I remember years later your mom mentioning that this woman was on Broadway in a groundbreaking play."

A memory comes firing back at me. During my freshman year in high school, I signed up to be in the school musical—*The Music Man*. It was the first time I had ever participated in a school play.

At the time, Mom told me an old friend of hers from NYU was also going to be in a play—a play premiering on Broadway.

"Thanks, Pearl," I say.

"Please take care of yourself," she says. "I know your mom would want you to."

After hanging up, I dash back to the library and return to the desk where I left my things. I pull out a pen and notebook from my bag and search for every play and musical that premiered on Broadway in 1996—my freshman year in high school—the year Mom told me her friend was going to be on Broadway.

Thirty-eight productions come up that premiered in 1996. I go through each one alphabetically, starting with *A Delicate Balance*, which premiered on April 21, 1996, researching every cast member, including understudies, to see if any of them were graduates of the Tisch School of Arts.

When I reach the halfway mark on the list, *Jack: A Night on the Town with John Barrymore*, which premiered on April 24, 1996, I have a tally of thirteen actresses who made their Broadway debuts in plays premiering that year who also went to Tisch.

I keep going. By the time I reach the last play on the list, *The Three Sisters*, which premiered on November 7, 1996, I have twenty-seven women's names written down—but none of their names are Liz or Polly, like Pearl mentioned.

I need to get ahold of the 1978 Tisch yearbook—the year Mom would have graduated had she stayed at Tisch, to see if any of the twenty-seven actresses on my list graduated that year.

I stand up from the desk and approach a librarian who tells me that I need to put in a special request from archives if I want to get a hard copy of the yearbook but provides me with a link to view it online in the interim. I thank her, return to my desk, and access the 1978 yearbook through an archive collection online.

As I go through each of the graduates' yearbook pages, I see pictures of performances they were in and quotes they posted about their future, and I think about Mom, how she could have been one of them, wondering what happened to her that made her change the course of her life.

I click through yearbook page after yearbook page, focusing on the women—Trisha Fields, Belinda Henry, Meghan O'Hare—none of them are on my list of actresses who either appeared or understudied in performances in plays and musicals that premiered on Broadway in 1996.

The anxiety in my body starts rising again because there aren't many pages left in this yearbook. But when I turn the following page, I see Mom's face smiling at me! She's in the background of one of the pictures on Laura Poitier's yearbook page.

I immediately cross-reference Laura Poitier with my list of actresses and spot her name. She was an understudy for the role of Joanne Jefferson in *Rent*, which premiered on Broadway on April 29, 1996.

I zoom further into the picture where Mom is standing in the background and see a man beside her with his arm slung over her shoulder. It's the man that picked Mom up from our house—the one she lied about, who she said was her second cousin. The one that drove a VW with a surfboard on top. The one who she went out with and then returned home alone crying. The one that sounded a lot like the guy Margot Cadell was in a relationship with, according to her neighbors. Who *is* he?

I need to find Laura Poitier. Maybe she'll know who this guy is. And maybe she'll have answers for me about what happened to Mom while they were in school together.

I Google her name. She immediately comes up on the NYU university faculty page:

Laura Poitier, Chair of the Tisch School of Arts.

* * *

"University ID," a tall, stern-faced guard tells me.

"I'm a psychologist," I say. "Laura Poitier's office called me for a student emergency."

He looks at me dubiously. I pull out my driver's license, handing it to him. "Look me up. Dr. Beatrice Bennett," I say confidently.

He uses the walkie-talkie from his pocket to contact someone. I hear a woman on the other end talking to him, sounding confused, but she tells him to send me up anyway. He takes my information, including my psychology license number, and lets me through.

I take an elevator to the third floor and follow the signs leading me to Laura Poitier's office. An assistant sporting a ballerina-high bun and thick black-framed glasses greets me.

"Are you the psychologist?" she says, looking up from her computer screen.

"Yes," I say.

"What's going on?" she asks.

"I'm hoping to speak with Laura," I say. "She was a classmate of my late mother."

She narrows her eyes. "I thought this was about a student emergency."

"It's a personal one," I say. "The guard was confused."

"Oh. Well, Laura is tied up in rehearsals all day for our fall musical production. Her office hours are tomorrow between one and two PM."

She's running out of time.

"It's an emergency," I say again.

"You can leave me your name and phone number, and when she checks in, I'll let her know you came by."

"Okay," I say, handing her my business card. "Thank you."

I leave, determined to go to every classroom in every Tisch School of the Arts building until I find Laura Poitier.

I walk through a hallway to get to the elevator and pass a large sign for a rehearsal schedule taped to the wall:

Rent Rehearsals

Week of October 11th–15th

Studio Theater #1 721 Broadway

10 am – 10 pm

I exit the building and pull out my phone, typing the theater address into the Google Maps app. When I look up, I vaguely notice a guy who looks like the one I almost bumped into when I left the registrar's office. He's standing by a bus stop across the street.

Is he following me?

I push the thought out of my mind, following the app as it guides me through Washington Square Park until I reach Broadway. I scan numbers on various buildings looking for the theater address, when I spot an actor in costume slipping out of a back door in an empty alley, lighting a cigarette. This must be the theater.

I enter through the same back door he just exited. Once inside, I realize I'm in a dressing room. A few actors in costume and makeup that look like they're part of a nineties Central Casting call stare at me strangely.

"I'm a friend of Laura's," I say. "I think I came through the wrong door."

They nod, like my being here now makes sense.

I exit the dressing room and walk down a long hallway, passing restrooms and an empty concession stand, until I reach the front of the theater and step inside. The lights dim. About a dozen actors are on stage, including those I just saw in the dressing room.

"Actors, mark your place," a woman with a commanding voice says. She's sitting in the front row of the audience with her back facing me. All I see of her is a majestic braided hair crown wrapped around her head. "Music, please."

The music starts, and the actors begin singing the show's signature song, "Seasons of Love."

"Stop!" the woman calls out over the actors' voices.

The music abruptly halts, the actors stop singing, and the house lights come back up.

"The lighting's off-center," she says, turning around to face whoever's in the lighting booth above me.

That's when she sees me—standing alone in the back of the theater. For a brief moment, our eyes meet, and she stops in her tracks as if she's seen a ghost.

"Ten-minute break," she announces.

She stands up in a trance, walking toward the back of the theater, still staring at me.

"Are you Laura?" I ask her as she approaches me.

"You look *exactly* like someone I knew a long time ago," she says in disbelief.

It's not the first time I've been told I look like my mom.

"Irene Mayer?" I say.

She nods.

"I'm her daughter."

She sits on one of the chairs in the back of the theater, bends her head, and begins to weep.

Despite being accustomed to regularly watching people cry in my office, I'm unsure how to respond; I wasn't expecting this.

"I didn't mean to upset you," I say.

She shakes her head. "These aren't tears of sadness," she explains. "After I visited your mom in LA forty-plus years ago, she moved, and her number changed. I figured she'd gotten married and changed her name because I could never find her again. Over the years, I tried searching for her at the registrar's office and online but never came up with anything. Probably because I'm old and a Luddite. I never thought I'd hear from her again. How is she?"

"She died when I was in high school," I tell her.

"I'm sorry," Laura says, bending her head, taking in the news.

"Thank you."

She tries to gather herself, adjusting the braided crown on her head.

"I'm glad to meet you," she says. "Did you know that your mother had more talent than all of us combined in the tip of her pinky?" She lifts her left pinky finger.

"No," I say.

"In my twenty-seven years as a professional actor on Broadway, and twenty years of teaching acting to countless students, I've come across talent like hers maybe two or three times. I've always wondered what might've been had not she gotten caught up with, you know . . ."

"No, I don't know," I say.

"Uh," she stammers. "I assumed you did."

"Can you please tell me what that was?" I ask. "That's actually why I'm here—I'm looking for answers."

Laura looks uncomfortable. "It's not my place to . . ."

"Please." I dig in.

"I'm sure your mother carefully chose what she wanted to disclose to you."

"I was fifteen years old when she died," I say. "I think she would've told me more about herself when I got older had she lived."

"It's best you carry the memory of what you know about her rather than have it sullied by a stranger."

Sullied?

I'm tempted to tell her the truth, that Mom might still be alive, that I know something happened to her that might not only imperil her life again but is putting me in danger and possibly Eddie and Sarah too. But I can't. Laura would probably go to law enforcement, definitely contact someone at the university, and it would become breaking news in a New York minute. So I try a different tactic.

"I've struggled in my adult life," I say. "I think it would help me to know about my mom's struggles. Isn't that what the theater is all about? Isn't that what art is for? Making existence a little more bearable, knowing we're not alone in the human experience?"

Laura takes a deep breath in. "Let's just say your mother got involved with the wrong crowd who introduced her to bad things our freshman year."

"Do you know if she had a boyfriend back then?" I don't mention that I just stalked her yearbook page at the library.

Laura meets my eyes and pauses before answering.

"No," she finally says.

There's something she's not telling me. She must've known who that guy was. She stayed with Pearl and Mom in LA. Why won't she tell me?

"When your mom left Tisch, I tried to convince her to return," she says, changing the subject. "I told her what I believed—that she was destined for Broadway, Hollywood, the sky was the limit for her, but she was adamant that this wasn't the right place for her anymore."

Laura continues speaking in vagaries as I try to discern between the lines.

"Did you know she was hospitalized for a month after leaving Tisch?" I ask.

"I didn't," she responds with a tight smile.

Once again, I don't believe her.

"Listen, I'm so glad we had the chance to meet," she says. "But I better get back to rehearsal."

"Thanks for taking the time to speak with me," I say.

"It was a profound pleasure," she says.

I walk away and slip out of the back of the theater, thinking about what Laura might have been withholding from me and why.

My phone starts ringing. It's the NYU registrar's office. I pick up. "Hello?"

"I have an old address for your mom," Neil says. "From when she went to NYU. I found it after you left the office. Maybe someone there knows something about what happened to her. Probably a long shot, since it's been decades."

"I'll still take the address," I say. I have no other leads.

"It's not university housing. It's on 15th Street, near Union Square Park—313 East 15th street," he says.

"Okay," I say, quickly taking out my notepad and pen from my purse to jot it down. "Thank you again for helping me."

"No problem," Neil says.

After we hang up, I look up and think I see that guy again, the one from the registrar's office and the bus stop. He's about halfway down the block, leaning against an electric pole. He's in his thirties and doesn't look like a student. He meets my eyes and stares at me.

My heart begins to race. I instinctively turn around, walking in the opposite direction, camouflaging myself in the middle of a packed sidewalk filled with people.

* * *

As I walk up 15th Street, my cell phone starts ringing. It's Paul. I quickly answer, glancing behind me to see if the man is still following me. Thankfully he isn't.

"Should I still wait for you to eat lunch?" Paul asks.

"I only have one more stop to make," I say. "I'm going to see where my mom lived during college. I'll head back to your place right after. Feel free to start, if you're hungry."

"Okay," he says.

We hang up, and I reach the exact spot where the building for 313 East 15th street should numerically be, but the building doesn't exist. Instead, it's a parkette—a small lot of land filled with grass and benches in the middle of a dense city block. People are using it to walk their dogs. A young couple is sitting and laughing on one of the benches.

I look down at the paper again with the address Neil gave me, wondering if I wrote it down incorrectly. I quickly call him to verify that what I wrote was correct, which he does.

After we hang up, a large group of teenagers on a field trip led by a guide walk toward me. I immediately recognize their black shirts with *D.A.R.E.* printed in red, bold cursive font.

My mom used to volunteer for the organization—to my great embarrassment, because no teen wants their parents hanging out at their high school. When *D.A.R.E.* members visited my freshman year, she was on stage with them in the auditorium, facilitating a group discussion.

"Excuse me," the guide says, trying to move the teens around me. She leads them to a small monument by the entrance of the parkette that I didn't notice before.

"You're standing in front of a city landmark," she tells them, pointing to a gold plaque on the top of the monument. She reads its inscription out loud:

"In 1973, in a building located at this address, 313 East 15th Street, Alexander Valentine established one of the first halfway houses in New York City: Valentine's House. It remained on this site until 1992. This monument was erected by the New York Preservation Society."

The guide adds, "It wasn't only one of the first halfway houses in New York City. It was one of the first halfway houses in the world which served as transitional housing for people leaving drug and alcohol rehabilitation programs. There are now hundreds of halfway houses throughout the country."

She asks the teens if they have any questions, but they don't, so she points to a subway entrance up the block, and they all walk toward it.

After they're gone, I walk up to the plaque, reading over the inscription, honing in on the address—the one the registrar's office had on file for Mom.

I then notice an engraved sentence in tiny font below the inscription. A sentence the *D.A.R.E.* guide didn't read out loud:

This property is maintained by the generous donation of the Cadell family.

38

April 1998

WHEN I FINALLY returned to school, the kids who knew me thought I had had a mental breakdown because of what happened to my mom. They didn't know the truth about ED. And I didn't want to tell them, for fear they might say or do something that would send me backward.

"You look great," Cindy told me as I stood in front of my locker, storing a couple of books inside. She was a popular girl with a waif-like body who'd been on my soccer team.

Her comment about my appearance made my not-fully-recovered brain wonder if she'd said it because I looked like I had gained weight, momentarily drawing me back into ED thoughts. I had to visualize myself crumpling the thoughts up and throwing them in the trash.

"Are you practicing with us today?" she asked me.

I shook my head. "I missed a lot of schoolwork while I was gone. I have to catch up, so I'm not going to be on the team."

"Too bad," she said.

I had already decided I wouldn't return to playing soccer for fear of falling back into compulsive exercising. It was a funny thing. At the beginning of my illness, I was obsessed with soccer, the practice part of it, always running twice the laps the coach asked us to do, feeling upset when anything got in the way of it, like the occasional rain or the coach being out sick.

But now, I didn't care about soccer and wondered if soccer was something I had ever really wanted to do, or whether it had been a way to obey ED, who had always told me I needed to do it to burn as many calories as possible.

"My parents are out of town," Cindy said. "I'm having a party on Saturday night. You should come."

"Thanks for the invite," I said, closing my locker.

The bell rang, and I was relieved when we left for our respective classes.

Later that evening, when I was at my outpatient recovery group, I told them about the party invite.

"If you think there will be drugs or alcohol there, I wouldn't go," Samantha said. She was twenty-seven years old and had a history of addiction with ED. I learned from the group that eating disorder sufferers have up to a fifty percent higher risk of developing drug and alcohol addiction.

I knew Samantha was right, but it was hard to figure out how to be a teenager in high school again without participating in sports or going to parties. So I decided to go anyway.

I made Dad drop me off a couple of blocks away. He didn't know that Cindy's parents were out of town or anything about the potential minefield I was entering. He innocently thought it was good that I was trying to ingratiate myself into my old life again.

When I got to the party, Cindy's house was packed. There was alcohol everywhere. She was drunk in the corner with a football player and didn't even notice me as I stepped inside. Charlie, a guy from my chemistry class, came up to me holding a red plastic cup with beer.

"Where's your drink?" he asked.

Saying no to alcohol was easy because even though I wasn't actively restricting, I still wasn't in a place of embracing extra calories.

"I'm sober," I blurted out.

"Ohh," Charlie said. "That's why you were gone from school so long? Rehab?"

Before I could answer, another guy approached, holding a joint. "Wanna hit?" the guy asked Charlie.

"Sure," Charlie said. "But don't offer her any. She just got back from rehab."

I left the house and walked a couple of blocks, returning to the corner where Dad had planned to pick me up a few hours later. It was before cell phone days, so I just sat there until he arrived. Samantha was right. I shouldn't have gone.

"Did you have fun?" Dad asked me when he picked me up.

I nodded even though I felt utterly alone. I was beginning to realize I was going to need something to help me get through high school, something more than throwing myself into all the schoolwork I had missed. I had to find a purpose, a reason for waking up every morning, or ED would fill the void.

39

I SIT ON ONE of the benches inside the parkette, staring at Mom's bracelet on my wrist, running my finger over the engravings and the small scratch in the corner. I've heard of Valentine's House before. The last time was after my middle school graduation.

Mom, Dad, and I had just gotten through a two-hour outdoor ceremony under a beaming sun listening to speeches by honor students, counselors, and the principal, which culminated with me walking across a makeshift stage to pick up my diploma.

We went to a brunch place in Brentwood after to eat, our cheeks still red from the sun. As we got settled at our table, a woman with chunky vintage green and red bracelets and short curly black hair approached us.

"Is it you?" she asked Mom with a wide smile. "Is it really you?"

Mom's entire body stiffened. "I'm sorry, but I don't think I know you," she said curtly.

"You weren't at Valentine's House?" the woman asked her.

The name Valentine's House stuck in my mind because, as a kid, I thought it was such a neat name for a house.

"No," Mom said, clearing her throat.

"In New York City, back in the seventies?" the woman pressed.

"I went to college in New York, but I've never heard of Valentine's House."

"Oh," the woman said.

"Maybe you remember me from NYU?" Mom asked her.

The woman shook her head. "I didn't go to NYU."

"Mom, I'm hungry," I said. "Can we order?"

"Let's do that," Dad said.

"My daughter graduated from middle school today," Mom explained to the woman. "We're celebrating."

"Congratulations," the woman said.

"Thank you," said Mom.

The woman slowly retreated from us, but I remember Mom being distracted for the rest of the meal, half present, half somewhere else, every so often looking up at the woman who was seated at a table nearby with her friends.

After we finished eating and left the restaurant, we passed the woman who was standing outside waiting for her car at the valet station.

Mom smiled at her as we walked by her when I heard the woman whisper under her breath, "I'm glad things turned out well for you."

She isn't who you think she is.

The words echo in my mind like a sound bouncing off a cave's wall, reverberating over and over again.

Is this the trouble Laura Poitier alluded to that Mom got caught up in? Is this why I never saw her take a sip of alcohol? Why she specialized in treating addiction? Why she led a discussion with *D.A.R.E.* at my high school?

I think back on a conversation I had with her the year before she died, when we were discussing what colleges I might want to go to, and she shared with me how she got into the field of psychology.

"I lost both of my parents to cancer during my senior year of high school. Thankfully, a school counselor stepped in to help me. Talking with her gave me a window into what it meant to be a therapist. I thought I might be good at it," she told me.

"But you went to college for acting," I said.

"I did, but I tucked away that other experience in my mind and never forgot about it."

"When did you decide to switch from acting to becoming a psychologist?" I asked her. "And how did you decide to specialize in addiction?"

She paused for a long while. "I can't remember when I made the change," she finally said. "I decided to focus on addiction because twelve-step recovery programs integrate the psychological with the spiritual. And after losing both of my parents at such a young age, I relied heavily on my faith."

I took what she told me at face value. It felt effortless, and it made sense.

Now learning that she might've lived in a halfway house, she probably did rely heavily on her faith—but for her recovery. Her response to me was rooted in some truth. Lying by omission, lying without lies.

It's the same thing I did when Eddie asked me if I had ever wanted to have kids with Jay. I told him, "We had just gotten married," insinuating we weren't ready yet, without telling him what really happened.

I get up from the bench and return to the plaque.

This property is maintained by the generous donation of the Cadell family.

How can one of the main players responsible for the opioid epidemic in this country be funding a city landmark that was once used as a halfway house for drug addicts?

And why do the Cadells keep popping up whenever I learn something new about Mom?

My phone starts ringing—it's Jay.

I debate whether to answer because he warned me against doing what I'm doing. But I don't think he'd be calling me unless it was important.

"Hello?" I say, picking up.

"Hi," he says. "In case you were tempted to try to track down your mother, I just found out that my colleague who testified against William Jr. and Quentin Cadell had to move his wife and kids out of state because of dangerous threats against them."

This is why I can't give up. I won't be out of danger until I find out if Mom is still alive, and Eddie and Sarah may not be either.

"It turns out my mom was hospitalized for a month at Bell Hospital during her freshman year at NYU. She also lived in a halfway house—" I spill.

"Wait, did you say Bell Hospital?" Jay interrupts.

"Yes," I say.

"That was one of the first hospitals in New York State to create an opioid detox program. They were considered pioneers in the field," he says.

My stomach sinks. What I hadn't wanted to believe—that Mom might've been an addict—is growing harder and harder to run away from.

"I also found out that the halfway house she lived in is now a parkette maintained by the 'generous' donation of the Cadell family," I say.

"That's not uncommon. When the Cadells first started being scrutinized by the Feds, they funded halfway houses to shift the blame away from the fact that they were lying and hiding how addictive their drugs were. They tried to control the narrative, to position themselves as supporting the fight against addiction, to make themselves appear innocent. How did you find all of this out, anyway?"

I don't respond because I don't want to lie. But three ambulances roar down the street, giving it away.

"You're in NYC, aren't you," he says.

"Yes."

"I called because I was worried you might end up doing something like that," he says. "I know how much losing your mom impacted you, how much it ended up impacting us. But I don't think you realize how dangerous these people are, Beans. You don't owe her your life."

He doesn't realize that I won't get my life back until I find out if she's alive.

*   *   *

After I left the parkette, I Googled Alexander Valentine. He's a long-time art gallery owner in Chelsea—the Valentine Gallery on 21st Street. I have no idea whether he still works there, is retired, or is even alive. I also have no idea if he'll remember Mom.

The gallery is filled with human-sized neon orange, pink, green, and blue butterflies. Butterflies everywhere, hanging from the ceiling, in the windows, pasted to the walls.

There are no people inside except an older, elegant man with silver hair, dressed in a gray cardigan with tortoise-framed glasses, seated behind a wooden rolltop desk, reading a book in the back of the gallery.

He puts it down and looks up at me. "Good afternoon," he says.

"Are you Alexander Valentine?" I ask.

"Last time I checked," he says, smiling.

"I'm Beatrice Bennett," I say. "My mother was Irene Mayer."

He smiles, moving his glasses to the tip of his nose, looking at me over the rims. "You looked familiar," he says.

"You remember her?" I ask.

"She was one of the first residents we had," he says.

"So she *was* an addict?" I ask.

"Yes," he says.

Even though everything pointed to this, I didn't want to believe it.

As children, we hold our parents on a pedestal. As we get older, they become human. But for those of us who lose them when we're young, we never have the chance to integrate them into real people.

Alexander notices I'm upset. "I'm sober too," he says, trying to lessen the blow and normalize her being an addict. "Just celebrated my forty-fifth anniversary," he adds.

"Congratulations," I say. I can't tell if he thinks I said it out of anger, so I clarify. "I'm a psychologist, and I know how hard-fought recovery is. I've been on my own recovery journey too. I just never knew this about my mom until today."

"She was very motivated to get better," he tells me. "More motivated than most. Not sure if that helps you to hear. What brings you here?"

"She died when I was fifteen, and I'm trying to learn more about her. I've had my own struggles," I say.

"In my mind, the only thing holding her back was her boyfriend at the time," he says. "We advised everyone who entered the halfway house to hold off from relationships until they had at least a year of sobriety under their belt. Many folks bucked the advice. She wasn't the only one."

"Do you know who he was?" I ask.

"I never met him, but I remember her roommate wasn't a fan," he says. "Esther Hermes—a famous socialite at the time. She and your mom knew each other from Bell Hospital. They had detoxed together there."

Mom never mentioned Esther. Of course she didn't; she never mentioned she was an addict.

"I heard your mom still graduated from NYU after the semester she took off when she came to us. Is that true?" Alexander asks me.

I nod. "She became a psychologist. She specialized in addiction."

He smiles. "Good for her. I got out of the game, had to focus on my own sobriety. Can't help anyone if you don't help yourself first."

His words hit close to home. If and when all of this somehow blows over, I know I'll have to reckon with ED if I plan to return to my job helping others—and to my life with Eddie and Sarah, which now feels like a dream slowly slipping away.

I try pushing the thought out of my mind when my stomach growls loudly enough for Alexander to hear.

"We had a showing last night, and I have leftover food in the back. Can I offer you some?" he asks.

My phone starts ringing. It's Paul again.

"I need to go," I tell Alexander. "Thanks again for talking to me about my mom."

"I'm glad things turned out well for her," he says. "I'm sure they'll work out for you too. I'm not sure what kind of struggles you've had, but I'd be remiss if I didn't tell you that recovery is always possible. If you can quit for a day, you can quit for a lifetime."

I nod, remembering Benjamin Alire Saenz's quote from graduate school. I've yet to come across an analogous one for food.

The difference between alcohol and drug addiction and restricting food is that you can't quit food. You have to find a way to live with it. Choosing eating disorder recovery means choosing it multiple times a day, every time you eat, over and over again.

My stomach growls loudly again.

"Sure I can't offer you something?" he asks again.

I shake my head, hard. "I gotta go."

40

June 1998

M Y SOPHOMORE YEAR in high school had started with Mom alive and ended with her gone and me recovering from an eating disorder.

My return home after Better Horizons had been bumpy. Being in school felt like an ongoing contact sport. Navigating all the usual teenage stuff while ED was still in my ear was not easy.

Going to my outpatient recovery group three nights a week helped. Listening to older women discuss how their lives had been destroyed by ED served as a reminder of what was at stake for me.

But I also knew that big picture, I needed something to focus on, a sense of purpose, to maintain my recovery. I had tried joining various clubs at school—the debate team, the math club, a classic film group. But I still hadn't found anything that spoke to me deeply until I met Jessica.

One night, she arrived to speak with us when we were eating dinner at the outpatient recovery center. She had been a patient years before, sitting in these same chairs, when she was recovering from bulimia.

She shared her history with us, how she had first developed bulimia in high school after watching a TV show about eating disorders in which a girl described how she had made herself sick enough to throw up. Afterward, Jessica went to the bathroom, pulled her hair back, and used the same technique to make herself sick, which marked the beginning of a decade-long battle with the eating disorder.

"For a long time, I was obsessed with that TV show," Jessica told us. "I blamed my eating disorder on it. But after years of therapy, I understand that while it might've been the match that lit the fire, it wasn't the only reason. I have anxiety and perfectionistic tendencies, which made me vulnerable to developing an eating disorder. I now realize I have the power to choose recovery, even when it's hard."

Her words made me think about how much I had blamed my eating disorder on Mom's death. And I realized that, like Jessica, I would have to move past that narrative to maintain long-term recovery. This revelation was profound and wasn't my only one during her visit.

Another light bulb went off when she spoke about the therapist who changed her life. "I don't know what I would've done without my therapist," Jessica said. "She made me believe I could be someone in this world. Because of our work together, I wanted to help people the way she had helped me, so I went back to school to become a therapist. Without the sense of purpose my work gives me, I don't think I would've been able to maintain my recovery this long. Your life has to have meaning, not just to others, but to you too."

I thought about Dr. Larsen and how she had helped me. And I thought about Mom and all the patients she had helped in her career. Succumbing to ED would've meant Mom's death defining my life. But I wanted my mom's life to be her legacy, and choosing to follow in her professional footsteps meant just that.

After my sophomore year ended, I volunteered at a local counseling center near our house for the summer. Listening to other people's struggles didn't shrink the magnitude of my own, but it did help put mine in perspective and made me feel less alone.

I spent the remaining years of high school volunteering at the center before heading to UCLA for college, where I majored in psychology. Like Jessica, I had found my purpose.

41

"SOMEONE WANTS TO say hi to you," Eddie says, putting Sarah on the phone. Every Thursday, they have early dismissal at her school, so they're already home.

"Hi, Beans," she says.

"How was school today?" I ask her.

"It was Mackenzie's birthday. We had chocolate cake. I saved you some, but then I ate it," she says.

I flash to the first birthday party Eddie invited me to for a boy in Sarah's class about six months after we had started dating. It was the first time I was to meet her classmates' parents, and I remember how nervous I felt, unsure of whether I'd fit in.

When we arrived at the large backyard party in Cheviot Hills filled with balloons and a giant bouncy house, a Lululemon mom named Dedra immediately cornered me.

"Do you have kids of your own?" she asked, narrowing her eyes at me.

"No," I said, feeling the word catch in my throat.

"What do you do?" she continued.

"I'm a psychologist," I answered.

She nodded and took a sip of water from a pink hydro flask bottle that dangled on her right pointer finger.

"Well, you snagged a great guy," she told me. "I tried to set him up with my girlfriend, but he said he wasn't ready. I don't think he's been with anyone but you since Sarah's mom died."

Thankfully, at that moment, the birthday boy's parents carried a large, blazing cake into the yard, and I was able to excuse myself from the conversation, which felt more like an interrogation.

After everyone sang happy birthday, Sarah walked over to me and sat down with a slice of cake, while Eddie talked with a few dads.

She chatted about the bouncy house, and I felt so much joy sitting with her talking—the kind of thing I had ached to do with my mom for as long as I could remember.

But then what happened when I was pregnant crept into my consciousness. And I thought about how if Eddie knew the truth, how I'd been restricting food and lost the pregnancy, he might not have asked me to come to the party in the first place, how he might not want me to be in Sarah's life at all.

That's the problem with secrets. They don't stay in small corners. They permeate the air, smoldering until they engulf everything like a Malibu fire.

"Wanna bite?" Sarah asked me, moving her piece of cake in front of me.

I wanted a bite. I wanted to be normal. I wanted to believe I could be who she needed me to be at that moment, but I was too scared, too overwhelmed.

"Thank you," I said. "It's your slice. You should eat it."

"Why don't you get a piece?" she asked me.

"I'm full from lunch," I lied.

A few months later, I lied again at another one of her school functions when she offered me some of her food. My fears about whether I'd measure up as a mom hadn't dissipated. They'd only intensified.

But there was something else brewing underneath the fear. Something deeper. Something I struggled to get my arms around at the time—a feeling of worthlessness. I didn't deserve to be *anyone's* mother. Not after my ED-related miscarriage.

"Are you coming over for dinner?" Sarah asks me over the phone, pulling me out of my memory.

I guess Eddie didn't tell her that I left for New York. Maybe he didn't want to have to lie about why I'm here.

"I can't tonight," I say. "I'm sorry."

"Oh," she says, sounding disappointed.

"But I promise I will again soon," I tell her, wishing I could reach through the phone and hug her.

"Okay," she says. "Bye."

"Bye," I say.

Eddie gets back on the phone. "Paul just texted me that he's still waiting for you to eat lunch. It's almost two o'clock in New York."

"I've been immersed," I explain.

"What's going on?" he asks.

"I can't get into it right now," I say.

"Are you okay?" he says, now sounding worried.

"I'm fine, but I'm about to meet my mom's old roommate from New York," I say, standing in the lobby of an art deco-style building on the Upper West Side. Esther Hermes's building, which I Googled after leaving Alexander Valentine's gallery in Chelsea.

"Her college roommate?" Eddie asks.

"They lived together off campus . . ." I hedge, leaving out how they really met. "I'll call you when I get to Paul's."

"Okay, I'm waiting, and so is he," he says. "One other thing . . ."

"Yes?"

"I love you."

"I love you too," I say. "Both of you."

After we hang up, I think about how I'd give anything to be at his place—going over Sarah's spelling words with her, all of us eating dinner together, instead of where I am right now.

"Excuse me," a doorman dressed in a navy blue uniform with gold buttons says. He points to a Cell Phone Free Zone sign on his desk.

"I'm sorry," I say. "I'm off now. Will you please ring the Hermes residence?"

"And you are?" he asks.

"Irene Mayer's daughter," I say, hoping Esther still remembers my mom.

He dials an old-fashioned black phone on the reception desk, lets her know I'm here, hangs up, and says, "You can go up now."

"Thank you," I say, letting out a sigh of relief. Guess Esther remembers Mom. "What floor?"

"The penthouse."

I step inside the elevator and press the PH button, which I estimate is the eighteenth floor since the last numbered button on the panel is seventeen. I ride up to the top, and when the door opens, and I step out, I realize I'm standing in the middle of a kitchen.

A woman around my age, several decades too young to be Esther, is holding a bruiser of a baby boy spilling out of her arms.

"You're not Esther," I say.

"I'm her daughter," she says.

"Her daughter?"

"Yes, I'm Claire, and this is Louis, her grandson," she says, motioning to the baby boy. "My mom died last year."

"I'm sorry," I say.

"Thank you," she says.

"My mom died too, when I was fifteen."

"I know," she says. "I'm sorry. It must've been so hard to lose her at that age."

"You knew my mom?" I ask her, confused.

"I didn't know her, but I knew of her," Claire responds. Louis starts getting fussy in her arms. "Do you mind if we talk in the living room? All of his toys are there," she says.

"Okay," I say, following her into a massive living room with breathtaking, cinematic views of Central Park and baby toys littered all over the floor.

She picks up a clear teething ring filled with liquid from a pile of toys and hands it to Louis, who sticks it in his mouth and starts sucking on it.

"Please take a seat," she tells me, motioning to a long cream couch as she sits down with Louis on her lap.

I sit down next to them, taking in the majestic views. "This is a beautiful apartment," I say.

"Thanks, it was my mom's. I moved in with her after she got sick with MS so that I could help her, and stayed after she died," she says.

There's a loneliness in her voice. She's not wearing a wedding ring and hasn't mentioned anything about Louis's father or having a partner.

"What brings you to New York?" she asks me.

"I'm trying to learn more about my mom," I say. "May I ask how you knew about her?"

"Sobriety was a big part of my mom's life, so she talked about Irene a lot, who she always said was the one responsible for helping her get sober."

"Really?" I say.

"Your mom must've mentioned how they detoxed together at Bell," she says.

I don't tell her I just learned this fact less than half an hour ago.

"Mom said Irene was admitted first and further along in the detox process," Claire continues. "After Mom arrived and started going through withdrawal hell, ready to give up, Irene was the one there cheering her on, telling her it would get better, and it did. My mom told me she would've never gotten sober without your mom's help."

"Did your mom ever mention anything about a guy my mom was seeing while they were at the halfway house together after Bell? Because I just spoke with Alexander Valentine, the former clinical director there, and he said your mom wasn't a fan of his," I say.

"My mom never said anything disparaging about Irene. She was her hero. Everything my mom achieved in her adult life, from graduating from college to getting married to having a family to dedicating her life to philanthropy, she attributed to her sobriety, and your mom was always at the heart of that."

My mom, a flawed hero, apparently had redemptive qualities.

"Even after Irene left the halfway house, my mom said she still regularly visited her there to support her sobriety efforts."

I'm struggling to absorb what Claire is telling me. Why did Esther tell Claire about her past, but Mom never told me about hers? Was it because I was a teenager? Did she think I might not be able to handle it? It could've served as a cautionary tale at a time when kids experiment, had she been honest with me.

And why didn't Dad ever mention it? I was twenty-eight years old when he died. There was no reason by that time that I shouldn't have known.

Is it possible he didn't know? He must've. She never ever drank, volunteered for *D.A.R.E.*, and dedicated her career to helping other addicts.

Maybe he didn't tell me because he was trying to preserve my memory of her, of who I thought she was. But that doesn't make sense, because if he did know, he was obviously okay with who she was, including her past. He married her and had a family despite her history of addiction.

Maybe he kept it from me for a different reason, something related to her death. Something to do with the Cadells that might've compromised me . . .

"May I ask when your mom first spoke to you about all of this?" I ask Claire.

"In high school, before the congressional hearing in 1997," she says. "It was hard to avoid."

"Congressional hearing?" I repeat.

Her eyebrows raise. "You didn't know about it?"

I shake my head.

"It was the only topic of conversation in our house for months. Mom and Dad fought about it all the time," she says.

"What was the hearing about?" I ask.

"Congress asked patients who had gone through the first opioid detox program at Bell in the seventies, the one our moms were in, to testify in a hearing against TriCPharma. The Feds were trying to establish that the company knew from the start that their drugs were dangerous and addictive. The hearing wasn't compulsory. There were no subpoenas, so it was up to former patients if they wanted to testify, and my dad really didn't want my mom to. He'd heard rumors about the Cadells and was worried about potential retribution. But my mom wanted to anyway. Their drugs stole years of her life and destroyed her youth. She was a fourteen-year-old equestrian phenom headed for the Olympics and got in a riding accident, after which a doctor prescribed her the first generation of TriCPharma 'pain' drugs. She didn't get on a horse again until a decade later."

"I'm sorry," I say.

"Thanks," she says. "Mom and Dad argued a lot about her testifying. She kept saying it would be confidential, how they'd already given interviews about TriCPharma drugs to the head of the research department at Bell Hospital back in the seventies, and how there had never been any problems.

But Dad said this was different, that there were always leaks with congressional hearings, and if the Cadells ever found out that she testified, it could not only compromise her but also put our entire family at risk. One night they had a huge fight about it, and he asked her, 'Don't we matter?' After that, I guess something shifted because she decided not to go through with it."

A chill runs through me, thinking about the same exact fight that Mom and Dad had. It would have been at about the same time too.

"Irene testified though—"

She did?

"—and when she was killed shortly after, there was no doubt in my dad's mind that it wasn't a random hit-and-run accident. He was convinced it was because of a leak from the hearing, even though the testimonies were sealed. My mom was wrecked. She kept saying, 'It should've been me.' She said your mom was the bravest woman she knew."

"Do you know where this hearing took place?" I ask.

"At the Capitol. Your mom stayed in New York at a hotel near us. The night before she was supposed to take a train to DC, she met my mom. After they got together, I remember my mom coming home distraught. I wasn't sure if she was worried about Irene going through with it, or if she felt guilty that she wasn't testifying herself, or both. I had just started high school, and it felt like this dark cloud was hanging over my freshman year."

Wait a minute. The only trip mom took by herself in 1997 before she died was to go to her supposed NYU Tisch reunion. After the trip, she returned home with a bruised body, claiming she had been mugged by a cyclist that had crashed into her on his bike before grabbing her purse and warning me to stay away from New York.

This trip must've been when she went to DC to testify in front of Congress about her opioid addiction. Maybe she wasn't hit by a cyclist who mugged her. Maybe the Cadells roughed her up beforehand to try to scare her into not testifying.

"One of the senators that sat on the committee hearing still works on the hill—Senator Lyon from West Virginia," Claire says. "My parents donated a lot of money to politicians, but after Irene died, they stopped. Last year, before my mom passed, she mentioned that she'd heard the president might unseal the testimonies from the hearing. She wanted me to hear her hero, Irene, testify, and when it didn't happen, she tried tracking down Dr. Siegel. He was the researcher at Bell in charge of their detox unit. She was hoping to find the interviews he did with them back in the day so that I could hear your mom speak. But almost fifty years had passed, and he was long gone. Nobody at the hospital knew where the interviews were either."

Louis starts getting fussy again in Claire's arms. "I need to get his bottle," she says, handing him over to me without any warning and leaving me alone with him in the living room. I awkwardly take him in my arms and try bouncing him on my lap to calm him. But it doesn't work, and he starts to cry.

She quickly returns with a bottle of milk and a slice of chocolate cake that she lays down on the coffee table.

"It was his birthday a couple of days ago, and I have leftovers from the party. Can I offer you a piece?"

"No, I better go," I say. She takes Louis from my arms and puts the bottle in his mouth. "Thank you for speaking with me," I say.

"It's the least I could do," she says. "I'm not sure I'd be here if it weren't for your mom."

"May I use your bathroom before I leave?" I ask.

"Of course," she says, pointing to a door outside the living room.

When I step inside the bathroom, I stare at myself in the mirror, reeling over everything I've just learned, especially

Mom's decision to testify in front of Congress, implicating the Cadells in her opioid addiction, a decision that may have ultimately ripped our family apart.

I can't understand why she did it. Why didn't she take Dad's concerns seriously, as Esther did with her husband? Mom was an intelligent woman who must've known the risks it posed, not just to her but also to Dad and me. They fought about it. If she had listened to him, she likely never would've had to disappear, and I wouldn't be here right now.

While it was nice to hear Claire talk about how much Mom helped Esther, what about me? I was Mom's *daughter*. Why didn't I matter enough for her to make a different choice that might've kept our family intact?

In the end, she chose a path that may have been responsible for irreparably altering the course of my life. And now it seems, twenty-six years later, my life has been turned upside down again because of this decision she made decades ago.

I feel the heat in my chest returning. My anger bubbling over. Not just at her but at the hand I've been dealt.

Why couldn't I have had Esther Hermes as my mother, who was honest with her daughter about her struggles with addiction, the one who decided her family's safety mattered more than testifying in front of Congress? Why am I the daughter left tasked to solve the impossible riddle of what happened to my mom to get my life back?

According to Jay, the Cadells never let past vendettas go, which means they've been trying to find her for twenty-six years and won't stop until they do.

That last thought stops me, because I realize something.

If the Cadells have been searching for Mom since she disappeared twenty-six years ago, I would've noticed someone following me long before now, wanting to see if I've been in contact with her through the years.

But I didn't until last week after my car was broken into when I was with Sarah, which means their pursuit of her is new. So why now? Why are they after her *now*?

Maybe it has to do with what Claire mentioned about the rumor that the president might unseal Mom's congressional testimony along with the others. But that doesn't make sense, because even if she's alive, it's not in her power to stop the president from unsealing it.

Maybe there's something in it. Something she disclosed that they're nervous about her coming forward with if she's still alive and her testimony is released to the public. I have to find out what she said in it.

I pull out my cell phone and text Eddie:

My mom's roommate's daughter asked me to stay to eat.
Texting Paul now to let him know.

Eddie immediately texts me back: *Thanks for the update. Love you.*

I text Paul the same lie and tell him to eat lunch without me if he hasn't already.

I then splash cold water on my face and exit the bathroom. Claire is standing in the hallway in front of the elevator with Louis.

"I know how happy my mom would be about our meeting," she says. "I'm so glad I had the chance to meet you."

"Me too," I say.

The elevator arrives at the penthouse. I step inside, we say our goodbyes, and I ride downstairs to the lobby.

When I leave the building, I do something I'm not proud of. Something I know will not only worry both Eddie and Paul, but something they'd also be dead against me doing. I turn off my cell phone so they can't track me, and hail the first taxi I see.

"Where ya headed?" a driver with thick black eyebrows asks me.

"Penn Station," I say.

CHAPTER

42

September 2000

I T WAS THE fall of 2000 when Dad dropped me off at college for the first time.

I decided on UCLA not only because it was both of my parents' graduate school alma maters. It also allowed me to stay close to my eating disorder recovery community in Los Angeles, and to Dad, who I constantly worried about.

I felt incredibly guilty for moving out of the house and leaving him. A few years had passed since Mom died, and he had never gone on any dates or expressed interest in doing so.

I took some solace in knowing that he at least had his annual fall trip to look forward to. During my junior and senior years in high school, he went on a weekend road trip with his college buddies. He said the guys started the tradition to help support him after Mom died, and one of them had a house deep in one of the Northern California forests, off the grid, where they could completely disconnect from the world.

Even though I was probably old enough to stay back alone, I was recovering from an eating disorder, so he always asked my childhood nanny to stay with me. But she wouldn't need to this year because I would be at college.

After Dad finished helping me carry my boxes into my new dorm room and met my new roommate, we stood in front of his car, saying our goodbyes.

"When are you heading up north on your trip with the guys?" I asked him.

"A couple can't make it this year, so we're not going," he told me.

"Really?" I said, now even more worried that he didn't have it to look forward to in my absence. "Are you rescheduling it?"

"I'm not sure," he said.

"Maybe next year?" I said, feeling guilty about the empty house that awaited him.

He nodded. "Maybe."

I stood there biting my bottom lip, debating whether to come out with it.

"I don't think Mom would want you to be alone for the rest of your life," I said.

"I'm not so sure about that," he responded, half-chuckling.

"It's not funny," I said.

"Stop worrying about me. I'll be fine. Just take care of yourself. That's what matters most."

43

I STEP INSIDE PENN Station with its ninety-two-foot-tall ceiling and enormous glass skylight. I spot a large photography installation featuring the station's transformation dating back a hundred years to present day and a ticket booth next to it.

I quickly dash over. "When does the next train to DC leave?" I ask a woman with her hair pulled back in a red bandana.

"Regular or express?" she asks.

"Express," I say.

"Now," she says.

"One ticket, please," I say, handing her my credit card, which she swipes and hands back to me.

"It's gonna be close. Platform four," she says.

I scan the numbered signs, run toward number four, hop on an escalator, and race down the steps. When I get to the platform, the train is still there, and I jump inside the first door I see.

I walk through a couple of cars to get to my assigned seat before sitting down. Nearly every seat is taken.

The conductor speaks into the intercom: "Attention, passengers. We have a nearly full train today, so please don't block the aisles or doors. We'll be moving shortly."

The doors start to close when a man squeezes in just in time. The train begins to glide down the tracks as he walks toward me.

He sits on one of the few empty seats left across from me. When he rests his hands on his knees, I notice the small heart-shaped birthmark on top of his hand.

The back of my neck immediately breaks out in a panicked sweat. The train is already in motion. I can't hop off. It's also an express with limited stops, so the next one won't be for a while. Maybe I should stand up and move to another car.

"Hello, Beatrice," he says. "I'm special agent Jason Fields from the Federal Bureau of Investigation." He holds up an FBI badge.

I couldn't tell a real one from a fake one. It could be fake, or maybe he's a real agent with a real badge bought out by the Cadells.

"I'm working with Detective David Thompson from the LAPD on Cristina Cadell's disappearance . . ."

"I already told him everything I know when he came to my office," I say.

"I'm not here to question you." He lowers his voice. "Detective Thompson wanted me to let you know that you were right. He went back to the sailboat where Cristina's mother died to take another look. It appears someone tinkered with evidence to frame Cristina for Maria Cadell's murder, which makes sense because we still have no motive for why she'd murder her mother. Everyone close to both of them who we've questioned described an incredibly close relationship between the two."

I take in the information, unsure whose side he's on, not knowing whether to believe him.

"Why have you been following me today?" I ask.

"We wanted to make sure you weren't trying to meet with Cristina. It'll take a few days to put our case together, and she's still considered a fugitive. Trust me, you don't want to aid and abet a fugitive," he says.

"How would I be able to meet Cristina in New York when she's fled to Europe?" I ask.

"Rich people have a way of getting around. Nobody's sure if she's still there," he says. "You visited multiple hospitals today. We thought maybe Cristina was hospitalized, and you were trying to meet her at one of them. But I spoke with Ramona Marino at Bell Hospital, who told me you were looking for your late mother's medical records for your own health reasons."

I'm not sure if this is a ploy to get me to trust him more, to make me open up about Mom, or to give him information about what I may know about her whereabouts. I still don't know whose side he's on.

This is all too much. My hands start to tremble on my lap. I drop them by my side to hide my nerves, but not quickly enough, because he notices.

"Are you all right?" he asks me.

"I'm fine," I say.

"Where you headed?" he says.

"DC, like you," I answer.

"Why?" he asks.

"To advocate for mental health services for veterans. I'm a psychologist."

He looks down at the ground—on either side of me.

"No suitcase?" he asks.

I don't respond.

"By the time we get to DC, it'll be dinnertime," he continues. "How much advocating can you do at the Capitol after it closes?"

"I'm having dinner with a Senate staffer," I say. "You ask a lot of questions."

"Part of the job," he says, smiling for the first time, revealing a toothy grin.

I wish I could turn my phone back on and pretend like I'm texting someone to give him a hard signal that I have no interest in continuing this conversation. But I can't turn it on because then Paul and Eddie will know where I am, and I know they'd try to stop me from doing what I'm going to try to do in DC.

I look out the window instead, hoping Jason will get the hint that I don't want to talk to him. He takes the cue and pulls out his cell phone, leaving me alone, at least for now.

I don't stop staring out the window for the entire three-hour train ride as we pass wetlands, a baseball stadium, a giant sign on the Delaware River bridge that reads: "Trenton Makes—The World Takes," 30th Street Station, Philadelphia, an old cemetery, and the Baltimore and Potomac Tunnel.

As we pass landmark after landmark, I think about Mom, who made this trip decades ago when she went to testify against the Cadells. Was she scared? Why did she do it? Why was she willing to put our family at risk?

We finally arrive in DC, which has no skyline apart from the Washington Monument. When the train pulls into Union Station, I finally look away from the window and down at my watch. It's after six. I doubt anyone will be working at this hour, especially senators. I might have to go to a hotel room and wait until the morning.

"Good luck at your dinner," Jason tells me.

"Thanks," I say.

The train stops, and we both stand up when it abruptly jerks again. Jason bumps into me.

"Sorry about that," he says.

"It's fine," I say, slightly annoyed.

I get off the train and step onto a platform leading to Union Station.

I quickly look for an information kiosk and spot one next to an enormous arch with gold accents.

An older woman with dyed black hair and gray roots sticking out of her scalp greets me.

"Good evening. How can I help you?" she asks, adjusting a flower brooch on her jacket.

"I need to catch a ride to the Capitol," I say.

"The Capitol is a large place," she says. "Where exactly are you trying to go?"

"Where the senators work," I say.

"That would be the Capitol building. There's a large protest going on. Not sure how close you'll be able to get," she says.

"Can I walk there?" I ask.

"You could," she says. "It's a little less than a mile away, or you can exit that door and catch a taxi." She points to a glass door with a taxi sign above it.

"Thanks," I say and rush toward the door.

There's a line with a few people waiting when I step outside. I stand in the back and think about Eddie, how worried he must be that I've been out of touch for several hours, and I feel so guilty.

I try to remind myself that I'm doing this for us, so that I can get my life back and we can be together again. But it doesn't do much to assuage my guilt. I still feel awful knowing what I'm putting him through.

When it's finally my turn, I jump inside the taxi.

"Where ya goin'?" the driver asks.

"The Capitol building."

He pulls away and drives me down a long street until we reach it. The woman at the station was right—there's a massive protest going on.

As we get closer to it, I make out some of the signs the activists are holding:

OUR KIDS ARE NOT FOR SALE
I SPEAK BECAUSE THEY CAN'T
#SAVEOURCHILDREN

I pay the driver, get out of the car, and walk toward the building. A familiar woman is standing on a podium dressed in a suit, speaking next to half a dozen people.

"Child trafficking isn't a red or blue issue. It's a human issue. The passage of this bill is the beginning of the end of high-tech companies profiting off our children's bodies," she says.

I now recognize her—she's a senator from Hawaii.

"I'm proud to be joined today by some of my colleagues," she says, pointing to the people next to her. "Senator Judith Levine from California, Senator Hernando Rosario from Nevada, Senator Walter Lyon of West Virginia—"

I stop listening and immediately start wading through the crowd, trying to get closer to the stage where Senator Lyon—the only remaining member of Congress who Claire said was on the committee hearing that Mom testified in—is standing with a half dozen of his colleagues. For the first time in days, luck is on my side. He's the person who I came to DC to try and meet with.

The senator from Hawaii finishes speaking, and I hear some applause. I'm about halfway to the stage when I see the senators being directed off by security guards.

By the time I finally reach the podium, they're all off to the side, taking questions from reporters. There's a mousy-looking woman with glasses and frizzy brown hair dressed in a gray suit next to senator Lyon.

After the senators finish speaking with the reporters, the guards usher them back to the Capitol building, which is taped off. The mousy-looking woman stays back, next to the reporters, texting on her phone.

"Excuse me," I say, approaching her. "Do you work for Senator Lyon? I saw you standing next to him."

She looks up from her phone. "Yes," she says, pushing up her glasses to the top of the bridge of her nose.

"I have a question for him. Is there any way I can speak with him?"

"Any constituent question needs to be directed to his website—"

"It's not a constituent question," I interrupt. "It's about a congressional hearing that my late mom testified in. Senator Lyon is the only remaining member of Congress that participated in it. I'm trying to find out what she said."

I'm near tears. The day has caught up with me. First, learning Mom was an addict, then learning she chose to testify over our family's safety, and now realizing if I don't solve this riddle, I may never get my life back.

"The transcript might be available online," she tells me.

"It hasn't been unsealed yet," I explain.

"What hearing was it?" she asks.

"The TriCPharma hearing in 1997," I say.

Her eyes go wide. "I'm sorry," she nervously says and quickly walks away.

CHAPTER

44

July 2010

I HAD MAINTAINED MY recovery for over a decade through various support groups and one-on-one therapy. Don't get me wrong, there were many times when ED thoughts still floated through my mind, but I had a support system in place and ways to address them.

I hadn't relapsed once, not even when Dad was diagnosed with lung cancer the year prior. Thankfully, he was in remission after undergoing surgery and several rounds of chemotherapy.

Jay and I had recently gotten engaged and moved in together. We had graduated with our doctorates a couple of years before and had both gone into private practice.

He was at a conference out of state, and I was in the middle of a workday, writing patient notes, when I got a call that Dad was at the hospital again. He had collapsed at work, and an ambulance had taken him there.

I immediately left my office and went to Cedars Sinai Hospital, where he was admitted. As I anxiously rode the elevator up to his room, I wondered what was going on.

As soon as he saw me, he smiled. "Aren't you supposed to be working? You playing hooky to be with your old man?" he joked.

"What's wrong?" I said, sitting next to him on his hospital bed.

"The damn lung. It's giving me problems again. They ran some scans. I'm waiting to hear back."

Just at that moment, a doctor walked in with a grave look on his face.

"This is my daughter," Dad said proudly to the guy.

"Nice to meet you," the doctor said to me before turning back to dad. "I need to speak with you privately."

"Anything you have to say to me, you can say in front of my daughter," Dad told him.

The doctor took a breath in. "We got the results of your scans. I'm sorry, but the cancer has returned."

I closed my eyes, taking in the terrible news.

I had accompanied Dad to every one of his cancer treatment appointments, acting as a surrogate for my mom. On his final day of chemo, I was there, holding a graduation balloon with *Congratulations!* written on it that I'd picked up for him at the supermarket.

But now the cancer was back. I reminded myself that we had licked it before and would do it again.

"Can you please send copies of the scans to his surgeon and oncologist?" I asked the doctor.

"I'm afraid the cancer has metastasized throughout your body," the doctor told Dad.

"What?" I asked, confused.

"It's a quality-of-life issue now," the doctor clarified.

I looked over at Dad, who was quiet. He had registered the doctor's words.

"You can continue with treatments that will probably make you feel sick, but it won't change the outcome," the doctor continued. "You should consider how you want to spend the time you have left. I'm sorry."

It felt like a dream. It couldn't be real. Was I now going to lose Dad too?

After the doctor left, I hugged Dad, and he held me in his arms.

"I promise you'll be okay, Beans. You have Jay and your career, and you know how proud I am of you. That will never change, even if I'm not around."

It hit me, the gravity of the news, and I started to cry.

"I know I wasn't the easiest daughter," I told him. "I'm sorry for what I put you through."

"It wasn't you, Beans," he said. "It was the disease."

I still couldn't help but wonder if I was responsible for causing his cancer due to all the stress he'd endured because of ED.

Later that evening, the nurse finally kicked me out of the hospital room because visiting hours had ended. I left in a dreamlike state, in disbelief over the awful news.

That night I got a call at three in the morning that dad had taken a turn for the worse and that I should come to the hospital.

But the doctor didn't tell us it would be so soon. I would've never left him! I thought.

I ran to the hospital, terrified I might not make it to see him one last time and that I might be deprived of saying goodbye to him as I had been with Mom.

I sprinted into the building and rode up the elevator to his floor. When the doors opened, a nurse stopped me, told me it was after hours, and that I wasn't allowed in any patient's room. I explained the situation, but she told me she still had to verify what was going on before I'd be allowed into his room.

I wasn't about to wait, so I pretended I was going to the bathroom, and as soon as she walked toward a computer station to check something, I headed toward Dad's room.

When I turned the corner, I saw a woman's silhouette leaving it. Her back was facing me as she walked quickly down the hall. She wasn't dressed in medical scrubs. I wondered if she was a visitor who had gone to the wrong room. But it was after hours, so whoever she was, she wasn't allowed to be there.

As I watched her from behind, I realized she looked like Mom, the way I had remembered her. She ducked into a stairwell. I ran down the hall, trying to catch her. But when I opened the stairwell door, she was gone.

And by the time I got to Dad's room, he was too.

CHAPTER

45

I FOLLOW THE MOUSY-LOOKING woman with glasses and frizzy hair away from the crowd.

"Do you know something about the hearing?" I call out to her. "I just want a minute of your time."

"Please stop following me," she says as she ducks into a stairwell of an adjacent building.

I follow her anyway, down the stairs until we reach an underground parking lot. She stops in front of a blue Acura, finally turning to face me.

"I'm sorry, but I can't help you," she says.

"Please, I'm begging you. I came all the way from Los Angeles to try to talk to Senator Lyon about my mom. She died when I was fifteen, and I recently learned she was an addict. I've struggled with addiction, and knowing more about her history might help me with my recovery."

She meets my eyes. That's when I notice the tears in hers.

"My younger brother, Joey, died from an overdose," she says.

"I'm sorry for your loss," I say.

"Thanks," she says.

"Is this your car?" I ask her.

She nods.

"Can we sit down and talk? I promise I won't take more than a few minutes of your time," I say.

She nervously bites her bottom lip before unlocking the car. She sits in the driver's seat, and I quickly open the front passenger side, sitting next to her before she can change her mind.

"What's your name?" I ask her.

"Dawn," she says.

"Nice to meet you, Dawn," I say. "I'm Beatrice."

"I really can't talk about the hearing," she says. "I could get in trouble with my job."

"I get it. I'm a psychologist, and I'm bound by confidentiality in my job too. I promise I won't tell anyone anything you tell me. I have no need to. This is just for me to know, for my recovery."

There's a long stretch of silence between us before she speaks again. "I watched the hearing," she finally says.

"You did?"

"Yeah, but I don't remember what your mom said or anyone's specific testimony. I just remember my main takeaway—that TriCPharma is an evil company, which I already knew," she says.

"What do you mean?" I ask.

"I came to Washington to work for Senator Lyon so that I could help in the fight against the opioid epidemic. We're both from West Virginia, which I'm sure you know has one of the country's highest rates of overdose deaths. He told me I'd have a front-row seat at the table when it came to enacting change. But after I started the job, I found out he gets more campaign contributions from TriCPharma than any other member of Congress."

Oh no—*he's in with the Cadells too?*

"Really?" I say.

She nods, resigned.

"Why do you think he wanted you to work for him, given your history with your brother?" I ask.

"To silence me. I'm from his state, and with my background working for a different senator, I could've made a big difference in the fight against TriCPharma and companies like them, which would've caused him headaches since he's in their back pocket."

"I see," I say.

"After finding out about his connection to TriCPharma, I watched every congressional opioid hearing he participated in. I wish I had seen them before I took the job because I would've known he's always been their puppet. Now it's too late, and I'm stuck."

"You can quit," I suggest.

She shakes her head. "If I quit, he won't give me a recommendation to work anywhere else. Or worse, he'll have me blacklisted from getting another job on the hill. My family's poor. I send money back home to make my parents' lives easier. They went through hell after losing my brother. That's why I didn't want to talk to you. If Senator Lyon knows I'm giving up information about TriCPharma, he'll fire me."

"I'm sorry," I say. "I wish I could help."

"That's kind of you," she says. "I just wish I could've made a difference . . . for Joey."

"I bet wherever he is, he's thankful that you tried," I say.

She smiles at me through her tears. "I can show you the hearing if you want," she says.

My mouth drops open. "You have it?" I ask.

"I downloaded it on my laptop at home," she says. "Senator Lyon's a dinosaur. They're all dinosaurs here. He doesn't even know how to download. I've been tempted to release it to the press, but since it hasn't officially been unsealed yet, I could go to prison if anyone found out it was me."

* * *

I sit at a small dining room table in Dawn's modest one-bedroom apartment near Capitol Hill as she positions her open laptop in front of me.

"Can I offer you any food or water?" she asks.

"Water, please," I say.

She goes to the kitchen, and I start playing the hearing.

A much younger Senator Lyon is overseeing it. Witness after witness speaks about how they were affected by TriCPharma's opioid drugs—husbands who lost wives, wives who lost husbands, children who lost their parents, parents who lost children—when Mom is finally called.

I gasp at the sight of her. Despite the decades that have passed since I last saw her, and the computer screen now between us, she still feels closer to me than she has in years.

"Good morning Chairman Lyon, Ranking Member Mobley, and Members of the Subcommittee," Mom says clearly and confidently. "Thank you to Congress for asking me to participate today to discuss the opioid crisis in the United States and the Cadell family's role. I'm here as someone who was once addicted to TriCPharma opioid drugs and now is a clinical psychologist specializing in treating addiction."

Hearing her voice after so many years, talking about something that impacted her so deeply, something she never shared with me, feels surreal. Like she's come back from the dead in a different incarnation than the mom I thought I knew.

"First, I'd like to speak about my experience as a young college student who became addicted to TriCPharma drugs. I've always suffered from anxiety, and during college, I had a boyfriend who told me he had pills to help calm me."

Alexander Valentine said that Esther Hermes didn't like Mom's boyfriend. This is probably why. Whoever this guy was, he turned her onto these drugs.

"At first, they did calm me. But as is the case with opioids, I needed more and more to get the same effect, and increasingly became nonfunctional when I wasn't taking them.

"Detoxing at Bell Hospital in New York City at the age of eighteen was one of the most wrenching experiences of my life. It was a time that should've been filled with hope and promise about my future. Instead, I was in a detox unit, going through the physical anguish of withdrawal."

Dawn approaches me, handing me a glass of water. I momentarily pause Mom's testimony.

"I haven't seen a video of my mom since she died twenty-six years ago," I let Dawn know, swallowing past the lump in my throat. "It's also the first time I've ever heard her speak about her struggles with addiction."

"That must be hard," she says.

I nod and take a sip of the water before resuming the testimony.

"After I was discharged from Bell, I went to a halfway house. The subsequent years of my life were challenging, requiring intensive therapy and an enduring commitment to my recovery to rebuild my life.

"I'm here today because the Cadell family robbed me of my youth. And tragically, their drugs have become more ubiquitous since I was an eighteen-year-old college student. As a clinical psychologist in Los Angeles, I have witnessed the devastating toll they continue to take on families, destroying lives and stealing loved ones in their prime.

"Last year, I attended a funeral of a patient who died from a TriCPharma overdose after being prescribed one of their pain drugs for a back injury when he could've been treated with over-the-counter ibuprofen. Chronic pain is a serious quality of life issue. But these drugs are being grossly overprescribed at dangerous doses because the Cadell family has only ever had one goal—to ensure as many people become addicted to their drugs as possible so they can turn a profit.

"It's time to end their callous, immoral, criminal enterprise. Doctors take a Hippocratic Oath: Primum non nocere. First, do no harm. Prescribing TriCPharma drugs is harmful to patients. It's time we all stand up to the Cadell family."

And it's over. I close the laptop.

"I need some air," I tell Dawn and walk toward a small balcony off the living room.

When I step outside, I close my eyes, trying to put aside the shock of hearing Mom discuss her experience as an opioid addict, focusing on her testimony to see if I can extrapolate anything that might lead me to her.

Nothing she said struck me as any different from what countless other opioid victims have reported through the years. Nothing that would make the Cadells nervous if she ever came forward, assuming the president unseals the hearing.

The only thing that stood out was her palpable anger toward the Cadells, which felt personal. I guess it *was* personal. They stole her youth.

But her testimony somehow felt different from the others, who spoke broadly about the opioid crisis and their grievances with TriCPharma as a company. Mom seemed intent on personally hanging the Cadells, calling them out repeatedly.

The only personal connection I know of that she had with the family was with her former patient, Margot Cadell. Maybe Margot told her things during treatment that Mom couldn't disclose in the hearing due to patient confidentiality. And maybe those things were so egregious that it propelled her to testify, despite knowing the danger it posed to Dad and me.

"I put this together," Dawn says, stepping out on the patio. She's holding a plate of cheese and crackers.

"I don't have much of an appetite now," I say.

"I understand," she says. "It must've been hard to watch the hearing since you mentioned you only recently learned about her history with addiction."

I nod. "I'd never heard her speak about it before today."

*   *   *

Dawn and I stand outside of her apartment building. She offered to call me a Lyft to take me to Union Station after I lied and told her my phone battery died. I'm not turning my phone back on until I get back to New York.

The guilt is hitting me hard now, how I've gone off the grid for hours. I can only imagine how worried Eddie and Paul are. And I have no idea how I'll explain what I've put them through, especially when I've come up empty-handed. Nothing I heard in Mom's testimony has brought me any closer to finding her if she's alive, and I have no clue what to do now.

The Lyft car pulls up.

Dawn gently puts her hand on my shoulder. "I hope hearing her words helped you," she says.

As difficult as today has been, at least the people I've met have been kind.

I thank her and say goodbye, then get in the car, startled when I realize someone is sitting next to me in the back seat. It's . . . *Paul?*

"Didn't mean to scare you," he says as the Lyft driver pulls away.

"I'm so sorry for going off the grid. I knew you and Eddie wouldn't have been okay with me catching a train to DC," I say, then stop. Something isn't adding up here. "Wait, how did you find me?" I ask, pulling out my cell phone that's still turned off. "How are you in my Lyft?"

He takes the phone from me and points to the square tile on the back that he attached this morning. "The tracker works whether your phone is on or off," he says as he removes it.

"I better call Eddie now," I say. "He must be so worried. It's been hours since we last spoke. Did you tell him where I was?"

"Not exactly," he says.

"I need my phone to call him," I say.

"That won't be possible," he says.

"Why not?" I ask, confused.

He doesn't respond.

"What's going on?" I ask, starting to worry now.

He still doesn't answer.

I start panicking. Something must have happened. If he's reluctant to tell me, it must be bad.

"Is Eddie hurt?" I ask. "Is Sarah?"

He won't even look at me now.

"Tell me what's going on, Paul!" I raise my voice.

He turns to me with an icy metallic stare. "Paul is in Durham, North Carolina, with his husband, Anthony, visiting his father, who's recovering from heart surgery," he says flatly.

"What?" I say, dumbfounded. No, Eddie said Paul texted him that his mom asked them to visit this weekend instead . . .

Oh my God.

The man sitting next to me isn't Paul.

"Paul's phone and house keys were stolen at the airport before he got on the plane last night," he says. "Your boyfriend has been texting me."

Fuck, fuck, fuck!

Where is he taking me? Who *is* he? He must work for the Cadells . . .

God, I've been so stupid.

Everything this impostor told me today has been a lie. His story about being a gay bullied teenager, how Eddie invited him back home during their college breaks . . . I wonder how he found out they were roommates—probably through reading some of Eddie and Paul's old text messages on Paul's phone.

That's why there weren't any pictures of Anthony and Paul at the house. This guy probably hid them, so I wouldn't know he wasn't Paul. He only left out pictures of their dog that he said died. But the dog's probably alive and in a kennel somewhere since Paul and Anthony are in North Carolina.

And all day this impostor has been tracking my movements, probably trying to see if I was communicating with Mom. He must work for the Cadells.

"Who are you?" I ask, panicked, my voice cracking, my dry throat struggling to produce words.

Suddenly all of the car doors lock. I look out the window and realize we're well past the well-lit part of DC, driving through a dark, desolate area without lights.

"Where are you taking me?!" I shout.

The driver violently pulls over to the side of the road and turns the car off.

The man next to me grabs my wrists, squeezing them hard, and looks me right in the eyes. "Shut up," he says.

The driver turns the engine back on, and the car starts moving again.

I sit quietly, shaking in place. I'm being kidnapped.

But unlike when I was fifteen years old and abducted in the Santa Monica mountains by the ninja men who returned me to Better Horizons, this time, I won't be returned. I know that, deep in my bones.

I wonder if, by now, Eddie knows he's been communicating with a fraud. He must be so worried.

And then I have the most terrible thought of all—what if the agent that Paul dispatched to Eddie's house to protect Sarah and him wasn't sent by Paul and sent by the man sitting next to me?

I turn to the man to plead with him. "I was trying to find out if my mom was still alive because I realized I was being followed and thought the fastest way to get you guys to stop was to tell her she needed to disappear again if she was. I have no other motive. I just want to be able to return to my life. Please let me go. I won't look for her anymore. I promise."

"We gave you an off-ramp on the airplane with the text. You didn't take it. Now you know too much. Can't have loose ends running around," he says, his voice dripping with acid.

I think about Mom, how she fled decades ago to protect me from whatever this is, how Dad tried too, keeping her past a secret from me until the day he died, the burden it must have been for him. And how in the end, none of it was enough; it all still caught up with me.

I start to cry.

I think about Eddie and Sarah. How much I love them. How worried I was that I wouldn't measure up as a mom to her, convinced I didn't deserve to be one because of what happened in my first marriage. And now I want that chance more than anything.

"Do you have a family?" I ask the impostor between sobs. He doesn't respond. "Because there's a seven-year-old girl who needs me. I'm the closest thing to a mother she's had since her mom died. I beg you, for her sake, to please let me go."

He turns to me, about to say something, when the car hits something in the road, making it swerve out of control. He's thrown against the side door. His shoulder bangs into it. I grab onto the seat in front of me, trying to stop myself from being tossed around, squeezing my eyes shut, too terrified to watch what's coming next.

"What the fuck!?" the driver shouts, trying to regain control of the car, which keeps spinning. After a few donuts, it finally stops. The driver turns off the engine and immediately gets out.

I look out the window and watch him walk around the car, inspecting it. I turn to the man next to me, who, despite being thrown around, is still clutching my phone.

I consider whether I should try to grab it from him, but he's stronger than me, and so is the driver. They'd wrestle it away before I could try and make a call, assuming there's even reception here. We're in the middle of nowhere.

Every article I've read about what you should do if you're kidnapped says you must never let the kidnappers take you to another location because there's much less of a chance of survival if they do. I need to do whatever I can to break free before they take me anywhere else, even if it means jumping out of a moving car and rolling onto a highway. The problem is there's nothing around here, so even if I try to make a run for it, there are no people who could come to my rescue.

The driver opens the front door and returns to his seat. "Some asshole dropped a box of three-inch nails. One of my tires is almost completely flat," he says.

"Do you have a spare?" the impostor asks.

"Had to use it last week," the driver says.

"Jesus, PJ. You gotta replace a spare after you use it."

"Sorry," PJ says. "We can probably make it to a gas station. I can deal with it there." He pulls out his phone, looking at Google Maps. I guess there is cell phone reception here. "The nearest station is a quarter of a mile away."

"I'll text Ivy and have her meet us in case we need to use her car," the impostor says. He sticks my phone inside his jacket pocket and pulls out his own.

PJ turns the engine back on and starts to drive again.

My heart thumps so loudly in my chest that I can hear it. The box of nails in the road nearly killed us, but it also may have saved me. Now we have to go to a gas station with employees and customers where I can try to make a run for it.

I look over at the man sitting next to me and at the white glare from his phone. He doesn't realize I can see his texts.

Car trouble. Meet us at the next station, he texts.

Three blue dots appear, and then a response from Ivy, whoever she is:

On my way. FYI I don't think she's seen Isaac Siegel's interview.

Siegel . . . Why does that name sound familiar?

It's hard to focus through the gallons of cortisol shooting through my veins. But I know I've heard that name before, and I think it might've been earlier today.

I go through everyone I've met since I arrived in New York City—Ramona at Bell Hospital, Neil at the NYU registrar's office, Laura Poitier at the Tisch theater, Alexander Valentine the art gallery owner, Claire at her penthouse.

That's when I land on it—Claire brought up Dr. Siegel. She said that Esther had tried to get a hold of the interview Mom had done with him at Bell hospital in the seventies so Claire could hear her hero testify.

Who's Ivy, and how does she know about this interview from fifty years ago, let alone what Mom said in it and whether I've seen it or not?

The gas station's overhead fluorescent lights shine brightly into the car as we pull up next to a gasoline pump. Another car is already there—a black BMW. We park right behind it.

A woman jumps out of it and approaches us. This must be Ivy. She's wearing tight black leather pants and has straight blond hair that crawls down her back well past her waist, like a Hollywood supervillain.

As she gets closer, she starts to look familiar. Almost as if mousy Dawn didn't have glasses or brown frizzy hair . . .

It *is* Dawn. She's in on it.

And she has an in with Senator Lyon. Jay was right—the Cadells have infiltrated the highest levels of government.

My heart sinks. How could I have been so naïve, believing her story about her dead brother who overdosed? How grateful I was for her kindness, when it was all a ploy to trap me. She showed me Mom's testimony to get me to trust her so that she could fish for information—to confirm that I hadn't seen Mom's interview with Dr. Siegel. And because I told her Mom's congressional testimony was the first I'd ever seen her speak about her addiction, she got the answer she needed—that I hadn't seen the other interview.

PJ opens the glove compartment and grabs a strap of rope. He gets out of the driver's side, walks around to my door, and opens it.

This is my one chance to escape, so I immediately start kicking, screaming, and trying to escape. "HELP! HELP! HELP!" I scream.

The impostor next to me yanks me back by my hair, making me scream even louder.

"I'd keep it down," he says, pointing something into the small of my back. Something that feels like what I imagine a gun might feel like.

"Give him your hands," he says, motioning to PJ, still holding the rope.

Fearing for my life, I put my hands in front of me. I stare at Mom's bracelet on my wrist, my name and birthdate engravings, and the small scratch on the lima bean charm, until it all disappears underneath the rope. After PJ finishes tying my hands, he closes the car door and walks toward the gas station store.

The impostor turns to me and says, "I better not hear a peep out of you. And don't bother trying to get anyone's attention. The windows are tinted. Nobody can see inside."

He gets out of the car and walks up to Ivy. She smiles at him and gives him bedroom eyes. He leans her against the BMW, and they passionately kiss as if kidnapping someone is a huge turn on for them.

This is my last chance to escape. There's got to be an employee inside the store that could help me. But they won't be able to hear me if I kick and scream inside the car; the impostor kissing Ivy, who has a gun, will.

My best bet is to open the car door and make a run for it. With my hands tied, my feet are my only option. I lift my left foot, trying to kick off my shoe so I can use my toes to open the door, but the shoe won't come off.

I try bending my ankle on the ground, using the carpet as leverage to get it off. It's the same ankle still sore from when I slipped trying to chase Cristina Cadell out of my office. The car's rug burns against my ankle. The shoe about halfway off when another car pulls up next to ours.

The driver gets out, and I gasp. It's Special Agent Jason from the FBI.

Oh God, he's in on this too. He surveys the station, glancing over at Ivy and the impostor still kissing next to the BMW, but doesn't say anything to them and walks toward the store instead.

He steps inside for a moment but then quickly exits, approaching Ivy and the impostor, showing them his FBI badge.

Wait, so he *isn't* in on this?

I start kicking and screaming to let him know I'm inside the car. He registers the noise, pulls out a concealed firearm from his pants pocket, and runs toward me in the car.

"HELP! HELP! HELP!" I keep screaming.

Ivy and the impostor jump in her BMW just as PJ walks out of the station, holding a pack of gum in his hand and popping a piece in his mouth.

"They got an extra tire—" PJ calls out to them when he sees Jason with his gun drawn, moving around the car I'm in.

PJ runs to the BMW and jumps inside, barely making it, as Ivy and the impostor peel away.

Jason quickly turns in their direction and fires a couple of shots toward the BMW's tires, trying to stop them. The sound moves through me like a violent earthquake.

But it's too late. They're gone.

"Help!" I scream again and again.

Jason returns to the car, carefully casing it, listening to me scream in the back seat, before moving to the front driver's side, unsure if anyone's there because of the tinted windows.

He tries opening each door handle but they're all locked, so he bashes the driver's side window with his gun. The glass shatters, pouring into the front seat. He looks in the back seat and discovers me alone with my hands tied.

His face melts in relief. "You're safe now," he says.

"But you're not," I whisper.

CHAPTER

46

September 2012

AFTER DAD DIED, I struggled. Coming to terms with being parentless was overwhelming, and I knew I was at risk for relapsing, so I went to biweekly therapy sessions and two different eating disorder recovery groups.

I also threw myself into my work, building my private practice, spending time with Jay and his parents, trying to keep myself busy.

Jay and I had talked about getting pregnant, but I wasn't sure if I was ready. I decided to go off birth control to see what would happen. I had multiple friends who had struggled to get pregnant, so I assumed it would take a while. But it didn't.

On my thirtieth birthday, we had plans to go for dinner at Shutters on the Beach in Santa Monica. Jay had told me he had a surprise he was planning to give me after we finished eating. I didn't tell him that I had one too.

We sat outside next to the Pacific Ocean, looking at the surfers in wetsuits paddling out on their boards to catch a few more waves as the sun set.

After I blew out the candle on a slice of red velvet cake, Jay took out an envelope from his pocket and handed it to me.

"Happy birthday," he said.

I opened it to find two plane tickets to Rome for the summer. He knew it was the last trip Mom, Dad, and I had gone on together before she died. Tears bubbled in my eyes, thinking about how much I missed them and how much I would miss them in this next chapter of my life.

"Thank you," I told Jay. "But we might have to hold off on the trip."

"What do you mean?" he said.

I took out an envelope from my bag and handed it to him. He opened it and pulled out a pregnancy stick test with two pink lines.

"You buried the lede!" he shouted, jumping up from his chair.

He pulled me into a hug, beaming, happier than I'd ever seen him, and kissed me deeply. Every hope and dream we had for ourselves and our future was in that kiss. I imagined all the holes left inside me after losing Mom and Dad, now filling up with our growing family.

After a minute, Jay pulled away. "Do you hear that?" he asked me.

"What?" I asked.

He pointed to the outdoor speakers. "The song that's playing . . ." he said.

It was "Angie" by the Rolling Stones.

"If it's a girl, we'll name her Angie," he told me.

CHAPTER

47

S PECIAL AGENT JASON unties my hands and lets me out of the car as the gas station attendant runs out of the store after hearing shots fired.

Jason shows him his FBI badge, explains the situation, and tells him his backup got delayed due to the protest in the Capitol.

The attendant returns to the store, and Jason asks me, "Are you okay? Did they hurt you?"

"They didn't," I say. "How did you find me?"

He takes my purse and pulls out a small black dot that looks like a tiny beetle.

"This little guy helped," he says.

I remember when he "accidentally" bumped into me on the train. He must've dumped the bug into my bag then.

"Even though you said you didn't know where Cristina Cadell was, I wasn't convinced. I thought you might still be able to lead us to her. We need her help in our case against her father. The Cadells are worried about what she might've told you. That's why they hired those guys to go after you," he says.

I shake my head. He still doesn't know anything about Mom and the real reason they've been following me. Why would he? She's just a random woman who died decades ago, and Cristina is the shiny object, a fugitive and heir to the billion-dollar Cadell fortune who can help them bring down the family.

"Am I being recorded right now?" I ask Jason.

"No," he says.

"After what you did here today, the Cadells will know you're not on their side," I tell him.

"You don't think they already know that?" he asks.

"It's not just them," I say. "They've infiltrated people at the highest levels of government. I saw the woman who just drove away in the BMW talking to a senator—Senator Lyon of West Virginia. I'm sure there are people you work with at the FBI, high-level people, maybe even your bosses, who the Cadells own. Once they find out what you've done here, you'll be persona non grata—or worse."

"I swore an oath to defend and protect the constitution. That doesn't waver, no matter how dangerous the criminals are that I come up against, even if they're on the inside. Detective Thompson and I aren't going to stop until we find Maria Cadell's real killers," he says.

"If you have a family, they'll go after them too, same with Detective Thompson," I say.

He shrugs, unmoved. "Growing up, I never had a family. I was bumped around from foster home to foster home until I was nine, when a teacher at school reported to child services that my fourth foster father was abusing me. A detective assigned to my case didn't stop doing his job, despite my foster father's threats against him and his family. That detective saved me, adopted me, brought me into his family, and treated me as if I were one of his own children. He was the best father anyone could've asked for, the best man I've ever known, and the one who taught me about the gravity of the oath I swore."

I'm not going to be able to get Jason to walk away from this.

"The most important thing now is to secure your protection," he says. "The Cadells operate like the mob and will keep going after you as long as they think Cristina divulged information to you about her mother's murder."

"What do you mean by protection?" I ask.

"When we get back to headquarters in New York City, my colleagues will discuss your options with you."

More police cars start to pull up. Officers get out and draw yellow tape around the gas station.

"I gotta talk to my colleagues," Jason tells me.

"They stole my phone," I say. "I need to call my boyfriend in LA to tell him I'm okay."

"I have an extra burner in my car," he says. "Hang on."

He walks to his car, pops open the trunk, pulls out a burner still in the store's plastic packaging, and walks it back to me.

"Here," he says, handing me the new phone. "Never been used."

"Thank you," I say.

"I'll be back soon," he says.

"Okay."

He walks toward the other officers, and I call Eddie, who immediately picks up. "Hello?" He sounds worried.

I panic, scared that the agent stationed in front of his house is a fake and might've hurt either of them.

"Are you and Sarah okay?" I ask.

"We're fine, but I've been trying to call you for hours and couldn't get through. Are you all right?"

Thank God they're all right. I can't tell him what's happened—it'll worry him more. "Yes, I'm okay," I say.

He breathes an audible sigh of relief. Then he says in a rush, "The person you're dealing with isn't Paul, Beans. I was on Instagram this afternoon and saw pictures Anthony posted of Paul and him with Paul's dad at the hospital, so I immediately reached out to him. Turns out someone stole

Paul's phone and keys right before they got on the plane, which means I've been texting with someone else. Thankfully, Paul sent out his colleague to my place before he left, so the guy guarding my place is legit. But whoever picked you up at the airport isn't Paul. They probably work for the Cadells. Did you ever go back to Paul's place?"

"No," I say, trying to sound as normal as possible.

"I'm so sorry, Beans," he says. "I had no idea."

"It's not your fault," I say, feeling guilty. He's beating himself up for not knowing that I was dealing with an impostor, while I went to DC behind his back, and I'm now keeping from him what's happened.

"The FBI has locked down Paul's place. He and Anthony are heading back from North Carolina now. Where are you?"

"I couldn't find a flight back to LA until the morning and decided to stay at my mom's old roommate's place," I lie.

"You're calling from her place?" he says. "I don't recognize this number."

I swallow hard and muster another lie. "I picked up a burner to be safe," I say

"Smart," he says. "I'm so glad you're all right. Call me when you get to the airport in the morning. I love you."

"I will," I say. "Love you too."

We hang up, and Jason walks back to me. "Time to go back to Manhattan," he says.

We get in his car. Billy Joel's greatest hits play in the background as he drives.

I look out the window and register how I'm feeling for the first time in hours. I'm thirsty, I really need to use the bathroom, and I'm so tired.

I want to go home to my old life, but this nightmare is far from over. I don't even know if I can trust Jason. I think he's on my side, but after everything that's happened today, I'm not sure I can trust anyone.

"What did you mean about securing me protection from the Cadells?" I ask again.

"My colleague from the US Marshals office will speak to you about WITSEC when she arrives at headquarters," he says.

"WITSEC?" I repeat.

"Witness protection," he clarifies.

"You mean where I abandon my life and start over in a dirt-filled town in the middle of nowhere with a new identity?"

"I know it's not what anyone wants to do, but it's how you can best protect yourself and the people you care about, at least for now," he says.

If Mom is still alive, she didn't choose that option when she left Dad and me, or Jason would know about her and the real reason the Cadells are coming for me now. And after the last few days, I understand why she wouldn't have. The Cadells have penetrated the highest levels of government, which means she wouldn't have been safe entering a government program like WITSEC.

And Jason telling me I'm still in danger is nothing I don't already know. But he doesn't know the real reason why or that the people I love, Eddie and Sarah, will be too, as long as the Cadells think I'm a loose end that knows too much—a loose end without any *leverage*.

But I'm about to try to change that. Because I know the one thing that might give me leverage over them, the one thing they're worried about me uncovering—whatever happened in Mom's interview with Dr. Siegel.

Everything hinges on this now. As soon as we get back to the city, I'm going back to Bell Hospital to track it down.

48

October 2012

THE OB/GYN APPOINTMENTS came fast and furiously, and I was always weighed. Given that weight gain and pregnancy go hand-in-hand, and that it's not only unavoidable but also necessary, I thought I'd be okay with it.

At first, I was, but when I began struggling to eat due to my pregnancy-related nausea and experienced an energy deficit, ED resurfaced. And I found I was no longer comfortable with my changing body.

As my thighs swelled and my stomach grew larger, I scoured the internet for pregnancy charts, wanting confirmation that I was at the lowest point of the acceptable weight gain guidelines. I also began seeking out other pregnant women to compare my weight gain to theirs to make sure mine was less. I'd stare at their stomachs, needing that reassurance.

"You've lost weight since our last appointment two weeks ago," Dr. Dina, my OB/GYN at the time, told Jay and me during a pregnancy well-visit appointment. "I want to run some tests to ensure there's nothing wrong, no fetal abnormalities or genetic defects."

Jay was sitting next to me silently, but I knew what was on his mind.

He finally came out with it. "I don't think Beatrice is eating enough. She's also exercising more than before she was pregnant."

"Oh?" Dr. Dina said, looking up at me from her chart.

"I think she might be relapsing."

I sat there in disbelief as the words came out of his mouth, remembering how happy he'd been when I first told him I was pregnant. Now there wasn't any joy on his face, only worry.

"I had anorexia in high school, but I've been in recovery for over a decade," I told Dr. Dina.

It had been fourteen years since I had left Better Horizons, and I had successfully maintained my recovery until this point, even after losing Dad, so I thought I had ED licked.

But the truth was over the last year, I had stopped going to individual therapy and had been going to my eating disorder support group less and less, showing up monthly instead of weekly.

I was slipping in my recovery without realizing it, and ED was there the whole time, patiently waiting for a chance to creep back into my life.

"I'd still like to run the tests," Dr. Dina said. "I'm also recommending that you speak to a psychiatrist."

"That's completely unnecessary," I said defensively. "I'm a psychologist. I'd know if I had a problem." The thought that I might be putting my pregnancy at risk was too much to bear.

"It isn't a choice. Otherwise, I'll have to call social services," she warned.

I was stunned. After a career where I had made occasional calls to social services to report parents who had endangered their children, it felt inconceivable that someone could potentially report me for doing the same.

I looked over at Jay, who seemed relieved by what Dr. Dina had said, and I was angry at him for disclosing what he had. But really, it was ED who was mad because he was being boxed in.

A couple of days after the visit to the doctor, I woke up with intense cramps. When I went to the bathroom, the toilet bowl was filled with blood.

And I fainted.

CHAPTER

49

Day Four

F BI HEADQUARTERS ARE in a gray, nondescript high-rise
building in a sea of gray, nondescript high-rise buildings
in midtown Manhattan. Unlike the others that barely have
any lights on at this late hour—2:07 AM—this one's lit up
like a Christmas tree and bustling.

I'm sitting on a chair in a small room with harsh fluorescent lights. Jason is standing in front of me.

"Someone from the US Marshals office will be coming
by soon to discuss WITSEC with you," he says. "Want something to drink?"

"No, but I'd like to use the restroom," I say. "I haven't
used one in hours."

"Of course, it's the last door on your right," he says,
pointing down the hall. He has no reason to believe I might
walk out of here, so I continue acting like I'm not planning
to. I don't have time to waste arguing over WITSEC with his
colleagues.

She's running out of time.

I can only pray that if Mom is still alive, she hasn't been
found yet, which is why those thugs tried to kidnap me in DC.

I walk down the hallway and make a right, but instead of going into the bathroom, I duck into the first stairwell I see, run down five flights of stairs as quickly as possible, straight through the lobby until I'm in front of the building.

Several taxis are driving down the street in the city that thankfully never sleeps, and I immediately hail one.

"Bell Hospital," I tell the driver as I jump inside. "Quickly, please."

"Medical emergency?" he asks.

I nod, he puts his foot on the gas, and we peel away.

* * *

A woman with pursed purple lips sits behind the information desk at the hospital entrance, playing Animal Crossing on her cell phone.

I stare at a row of television screens hanging behind her, tuned to different news channels—NY1, ABC, MSNBC—covering Cristina Cadell's flight from justice for her mother's murder. Footage plays of the Cadell brothers with a group of reporters. Quentin Cadell implores the public for tips about Cristina's whereabouts while his older brother William Jr. stands behind him. They're still intent on framing Cristina for her mother's murder.

The woman with the pursed lips looks up at me. "What can I do for you?" she asks.

My gaze moves away from the television screens back to her.

"I'm trying to get the contact information for Dr. Siegel, who worked in the opioid detox ward in 1974," I say.

She looks at me as if I'm not in my right mind. "You know that was fifty years ago?"

"Yes," I say.

"The hospital doesn't keep contact information that long. Try Google."

I can't Google anything on the burner Jason gave me. I glance over at the computer screen in front of her.

"May I use your computer to search for him?" I ask.

She gives me another funny look. "Not allowed, hospital policy," she says. "There are computers at the New York Public Library. You're free to wait at the coffee shop behind me until it opens."

I consider my options. At this point, Jason probably has a slew of FBI agents fanned out throughout the city looking for me, worried the Cadells have kidnapped me again. I know from my work as a therapist that the first places authorities look when people disappear are hospitals, so if I stay here, it's just a matter of time before they find me.

Maybe I should go back to Claire's place. I bet she'd help me, but it's the middle of the night, and I don't want to wake her baby or entangle her in the Cadell web I'm caught up in. Esther Hermes spared her family for a reason.

"Thank you for your time," I say to the woman.

I walk out of the hospital and notice an open FedEx store across the street. I dash toward it.

When I step inside the store, there's only one employee there. He's standing behind a cash register with his eyes closed, headphones on, singing "Ain't No Sunshine" by Bill Withers.

He's so enraptured with the music that he doesn't notice me. I walk up to him, waving my hand until he finally does. He drops his headphones down to his neck.

"My cell phone broke, and I need to do a Google search. May I use one of your computers?" I ask him.

"We're having Wi-Fi issues. A guy's supposed to come in the morning to fix it. I can search on my phone for you if you want," he offers.

I nod in thanks. "I'm trying to find the contact information for Dr. Isaac Siegel of Bell Hospital."

"How do you spell his last name?" he asks.

I try to remember how the impostor spelled it in the car. "S-I-E-G-E-L," I say.

"That was easy," he says. "Only one Isaac Siegel from Bell and only one address for him."

"What's that?" I say, grabbing a pen and a piece of paper lying on the counter.

"657 East 63rd Street."

*　*　*

The dilapidated brownstone wedged between two high-rise buildings on the Upper East Side looks condemned. Some of the windows have holes covered in duct tape. The doorbell has a handwritten sign that reads BROKEN in all caps.

I loudly knock on the door despite the late hour, not worried about neighbors being woken up because nobody in the high-rise buildings on either side can hear me.

After about a minute of knocking and no response, I make a fist and start banging on the door. When that doesn't work, I lift my foot and start kicking it forcefully. Finally, a light turns on inside, and I hear footsteps shuffling toward me.

"Go away," an old man says. "I have a Taser."

"Dr. Siegel?" I say.

"I told you to go away," he says.

"So, you are Dr. Siegel?" I ask.

He doesn't respond.

"My name is Beatrice Bennett. My mother was Irene Mayer. You interviewed her back at Bell Hospital in the seventies."

"Go away," he says again.

How do I get him to open the door to speak with me? I take out my driver's license and slide it under the crack of the front door.

"You have my license. If you don't open the door and return it to me, I'll call the police and tell them you stole it."

He slips the license back underneath the door.

"Please," I say, softening my voice now. "I'm begging you. I need to speak with you."

"Go away," he says for the fourth or fifth time.

I look around the dilapidated building, searching for any reason to force him to open the door and speak with me. That's when I spot it—a messy electrical panel on the side of the brownstone. There's no way it's up to code. Living in Los Angeles, with constant fire dangers, I know the electric company comes out 24/7 if there are any potential fire hazards.

"I don't think your electrical panel is up to code," I say. "It looks hazardous. I better call ConEd to let them know. I'm sure they'll send city inspectors to check out the rest of your house. Who knows what they might uncover—"

The door slowly opens, only a couple of inches, revealing a slouched man with a full head of gray hair, holding what looks like a cigarette lighter.

"What do you want?" he says, angry.

"To speak with you. Inside," I say.

"No," he says.

"Then I guess I have to call ConEd," I say.

He begrudgingly moves a couple of inches, letting me into the front hall.

I take in the brownstone, which has seen better days. Wallpaper is peeling off of the walls. There are several rusty orange rain stains on the ceiling.

"Can we please sit down and talk?" I ask him.

He sighs heavily, pointing me to a dining room with piles of books and papers everywhere.

"Here," he says, lifting a pile of newspapers from a chair. He sits across from me at the table, still clutching the Taser lighter in his hand like it's a weapon he's prepared to use against me.

"I'm here because of my mother, Irene Mayer," I say. "She was one of the first opioid patients that detoxed at Bell Hospital. You interviewed her, and I'm wondering if you remember what she told you."

"No," he says, curtly. "I interviewed a lot of patients."

"Do you know where the tapes of the interviews are?" I ask.

"The hospital kept them when I left. Anything else?"

I don't know whether I believe him or not. His only goal seems to be to shut down this conversation as quickly as possible and get me out of here.

"Why did you leave?" I ask.

"That was a long time ago. Doesn't matter now," he says.

"Was it because of the Cadells?"

"I don't have the tapes you're looking for," he says.

As a psychologist, I'm trained to notice when people are avoiding something. And Dr. Siegel just skipped over answering my question about whether the Cadells had something to do with his departure from Bell Hospital. Instead, he repeated his line that he doesn't have the tapes.

"Did they threaten you?" I press.

"You know what?" he says, shoving the table angrily to the side before standing up. "Just get out of here. I don't care if you call the electric company."

There's a saying in my field: The more hysterical people become, the more historical the material is. And there's something about what I just said that upset him deeply, dating back many, many years ago to when he was a young researcher.

"The Cadells didn't send me, if that's what you're worried about," I say. "Look me up. I'm a psychologist trying to find out if my mother is still alive. She died twenty-six years ago, but I recently learned that she might've had to disappear because of that crime family. And there's something in the interview you did with her that they're worried about me finding out. Something that may damage them and that may lead me to her if she's still alive."

He meets my eyes for the first time. "I'm sorry, I can't help you," he says with a notable shift in the tone of his voice. Almost like he wishes he could, but something's stopping him.

Maybe he doesn't trust me enough yet. Getting people to trust me is a skill I've had to cultivate over the years. Patients need me to bear witness to their most traumatic emotional injuries so they can heal. But they won't open up to me unless they feel safe in the therapeutic relationship, so I've learned how to align myself with them. Once they feel they can trust me, they do.

I need to do this with Dr. Siegel. I need to find a way to make him feel like he can trust me. There's clearly something he wants to tell me.

I look around the dining room for clues that might help. The dated furniture, a wooden cabinet filled with china, seemingly endless piles of papers everywhere—on the ground, chairs, and the table.

Over a couple dozen framed photographs of Dr. Siegel and his wife are mounted on the walls. The pictures tell a story—a love story.

They start with the two when they're young, in their twenties, traveling the world, happy, and in love. A photo of them on a camel together in front of the pyramids in Egypt. Another of them side by side, smiling in front of the Alhambra Palace in Spain. Yet another of them making goofy faces at Caesars Palace in Las Vegas.

Then come the wedding pictures. The two of them standing under a chuppah, holding hands. She's dressed in a traditional white gown with a veil. He's dressed in an old-fashioned tuxedo, beaming. There are several pictures of their wedding party, family, and friends surrounding them, smiling and laughing, a sharp contrast to his now isolated, solitary existence.

There's a picture of them standing on the stoop of this townhouse, smiling with their sunglasses on, boxes on each side of them. There's another picture of them in their backyard garden, reading newspapers on lounge chairs, with coffee cups on side tables.

But then the pictures change.

His wife's smile comes less frequently. She's seated and looks tired, as if standing might be more than her body can bear.

The final picture is a small one around Christmastime in front of a fireplace mantel decorated with stockings. She's sitting on a chair, visibly too frail to stand, looking far older than her years. Dr. Siegel is standing next to her with his hand on her shoulder, still the ever-doting husband.

"I can see how much you loved your wife," I say, pointing to the photographs on the wall.

He doesn't respond.

"I hope I'm not speaking out of turn, but it looks like she was taken away from you in the prime of her life. My mom was around the same age when she was taken from me. She was my world—and the Cadells might've stolen her from me."

Dr. Siegel's face suddenly turns beet red. He tightly clenches his hands into fists and slams them on the table, dropping the Taser lighter on it.

"They killed her!" he shouts.

A gasp escapes me. "What happened?" I whisper.

He slumps back down in his chair with tears in his eyes, all the fight beaten out of him.

"I was a researcher at Bell doing patient interviews when I discovered the truth about TriCPharma drugs, the lives they stole, the families they ruined. Once the Cadells learned about my interviews, they came to the hospital asking me to stop. They said they were tinkering with a new formula to make the drugs less addictive. I was raised in the Bronx and could smell a con a mile away. I knew they were lying, but I was young and filled with bravado. Thought I could change the world by bringing down the bad guys, even when they threatened me. So they moved on to my precious Amelia, harassing her every time she left our house."

"They killed her?" I ask.

He nods with watery eyes. "That morning, she called me from her office saying a guy had followed her to work. She saw him leaving the bathroom on the same floor as her office. She wanted to come home but had an important client meeting, so we planned for me to meet her at her office building right after it finished, and we'd walk home together. I wanted to protect her from being harassed. I never dreamt they'd . . ." He trails off in despair.

"What did they do?" I prod, because I need to know, and time is running out.

"A couple of hours after she phoned me about the guy that followed her to work, I got a call that she'd been admitted to the hospital because she 'accidentally' tripped in her office, hit her head on her desk, and suffered a brain injury."

"Oh my God."

"I ran to the hospital. The doctors didn't know if she'd make it. She survived but had no memory of what happened. She also had no memory of how to do basic things like eat and talk," he says, pointing to the pictures on the wall of her deteriorating. "I brought her home and tried so hard to bring her back to health, but she died a couple of months later in her sleep, of a stroke, common after a brain injury."

"I'm so sorry," I say. "Did you ever tell the police about how she had called you and told you she'd been followed to work?"

The tears in his eyes dry out. He looks at the pictures of his late wife with hardened eyes. "I tried, but it didn't matter. The Cadells pulled all the levers. If they wanted to make a police investigation go away, it went away. Amelia would still be alive if it weren't for them . . . and me. I'll never forgive myself."

I look at this elderly man sitting before me, recalling his late wife. I think about all the years they missed out on together because of this evil family, and I feel heartbroken for him.

"It wasn't your fault. It was the Cadells."

He meets my eyes like he's mulling something over.

"I have the interviews," he finally says.

"Here?" I ask, the word catching in my throat.

He nods.

"Can I see my mom's?" I say, almost breathless.

"Come with me."

He stands up from the dining room table, passes the pictures of his wife on the wall, and stops at the very last one—the one at Christmastime, where she's seated next to him, and he has his hand on her shoulder. He kisses his fingers and places them on her before moving on.

I follow him out of the dining room, up two flights of stairs, and into an attic. It's filled with dusty boxes and old furniture, including broken lamps, a dresser missing a drawer, and a faded yellow old mattress.

He walks toward the back, stopping underneath a leaking window. There are a few wooden floor panels covered in black mold. He pries one open from the ground with his hands, revealing a hollowed-out secret compartment with dozens of VHS tapes.

"After Amelia's accident, I left my job at Bell and became an accountant. I took the tapes with me. The hospital didn't want the interviews. They knew the dangers holding onto them posed and told the Cadells I had them. I considered contacting the press, but I was worried the Cadells might target Amelia's parents, who were devastated after their precious daughter died. So I kept them and built this compartment to hide the interviews. I figured the mold would be a good deterrent if they ever came by looking for them."

"Did they?" I ask.

He nods. "More times than I can count. They hired people to break in when I wasn't home and ransacked my place over and over again, searching for the tapes. I filed multiple police reports, even though I knew nothing would ever come of them. Eventually, they gave up and stopped breaking in. I thought maybe one day after I died, someone might discover the tapes and release them to the world, and the Cadells would finally get what they deserve."

"Thank you for protecting them," I say. "May I take a look?"

"Go ahead."

I get down on my knees and sift through the tapes. They're labeled with patient names, patients whose lives were destroyed by TriCPharma drugs. I go through several dozen tapes and come across Esther Hermes's, but I don't see Mom's. I keep looking until I spot one wedged in the back corner. It's stuck. I have to jimmy it to get it out. When I pick it up, I see the name—Irene Mayer.

"This is my mom's," I say.

"I'm not sure what kind of condition it's in," Dr. Siegel says. "After I left Bell, I became an accountant. I haven't watched these interviews since. I have a VHS player downstairs. We can try playing it."

"Okay," I say, standing up, patting the attic's dust off my hands and knees. I follow Dr. Siegel back downstairs into his study, where there's a desk, chair, small sofa, and an old television on a stand with a VHS recorder delicately balanced on top of it.

I hand Dr. Siegel the tape. My hand shakes, and Mom's bracelet with the lima bean and its engravings and scratch tremble on my wrist. I've barely eaten the last few days, and I'm on the precipice of possibly learning what the Cadells are so nervous about me uncovering—the only possible leverage I'll have to reclaim my life.

Dr. Siegel inserts the tape into his VHS player and presses the play button. The film quality is grainy with light streaks on it.

A much younger Dr. Siegel is seated at a small table in a nondescript room, speaking into the camera, which is shaky at first but quickly steadies.

"Today's interview is with Irene Mayer, who was admitted to the hospital three weeks ago. How are you doing today, Irene?" he says.

The camera clumsily moves to my very young mom, dressed in a mint green hospital gown, seated across from Dr. Siegel behind the same table.

"Okay," she says.

"Can you tell us what brought you to Bell?"

"I'm a freshman at NYU. I've always had anxiety. A friend, well, a boyfriend, told me there was this pain medication that might help me, so I tried it and got addicted," she says.

This is the boyfriend that she also mentioned in her congressional testimony.

"What has the detox process been like for you so far?" Dr. Siegel continues.

"Like someone pulled out the insides of my body, hammered them over and over again, and then stuffed them back inside of me. I wouldn't wish this experience on my worst enemy," she says.

"I'm sorry," he says.

"But I'm also grateful to be here, for a chance at recovery," she says.

So far, I don't understand why the Cadells would be worried or care about me seeing any of this. If anything, Mom seems less intent on personally hanging them in this interview than she did in her congressional testimony.

I pause the tape and turn to Dr. Siegel. "Can I ask you a question?"

"Sure," he says.

"Why do you think the Cadells would care about this interview now?"

"An old lawyer friend of mine once told me these interviews establish decades-old misconduct on the company's part, which could impact sentencing if the Cadells are ever brought to justice."

Claire mentioned that, too, about the congressional testimony. But if that were the case, why aren't they worried about all the other patients Dr. Siegel interviewed at Bell, like Esther? They never went after her. Why are they focused on Mom and what she said? Maybe there's still something to come in the interview.

"Let's keep going," I say, turning it back on and focusing my attention on the television.

"Can you tell me what this experience has meant to you as a freshman in college?" Dr. Siegel asks Mom.

"It's changed me. I have this vulnerability now. I don't mean to sound negative, but I know I'll have to grapple with this addiction for the rest of my life. It feels unfair to be dealt this hand at my age. Had I known how addictive TriCPharma drugs were, I never would've taken them in the first place," she says with a pained, regret-filled look.

"For others struggling with opioid addiction, what would you like to say to them?" he asks.

"That there's hope. There's always hope for recovery." It feels like she's speaking to me through the screen about my own recovery and the eating disorder that first took root inside me after she was gone.

"We're glad you're here with us," Dr. Siegel says.

She nods. There's still nothing jumping out at me in this interview. Nothing that gives me any leverage over the Cadells or leads me any closer to her if she's still alive.

"Irene," a woman calls from off-screen.

"Looks like the nurse needs you," Dr. Siegel says to Mom. "We can finish the interview later or tomorrow."

"Okay," Mom says.

She pushes her chair away from the table and stands up. And for a split second, right before the video turns off, I see it—*her pregnant stomach.*

"I didn't remember she was pregnant," Dr. Siegel says as I stare at the screen with my jaw wide open. "Did you know about her pregnancy?"

I shake my head, still unable to form words, in complete and utter shock, staring at my mom's stomach. She looks four or five months pregnant.

What Alexander Valentine said comes firing back at me, how Mom was more motivated than most to recover at the halfway house. This was why—she was going to have a baby. A baby she wanted to give the best possible chance to have a healthy outcome.

Sadness hits me, a sadness I know too well. Mom must have ended up miscarrying. She tried to get healthy for the baby, but it was too late. *This* is why she told Pearl she was thankful to leave New York behind her—the pain of it all. It's also probably why she was so eager to hang the Cadells in her congressional testimony. They hadn't just stolen her youth; they also had stolen her pregnancy.

"I guess this is what the Cadells are nervous about me finding out," I finally say to Dr. Siegel. "It wasn't what she said in your interview. It was the fact she was pregnant and miscarried because of their drugs."

"Maybe," he says quietly.

"But since then, there have been other women that have miscarried because of TriCPharma. Why do they care about my mom? It's also strange she didn't mention it in her congressional testimony. If she wanted to make the Cadells look bad, why didn't she disclose she miscarried to congress?"

"Maybe she didn't," he says.

"What?"

"Maybe she had the baby," he says.

His words don't register.

"You think my mom had a secret child and never told my dad or me about it?" I ask.

"I interviewed a lot of addicts at Bell. Many of them had done things while they were using, things they didn't necessarily advertise," he says.

I shake my head, adamant. "There's no way she could've kept another human being a secret from us for that long."

"Maybe she gave them up for adoption," he says.

"If that's true, why would the Cadells care about me finding out about it now? And how can I find out if this person even exists? I can't look up a birth record without a name, and I don't know who the father is."

"Google?" he says.

I stand up. "Can I use your computer?" I say, pointing to one on his desk in the corner of the office.

"Sure," he says. He walks to his desk and turns on the computer.

I try Googling "Irene Mayer and children." There are several Irene Mayers, but all that comes up for Mom are a couple of dated grainy pictures of her, Dad, and me that Dad probably posted on his Facebook page before he died. There's nothing about her having another child or, for that matter, ever being pregnant before me. This part of her life was erased like she was twenty-six years ago.

Dr. Siegel returns to the VHS player and ejects the tape from it. "I want you to have this," he says, handing it to me.

I shake my head. "I think it'll be safer with you." I notice a white label on the front of the tape with a typed address: 234 Howard Street.

"Was that your old office?" I ask him.

"No," he says. "It was probably your mom's address at the time."

"But she lived in a halfway house after she was discharged from the hospital. NYU had the address in their records."

"Apparently not forever," he says.

I remember Claire said that Mom left the halfway house before Esther did. Maybe this is where she moved to after.

"Where's Howard Street?" I ask Dr. Siegel.

"Near Little Italy," he says.

"I need to go there to find out if anyone knows anything about what happened with her pregnancy that might help me understand why the Cadells didn't want me to find out about it now," I say.

"Look," he says. "I'm rooting for you, but that was fifty years ago. Anybody that lived there back then is long gone by now."

I shrug. "You're not."

50

I'M SITTING ON a stoop in front of a reddish brownstone building—234 Howard Street—at 4:35 a.m. It's a quiet residential block filled with brownstones. Unlike Dr. Siegel's street, here I can't bang on any doors or ring any bells without waking up neighbors who will post the intrusion on the Nextdoor app or call the police. And by now, God knows how many people Jason has fanned out throughout the city searching for me.

My only play is to lie low for another couple hours until daylight. Then I'll try ringing the intercom, or maybe someone will walk out of the building to go to work.

I close my eyes, rubbing my pulsing temples, in disbelief over what I've learned about my mother over the last twenty-four hours. She was an opioid addict and *pregnant* with another child before she had me. And she never told me about any of it. It's as if she constructed a persona of who she wanted me to believe she was. Or maybe she was trying to protect me, not wanting to bring me into the Cadell fold. Maybe it was both.

The sound of a police siren approaches, and I immediately jump to my feet, trying to open the front door of the building, but it's locked. I frantically try several other doors on the block that are also closed until I find one that someone accidentally left slightly ajar. I sneak inside just as the police car zooms by.

I wait a few minutes until it passes, making sure there aren't any more cars behind it, before stepping outside to return to 234 Howard Street.

I'm about to sit down again on the stoop when a man in blue medical scrubs walks toward me.

"Do you live in this building?" I ask him.

"Is there a problem with the sewer line again?" he says. "Did it back up?"

"No," I say. "I'm Dr. Beatrice Bennett. In the seventies, my late mother lived here. I'm trying to see if anyone still lives here from back then that might've known her."

"My grandmother might've. She bought the building in 1960," he says.

The tears come quickly. Maybe it's the lack of sleep. Maybe it's the lack of food. Maybe it's knowing my mom isn't close to who I thought she was, and I'm not any closer to finding out if she's still alive or getting my life back because this man's grandma is long gone. Whatever it is, I'm having a hard time keeping it together.

"I'm sorry," I say, swiping the tears away from my cheeks. "I just found out that my mom was pregnant back then. I'm an only child, and I might have a half-brother or sister out there somewhere, but I don't know how to find them."

"You don't know who the dad is?" he says.

I shake my head.

"I think there are some old photo albums of the building in the basement. There might be pictures of tenants in them, but I don't know," he says, looking down at his watch. "It's too early to wake up my grandmother and ask her."

My eyes go so wide like I may never blink again.

"Wait, your grandmother's still alive?" I ask.

"Yeah, she lives in the apartment below me. I moved in last year to help her with the building. She's old."

"Really?" I say excitedly.

He nods. "I can look for the photo albums in the basement if you want."

"I'd really appreciate it."

"Come on in," he says warmly. "I'm Henry, by the way."

"Thanks so much. I'm Beatrice."

He opens the front door and leads me down a flight of stairs to a basement with a large metal storage unit which he unlocks with a key. Inside are a couple of dozen dusty cardboard boxes. They're stacked and labeled with black Sharpie marker. He looks around until he spots three boxes labeled **PHOTOS**.

"Let's see," he says, opening one of the boxes. It's filled with family photo albums. "I haven't seen these pictures in years." He opens another box—more family albums. He goes through them quickly, checking the dates and setting them aside. "Let's try this last box," he says.

He opens it, and on top is a thick, brown, old-fashioned three-ring photo album. Its cover picture is of a woman with black hair proudly standing in front of the building we're in.

"This is my grandmother," he tells me, pointing to her. He opens the album. Inside are pictures of the building undergoing interior renovations.

He reaches for another album in the box, opens it, and it's filled with photographs of tenants standing in front of their respective apartment doors. Each picture is meticulously labeled with names and dates, beginning in the 1960s.

"Wow, I didn't know she had all of these pictures. I think this is the photo box you're going to want to look through," he says, closing the album. "I'll carry it upstairs for you."

I follow him up three flights. He lets me inside his place and drops the box filled with the photo albums on a coffee table in the living room.

"I don't mean to be rude," he says. "But I just finished an overnight shift at the hospital, and I need to shower and change."

"Thanks again for taking the time to help me," I say.

"My grandmother wouldn't have it any other way. Her tenants have always been like family to her. Feel free to sit on the couch and look through them."

He leaves the room, and I take out all the albums from the box. I quickly go through each one filled with pictures of tenants and their respective apartments, making my way through the 1960s. Four albums in, and I get to one that starts in 1973.

I turn the pages until I reach 1974, searching for Mom. Finally I spot her—young, smiling, and looking more *pregnant* than she did in Dr. Siegel's interview, maybe six or seven months. She's standing in front of an apartment door with her hand placed on top of her growing stomach.

A man is standing next to her with his arm slung over one of her shoulders. The same man she was standing next to in the picture from Laura Poitier's yearbook page. The man who she told me was her second cousin.

The handwritten caption underneath the photograph reads: *Irene Mayer and "Baby Sally," 1974.*

Sally. Mom was pregnant with a girl.

Henry reappears in the living room dressed in regular clothes. "Any luck?" he asks.

"I found my mom," I say, pointing to the picture. "She's pregnant and standing next to a man, but your grandmother didn't write his name underneath the picture."

He looks at it. "Whoa, your mom was Irene Mayer?"

I blink, confused. "How do you know about my mom?"

"My grandma told me all about her. She didn't write the guy's name because she didn't like him," he says.

"Your grandmother talked to you about him too?" I say, pointing to the man standing next to Mom.

"She never stops. He was her only famous tenant."

Famous? The father of Mom's secret child was *famous?*

"Who is he?" I ask.

Henry picks up a copy of the *New York Times* next to the box of photo albums on the coffee table and hands it to me. The cover story, about the Cadell brothers seeking information regarding Cristina's whereabouts, includes a picture of Quentin Cadell and his older brother, William Cadell, Jr., talking with reporters.

"Oh my God," I gasp.

"My grandmother said he went by Billy back then," Henry says.

My throat goes dry. I can barely form words.

"My mom was in a relationship with William Cadell, Jr., and they had a baby together?" I say in disbelief.

"You didn't know about your mom and him?" he asks with a raised brow.

She isn't who you think she is.

"No," I say, struggling to take this news in.

"I know I said it was too early to wake up my grandmother, but if she knew Irene Mayer's daughter was here, she'd want me to wake her up—at any hour."

* * *

I stand beside Henry as he knocks on his grandmother's apartment door.

"Grandma, it's Henry," he calls.

I lean on the hallway wall to steady myself, my mind spinning.

If Mom had been in a relationship with William Cadell, Jr., how could she have later treated Margot Cadell, his cousin? That would've been a dual relationship, which is unethical for therapists to engage in. Maybe Margot *wasn't* her patient. Maybe they were just friends.

And William Cadell, Jr. is Cristina's father, which means Sally is a half-sister to both Cristina and me. Why didn't Cristina tell me about her? Does she not know?

"Grandma," Henry says as he keeps knocking. "I'm here with Irene Mayer's daughter."

Finally, a sign of life. We hear shuffling, before the woman from the cover of the photo album opens the door. Her jet-black hair is now white, and she's dressed in a white nightgown with small pink roses. As soon as she sees me, her eyes fill with tears, and she pulls me in close for a hug.

"I'm Carla," she says with her arms wrapped tightly around my waist.

"I'm Beatrice," I say, returning the hug.

She pulls out of the embrace and stares at me. "Sally's sister."

I swallow. "I just found out about Sally today. I'm wondering if you can tell me more about her."

Carla threads her arm in mine and pulls me inside the apartment. She leads me to the kitchen, with Henry following us from behind. The three of us sit around a small blue Formica kitchen table. An old-fashioned, clear, glass-domed cake holder with a partially eaten yellow cake lies in the middle.

"Would you like a slice of lemon cake?" Carla offers.

"No thanks," I say. "Henry kindly pulled out your old photo albums from the garage so I could look through them. That's how I learned about my mom's relationship with William Cadell Jr."

"Billy and Irene lived here together," Carla explains. "They met at Tisch. Your mom was studying to be an actress, and Billy was studying to become a director until his father made him transfer to Stern, the business school at NYU. He could never get out from underneath his dad's thumb. When William Sr. found out your mom was pregnant, he threatened to cut Billy off unless your mom had an abortion."

"It doesn't look like she did from the pictures," I say.

"Irene refused to. She told me she had lost her parents in high school and wanted a family of her own. I felt so badly for her. She was all of eighteen and going up against this rich, powerful family alone, who didn't want her to have their son's baby. When William Sr.'s threats against Billy didn't work to get her to terminate her pregnancy, he threatened to fight her for custody if she had Sally. He said they'd use the fact she had struggled with addiction—TriCPharma drugs—*their* drugs—to ensure she'd never get to be Sally's mom, even though he knew she'd gotten clean because she wanted to give Sally the best chance possible."

I sit quietly, thinking about Mom, a scared eighteen-year-old who'd lost both of her parents young, desperately wanting a family of her own, going up against this criminal family who was willing to stop her at all costs.

"She was willing to take the risk?" I ask.

"Yes, I think she hoped Billy's dad would eventually come to his senses and realize that her being in Sally's life was more important than whatever grudge he had against his son for having a child out of wedlock and in college."

"So she had Sally?"

Carla nods.

So Dr. Siegel was right. I do have a half-sister out there, who I might have the chance to know if I can find her. But why don't the Cadells want me to know about her?

"Unfortunately, Sally died a day after she was born at the hospital."

I barely register Carla's words. "What?"

"SIDS."

The pain hits me, thinking about the half-sister I just learned about that I'll never have the chance to know. A tear clips my cheek, adding to the countless tears I've shed in the last twenty-four hours.

"I'm sorry," Carla says. "I always wondered if the stress the Cadells put Irene under did Sally in. I tried to protect her when the Cadell thugs came by here, harassing her. By the end of her pregnancy, I made her sleep in my extra bedroom so they'd leave her alone. Billy was useless—he always followed his dad's orders."

"Thank you," I say quietly.

"After Sally's death, Irene couldn't get out of bed for days. She eventually broke up with Billy before leaving New York for good. I followed the lawsuits against TriCPharma through the years, always rooting for the Cadell family to be taken down. Years later, I made Henry search for Irene online since I'm old and not good with computers. I wanted to know what happened to her. He somehow found her obituary even though she had changed her last name, and I read about you and your dad. I was sad to learn she had passed but happy to know the pain of losing Sally hadn't stopped her from becoming a mom."

I close my eyes, but the tears still dribble out.

"Are you okay?" Carla asks me.

I nod, swiping the tears away.

"It's just a lot, learning about all of this."

"I understand. Just know you were wanted and, I'm certain, loved," she says.

"Thank you for sharing all of this with me. I have to get back to LA now."

"I'm so glad we got to meet."

I leave Carla's apartment, walk down the stairs in a daze, and step outside the building.

The sun is rising with a sharp glare. I left my sunglasses in my car in LA, so I shield my eyes with one of my hands.

I take out the burner Special Agent Jason gave me and text Eddie.

My mom had a baby with William Cadell, Jr.: "Baby Sally."
She died of SIDS a day after she was born in the hospital.

The Cadells don't want me to know about her. Not sure why.

Please let Paul know. Maybe he can find out why.

On my way to the airport.

I slip the phone into my bag and flag down the first taxi I see. It's still a ways down the street and one lane over.

As I watch, the taxi begins to veer out of control. The driver quickly changes lanes and nearly hits another car in the process. He's fast approaching me.

My last thought before everything goes black is that this is it—the moment the Cadells will take me out.

PART III
Intervention

We have met the enemy, and he is us.

—Walt Kelly

51

FIRST COME THE beeping sounds. Then the antiseptic smell hits me. I open my eyes and look down. I'm dressed in a pink gown, and one of my arms is connected to an IV catheter. I'm in the hospital. And I have no memory of how I got here.

A nurse with muscular arms walks into the room with a tray of food. "Oh good, you're up," she says.

"What happened?" I ask her.

"You fractured your skull on the concrete pavement and have a moderate concussion and seven stitches on the back of your head."

Now that she mentioned it, my head is radiating pain. Warm, hot pain, as if I were bleeding, even though I'm not anymore, according to her, since I now have stitches.

I lift my hand to feel them, but all I feel is gauze on the back of my head and Mom's charm bracelet still dangling from my wrist.

It comes back to me: the taxi.

"The doctor ran blood tests," she says. "Some of your levels are off."

"What do you mean?" I ask.

"You haven't been eating or drinking enough," she responds. "That's why you fainted."

"I wasn't hit by a taxi?" I say.

"No, but the driver called for an ambulance after you collapsed on the sidewalk," she says.

So it wasn't the Cadells who tried to take me out. It was ED. He's why I haven't eaten anything since I stepped foot in New York, except for a bite of bagel.

I look out the hospital window and see that it's dark out. "What time is it?" I ask the nurse.

"Seven, you've been sleeping all day," she says. "A visitor's been waiting to see you. I told him he needed to wait until you woke up so I could take your vitals."

A visitor?

Maybe it's Paul. The real one. Maybe he and Anthony are back from North Carolina now. But how would he know that I'm here? It's probably Jason. He finally tracked me down after I ducked out of the FBI headquarters. Hospitals are always the first place they look.

The nurse takes my vitals. "You're stable. You need to eat and drink now," she says, pointing to the tray of food in front of me—some kind of cheese sandwich, red Jell-O, and apple juice. "I'll get your visitor."

She leaves the room, and a moment later, Eddie appears at the door.

My heart leaps into my throat—it's not safe for him here! How did he even know where I was? And where's Sarah?

"Hi," I say, uncertain.

"Hi," he says, walking over to me and lowering his body into the chair beside my bed. "It's not the Four Seasons in Santa Barbara, but there's nowhere else I'd rather be."

I'd all but forgotten we were supposed to be at the Four Seasons this weekend, celebrating our second anniversary.

He takes my hands in his. "I'm so glad you're okay."

"How did you know I was here?"

"The hospital called me. They checked your purse, saw I was the last one you called on the burner, and tried me. I dropped Sarah off at my parents' and caught the first flight here."

"Is it safe for you to be here with me?" I ask him.

"It might not be yet, but I couldn't leave you alone in a hospital in another state," he says, choking up.

"Thank you," I say, grateful beyond measure to see him again.

"Paul's back from North Carolina. He looked into baby Sally." His voice sounds ominous. "She didn't die of SIDS."

I suck in a breath. "What do you mean?"

"She died in the hospital a day after she was born, but her death was caused by a TriCPharma drug—an opioid withdrawal seizure."

"Oh my God."

Even though Mom was in recovery by the time she had Sally, I know from my clinical training that opioid withdrawal symptoms in babies can last for months after a mother is clean.

"The Cadells paid off the hospital staff to tell her it was SIDS to keep the truth from her. They knew she could've sued them and brought their entire operation down."

This family is evil incarnate. To think how many lives could've been saved if TriCPharma had ceased to exist fifty years ago?

But I still don't understand why the Cadells care if I know about Sally now and why suddenly they've been trying to find out if my mom is still alive. People dying from TriCPharma withdrawal seizures has been a known fact for decades. It's not any news that could jeopardize them now.

"Why are the Cadells trying to find out if my mom is alive now?"

His phone starts ringing. "It's Paul," he lets me know, then answers. "Hi, I'm at the hospital with her. She just asked me why the Cadells are after Irene now. Can I put you on speaker?"

Eddie puts his phone on my hospital tray and presses the speaker button.

"Hi, Beatrice," Paul says over the phone.

"I'm so sorry about everything," I say. "I hope they didn't steal or damage anything at your apartment and that your dad is okay too."

"He is, thanks, and our apartment is fine," he says. "Listen, the Cadells are after your mom now because baby Sally was patient zero."

"Patient zero?" I echo.

"The first baby on record to die of a TriCPharma-related drug seizure, establishing half a century-long of wrongdoing on the company's part. Your mom found out the truth of what caused Sally's death from Margot Cadell."

Margot Cadell?

"Decades after Sally died, Margot also lost a newborn to a TriCPharma drug withdrawal seizure. The Feds found Margot's diary, where she wrote about her struggles with anxiety and the first time she used TriCPharma drugs to help calm her. She found samples at her parents' house after they had attended a TriCPharma conference. The drugs helped her feel better—temporarily—but quickly became addictive. Like Irene, she got clean before she gave birth, but it was too late. After she lost her baby, she was determined to take her family's empire down and hired a detective to find other women who'd lost babies to their drugs. That's when she uncovered what happened to Sally and that Sally's dad, her cousin Billy, had known the truth the entire time. She threatened to tell your mom if he didn't."

"Remember when we went to Malibu, and Margot's neighbors said she was in a volatile relationship with an older surfer guy?" Eddie asks me.

"Yes," I say.

"That was Billy. There are dozens of pictures of him surfing online. It wasn't Margot's boyfriend. They were cousins, and Billy was trying to stop her from telling your mom the truth about what happened to his daughter," Eddie says.

"So Billy knew all along?" I say.

"Yes," Paul says over the phone. He was at the hospital nursery when Sally became distressed and overheard the staff talking about her withdrawal seizure. William Sr. made sure Billy never told Irene because of the problems it would've caused for TriCPharma. But years later, she found out from Margot, and when the Cadells found out about their correspondence, they shut down all communication between the two."

That's why Mom's letter to Margot was returned unopened, the one I found in her box of letters. The Cadells made sure Margot never got it.

"How did you find all of this out?" I ask Paul. "Margot has been gone as long as my mom."

"The Cadells thought the secret of what happened to Sally died when Margot died. What they didn't know was that the father of Margot's baby, Chris, knew everything too. They wrongly assumed Margot didn't know who the father of her child was, but she did. Chris and Margot had had met at a Narcotics Anonymous meeting. She told him everything she'd learned about Sally before she died. She also told him that after the Cadells found out about her communication with your mom, Irene started facing death threats and even mentioned to Margot that she might be forced to disappear. He just gave up this information a few weeks ago," Paul says.

"Why did it take him so long to come forward?" I ask.

"Margot had been clean for several months and then suddenly overdosed after their baby died. The Cadells blamed her death on a drug relapse caused due to grief over losing her newborn. But Chris never believed it. He thought she was murdered for trying to get the truth out about the known dangers of TriCPharma drugs and feared for his own life, so he kept quiet until last month when he was dying of kidney failure and finally decided to tell the Feds the truth before he passed."

"Oh my God," I say.

"He called a few agents to his hospital bed and told them everything. They opened an investigation to look into Margot's death as a possible homicide and another one to find out if your mom was actually dead or if she had disappeared like she had told Margot she might be forced to do. Unfortunately, someone at the bureau leaked the information about the search for Irene to the Cadells. That's why you've been followed. They wanted to see if you were in contact with your mom to see if she was alive."

"So the Cadells are worried if my mom's still alive that she might come forward about Sally now because of the testimony Chris gave?" I ask.

"Yes. My colleagues at the bureau believe your mom is their best chance to finally take the family down. She's the only one that can testify about her relationship with Billy and what happened to their daughter, which will establish the Cadells knew about the dangers of TriCPharma drugs from the start. There's a lot at stake, not just for the family, but for shareholders and the survival of the company."

"What do you mean?"

"Billy is the current CEO of TriCPharma, which had a four hundred-billion-dollar market cap valuation last year, making it the fifteenth most valuable company in the world. His maintaining his position is critical to ensuring its stability. If your mom comes forward, he's done."

"But my mom might not even be alive," I remind him.

"The agency got a tip. There was a confirmed sighting yesterday," he says. "We're trying to find her now."

I gasp.

Mom really is alive?

Even after everything this week, it doesn't feel real.

The tears start to come. Eddie puts his hand on my shoulder and smiles, knowing what this means to me.

My head is throbbing, not just because I cracked it on the pavement. I pick up the apple juice from the hospital tray in front of me, hoping it'll help. My hand is shaking, so Eddie hands it to me, and I take a sip.

"I think Beatrice needs to get some rest now," Eddie tells Paul over the phone.

"Okay," Paul says. "I'll let you guys know as soon I have more news."

After we hang up, Eddie turns to me. "Once the Feds find your mom and explain everything to her, charges will finally be brought against Billy. He'll be ousted from his position, and the company's board members will want to move on, assuming TriCPharma can even survive. It's just a matter of time before you can safely return home to Sarah and me. But most importantly, you'll finally be able to reunite with your mom."

"I can't believe it," I whisper. She's been alive all this time. And she let me believe she was gone. After losing one daughter, she abandoned her second one. The pain is almost unbearable. I have so many questions. But I voice the easiest: "I wonder how Cristina found out she was alive."

"I don't know," Eddie says. "I'm so sorry the Cadells hurt you, but things are about to change."

I guess he didn't ask the hospital staff why I'm here, or maybe they didn't tell him.

He won't understand why you haven't been able to eat, ED tells me. *I'm the only one that understands you. The only one that ever has. That's why I never left you.*

I look down at my pink gown and don't say anything.

"You seem upset," Eddie says. "I know it's a lot to take in, but I promise this is all good news."

I still don't say anything.

"Are you upset because of Sally?" he asks. "I'm sorry you were robbed of knowing your half-sister."

It comes down to this. A choice I have to make—listening to ED, the monster who has stolen so much from me, who's telling me to lie—or telling Eddie, the man I love, the man who deserves to know the complete truth about me, the real reason I'm here.

Even if the fairytale ending he just laid out happens, I know there will still be bumpy waters ahead. And I also know that if I don't come clean, I'll be tempted to keep restricting my food as I try to wade through them. Secrets always beget secrets.

The hammering in my head is reverberating. It's not the concussion or the stitches. It's ED's voice and my own sparring.

"There's something I need to tell you," I finally say. "Something I should've told you a long time ago."

"Okay . . ." Eddie says.

"I was pregnant when I was married to my ex-husband."

He looks at me, confused, not understanding what this has to do with our conversation.

"The eating disorder I dealt with in high school after losing my mom resurfaced during my pregnancy. I had a hard time eating because of hormones, and it snowballed. I was also scared I wouldn't measure up as a mom."

"Oh, Beans, you're so great with Sarah. Any child would be lucky to have you as their mom." He says the words with so much conviction that they sting. Because I know what I'm about to tell him will probably make him question everything he's ever thought about me.

"If I'm completely honest, I don't know that I believed I deserved to be a mother," I say. "Restricting my food was how I coped. I had a miscarriage, and my marriage didn't survive it. After my divorce, I recommitted to my recovery, but . . ." I take a breath. "I've been struggling to eat since Tuesday when I found out my mom might still be alive."

He takes in the information, connecting the dots back to his original question. "So you're not in the hospital because of the Cadells?" he says.

"I fainted because I haven't eaten for the last couple of days. I don't want to make excuses. I just want you to know that after coming here alone, I realized my relationship with Sarah and you is what matters most to me in the world. Relapsing isn't an option because you two mean everything to me. You have my commitment that I'll fight like hell to always be there for both of you. I love you so much, and I want the chance to be a mother to Sarah if you'll still let me."

He doesn't say anything and glances at the hospital tray filled with food in front of me. The silence between us is heavy.

"I wish you had told me this before," he finally says.

October 2012

FIRST CAME THE beeping sounds. Then the antiseptic smell hit me. I opened my eyes and looked down. I was dressed in a pink gown, and one of my arms was connected to an IV catheter. I was at the hospital. And I had no memory of how I got there.

"What happened?" I asked a male nurse who was adjusting my IV.

"You had a miscarriage and lost consciousness. A D&C was performed. I'm sorry," he said plainly.

I wasn't pregnant anymore?

At first, I was too shocked to cry.

"Where's my husband?" I asked.

"He stepped out to make a call," he said. "Can I get you anything?"

I shook my head.

After he left the room, I thought about how the last time I had been admitted to a hospital was as a teenager when I had a feeding tube inserted. ED had stolen so much from my life back then, and now he had stolen my chance to become a mother.

I clutched my stomach. It felt smaller than before. That's when I started to cry.

A woman entered the room and saw me. At first, I couldn't place her because everything was fuzzy, except for the pain of the miscarriage, seeping into every cell of my body.

"Beatrice?" she said.

"Yes," I managed.

"It's me, Dr. Larsen."

I hadn't seen her in years, since I'd left Better Horizons. She looked different, older, with wrinkles and longer hair.

"What are you doing here?" I asked her.

"I was doing my daily rounds in the eating disorder unit and saw you on the chart, so I came to visit," she said.

I hadn't known I had been admitted to the ED unit. I looked down, too ashamed to meet her eyes.

"I'm a failure," I quietly said.

She approached me and gently put one of her hands on my arm like old times. It had creases and sunspots that hadn't been there fourteen years prior.

"You're not a failure," she told me. "Relapsing is sometimes part of recovery."

I nodded, my heart too heavy to respond.

"You've done beautifully for so many years. You mustn't let this moment define you," she said. "How you pick yourself up again will."

53

Special Agent Jason and his colleague, US Marshal Kira Frisk from WITSEC, are standing in front of my hospital bed. She's dressed in a black pantsuit and has notably small teeth.

When they first came into the room, they told Eddie they needed to speak with me alone. He seemed relieved to have a reason to duck out and told me he needed to head back to LA because of Sarah. I think our conversation upset him.

"We know why the Cadells were really after you," Jason says. "Your mother."

"Have you found her yet?" I ask.

They both look at each other, hedging.

"There's no easy way of saying this . . ." he says.

My stomach twists.

"A tip came in that she was in northern California, near the San Geronimo Valley. There was a sighting yesterday," he says. "But we just got word that remains were found nearby. They're doing more tests to verify. The initial DNA results look like a match."

"NOOO!" I wail out in agony. I've lost her all over again. A pain that knows no bottom.

"The sad truth is that if she hadn't gone off the grid on her own decades ago and instead worked with us to enter

WITSEC, this likely never would've happened," Kira tells me, biting her lower lip with her small teeth. "That's why you need to enter it. Even though it looks like your mother won't be able to testify about Sally, the Cadell brothers still have another reason to target you. They believe Cristina Cadell gave you information about her mother's murder."

I look around the hospital room, waiting for Dr. Larsen to make another appearance. Tell me how I can turn my life around again like she did at Better Horizons and after my miscarriage. But she's long gone, and I'm out of second chances.

"The bottom line is it isn't safe for you to return to your life in LA," Jason says.

"I'm not entering WITSEC," I tell them.

"I know this is difficult," Kira says. "But you have to consider other people in your life who you care about who might get hurt in the crossfire as the Cadell brothers continue to pursue you."

Mom is gone for good. It seems Eddie is now too. He doesn't want me in his or Sarah's lives anymore. My worst fears have been realized.

"I don't have people in my life who I need to worry about getting hurt," I say.

"What about the guy who was just in here?" Jason asks me.

"What about him?" I say coolly.

Jason gets the hint.

"How about your patients?" Kira asks.

"I don't know if I'm fit to be a psychologist anymore," I say.

"Then what will you do?" she says.

"I'm not sure."

"If you don't have anyone or anything to return to in LA, then why wouldn't you want to enter WITSEC and relocate?" she presses.

I think about how the Cadells have taken everyone I've ever loved or wanted the chance to love away from me.

"Because there's nothing left for them to take from me," I say.

"What about your life?" Kira says.

"What is a life without love?" I ask.

She and Jason look at me, perplexed.

I know their type. I've had their kind grace my office through the years. They are high-achieving people, used to navigating complex facts on the ground and calculating high-level risks, yet are ill-equipped to answer a question as simple as the one I just posed.

"Your phone was found in a dumpster off a tristate highway," Jason says awkwardly, handing it back to me.

I take it from him and lay it beside me on the hospital bed.

"Please consider what we've said," Kira says.

"I've made my decision. I'm not entering WITSEC. I want to rest now," I say.

After they leave, I text Eddie to thank him for visiting me. But he doesn't respond.

* * *

The night is dark and long. The hospital sounds that once terrified me—moans and cries coming from adjacent rooms, loud machines rolling down the corridors, I'm numb to now.

At some point, my phone makes a sound—a notification that it's Eddie's and my second anniversary.

Before our first trip to Santa Barbara last year, when we dropped Sarah off at Eddie's parents' place, his mom pulled me aside.

"Eddie's dad and I will be thrilled when you two tie the knot," she told me. "I know your generation takes things slowly, but my granddaughter needs a mother."

I knew what she said was true and decided I would finally tell Eddie about what happened in my first marriage while we were away and alone.

As we ate dinner on an outdoor wraparound patio at the hotel's seafood restaurant, I was summoning the courage to tell him the truth when he lifted his champagne glass.

"To finding you," he said. "The best thing that's happened to me since Sarah was born."

I swallowed hard, fearful of opening up because of how he might react to finding out about my ED-related miscarriage.

"You're the only woman I've dated since Helen died, and I know she had something to do with our meeting," he continued. "When I was younger, I had all hopes for what my future children would be like one day—smart, good in school, athletic. But after Helen died, I realized what I hoped for more than anything was that Sarah grows up to be kind, like you were to me at the bakery when we first met. Thank you for being kind."

Does a kind person keep secrets? I thought.

He clinked my glass. I sipped the champagne, trying to swallow down my guilt, unable to bring myself to tell him the truth about my past.

Later that night, I lay in bed, struggling to sleep, debating whether I should wake him up and finally tell him. But I didn't. Maybe if I had, he'd still be here with me.

The nurse comes in and turns on the light to check my IV. In the cold, harsh fluorescent hospital room light, I can't escape the fact I'm alone.

After she leaves, my phone makes another sound. A text from Sarah:

Hi Beans! Life360 says you're in New York!
That's so far. I miss you.

54

Day Five

I REST MY HEAD back on the airplane seat's headrest. The gauze is gone, and my hair is covering my stitches. The doctor referred me to have them removed in LA.

Unlike the red-eye flight I caught to NYC on Wednesday night when I was worried about my safety, now I don't care. Maybe someone followed me onto the plane. Maybe they didn't. It doesn't matter anymore.

I haven't heard anything from Eddie since he left me at the hospital yesterday.

I stare straight ahead at an old rerun of *Friends* playing on the aircraft's TV.

Eventually, the captain announces to prepare for descent, and we land into a rare LA storm. Rain hits the plane's windows. I have no umbrella or raincoat with me.

I take a shuttle to my car parked in a lot near the airport and drive myself home.

When I pull up in front of my house and get out of my car, I feel out of body, like I'm watching myself as a spectator, emotionless—depersonalization, as we call it in the field. Apart from being soaked from the rain, the only thing

I feel is a bit of throbbing in my head, remnants from my fall.

I roll my carry-on suitcase inside over a pile of mail slipped through the front door slot while I was gone. I turn on the living room light, half-expecting the place to be ransacked by the Cadells, but it isn't.

I head to my bedroom, wondering if someone's waiting for me, ready to take me out. I'm not scared, just numb.

When I step inside my bedroom, I realize someone *is* there.

I can make her out even in the darkness, sitting on the resting chair next to my bed. This time, she's not wearing a baseball cap. I turn on the light.

"I thought you were in Europe," I say.

"I needed to come back," Cristina says.

"Why?" I ask.

"When I was on my own, it was one thing. But I can't be a fugitive on the run with a baby," she says.

"A baby?" I say.

"I'm pregnant," she says. "My dad's at his house in Venice. I was going to go there and ask him to drop the fake charges against me for the sake of my future son, but I realized there's no point. I'm turning myself in. They'll take my son away from me after I have him in prison, so I came here to ask you if you'll make sure he knows the truth about his mom."

"The detective investigating your mother's death knows you're innocent," I tell her. "He found evidence that you were framed. They need you to help their case against your dad."

"It's useless," she says. "Once my father and uncle get ahold of him and threaten his life and the lives of his loved ones, he'll fall into place and help make it look like I murdered my mom when they're the ones that killed her to silence her because she knew too much about their operation. That's how it always goes. That's why my cousin Margot supposedly 'overdosed.' Did you find your mom?" she asks, pointing to Mom's bracelet on my wrist.

I shake my head, unable to say the word "remains" out loud.

"How did you get her bracelet?" I ask.

"My dad hired a PI to see if your mom was still alive, and the PI gave it to him as proof that she was. I don't know how he got it. I stole it from my dad's house to prove it to you. I'm sorry you couldn't find her. I was hoping you could warn her, so you wouldn't lose her forever like I've lost my mom." She's trying hard not to cry.

"Thanks for trying to help me," I say.

"I'm so worried about my future baby boy. God knows who's going to end up raising him. Please promise me you'll let him know his mom didn't do the terrible things they're going to say I did."

She stands up, revealing a small pouch sticking out above her pants waistline, not quite yet big enough to signal a pregnancy, looking more like she ate a large meal.

Suddenly she winces, grabs her stomach, and sits back down again. "I think he just kicked me for the first time," she says.

I remember what that first kick felt like. And I remember what my stomach felt like after the D&C. I think about the miscarriage I suffered because of ED that took hold of me after Mom was forced to disappear because of the Cadell family. And I think about how now I won't have the chance to be a mother to Sarah for the same reason.

I flash to Mom's pregnant stomach in Dr. Siegel's interview and think about Sally, who also died because of the Cadell empire, and how Mom was forced to abandon me because of them.

I look back at Cristina, who's rubbing her stomach, and think about her son growing up without his mother and her living her life in prison because of the Cadells, and something breaks inside of me.

A fury is unleashed. A fury that's been building since the day I said my last goodbye to mom. A fury that feels like it could power all of Los Angeles. *Not one more.*

I start walking out of my bedroom.

"Where are you going?" Cristina calls out.

I'm already down the hall.

"What are you doing?" she shouts.

I run out of the house as she chases after me.

"Where are you going?" she asks again as I get into my car.

"To pay someone a visit," I say.

CHAPTER

55

THE VENICE BOARDWALK is empty even though it's Saturday night. Usually, it would be filled with locals and tourists popping into the skater and surf shops, eating at restaurants a stone's throw from the Pacific Ocean. But the rain has cleared everyone out tonight.

Billy's address was easy to find through a quick Google search on my phone. Featured in the *Dirt* section of the *Hollywood Reporter*, which covers celebrities, professional athletes, and other moguls' real estate purchases and sales, it was described as a modern architectural stunner with walls of windows and sliding glass doors showcasing oceanfront views.

I pull up in front of a custom-made garage painted with four shiny-colored surfboards—blue, pink, orange, and yellow, bringing back echoes of 1970s Los Angeles, a stark contrast to the white sterile box of a mansion standing behind it.

I get out of my car and walk to the front entrance, where a very tall guard dressed in a long, black raincoat stands.

"I'm here to see Billy," I tell him.

"Is he expecting you?" he says.

"Yes," I say.

"What's your name?" he asks.

"Beatrice Bennett. Irene Mayer's daughter."

He makes a call on his phone. A moment later, the enormous wrought iron front door opens.

I step inside the house, and it's as sterile on the inside as on the outside. Sparse furniture. Little artwork. It feels like no one lives here, and nobody's here to greet me.

"Hello?" I call out.

No one responds.

Whoever picked up the guard's call must know I'm here.

I tentatively walk inside the house and notice several cameras positioned on the ceiling. I pass a large living room, dining room, bathroom, and bedroom when I see a bright light coming from a room at the end of a long hall. I tentatively walk toward it until I reach it.

When I peek inside, I see a man seated at a white marble desk in a large office with ocean views. His face and eyes are hardened compared to how he looked in the pictures with Mom when he was a fresh-faced NYU college student.

"Come in," Billy says. "Close the door behind you."

I step inside his office. There are no family pictures, no artwork except one huge Saint Laurent surfboard hanging on a wall, and no cameras either. Whatever happens here will stay here, like a vault.

Panic rises inside my body. Have I unwittingly surrendered myself to the enemy, raised my white flag, thrown my hands up in the air? This is the very last place on earth I want to be. But it's the only place I can do what I came here to do.

I walk toward a brown leather couch at least a dozen feet from Billy's desk and sit down. The distance between us provides little comfort.

"Why are you here?" he asks.

"I know about what happened to Sally," I say.

His stoic face remains expressionless.

"How you knew TriCPharma drugs caused her death," I continue. "How you were complicit in covering it up."

He gives me an icy look. "If you're here for an apology, you won't find one. Your mother was an addict. She wasn't fit to be anyone's mother. What happened was for the best."

Shamelessness is his superpower, and he has it in spades. It makes me burn inside.

"Was it also for the best that I lost her when I was fifteen because of your family?" I say.

"You have a lot of nerve coming here, talking about things you know little about when you should be thanking me," he says.

Anger flames inside me, and I can't hold back, even if it costs me.

"My life was irrevocably changed when my mom was forced to disappear because of your family, and not for the better. Don't you dare tell me I should be thanking you," I say.

"My father paid for your mother to go to the best detox program in the country at the time. She got a second chance at life because of my family. You wouldn't be sitting here now if we hadn't helped her."

I realize this is Billy's narrative. We all have them. The stories we tell ourselves. The plots we write ourselves out of during difficult moments in our lives when taking ownership of our roles is too much to bear.

I did it with ED for a long time, solely blaming my eating disorder on losing Mom. At a certain point, I had to take ownership of my role to reclaim my agency and understand the choice before me so I could choose recovery.

Billy's story is that his father saved my mom. A story he has undoubtedly told himself over and over again through the years until he absorbed it as the truth. Whenever the voice inside of him questioned whether his family's opioid empire played a role in his daughter's death, he has soothed himself with this story.

"You have her hubris," he says. "At least I knew I wasn't fit to be a parent as an eighteen-year-old kid."

"Maybe it wasn't that," I say. "Maybe your father made you believe that because he never wanted you to have Sally."

His eyes flicker with anger. I just poked a hole in his story. The one he's desperately clung to for decades. The one that built his house of cards.

"Why are you here?" he asks.

"To make a deal," I say.

"She's never coming back," he says it like he's trying to hurt me as retaliation, and it works. The words sear through me so deeply it takes my breath away. I try to maintain my composure.

"I'm not here about my mom," I say. "I'm here for Cristina."

"Cristina," he says, almost chuckling. "Why do you care about her after the so-called atrocity my family committed against you?"

"Because it's too late for Cristina and me. We both lost our moms," I say. "But it's not too late for your future grandson."

"Grandson?" he says, furrowing his brows, confused.

"Cristina is pregnant. She's having a baby boy. I'm here to make a deal, so he doesn't grow up without his mother."

Billy gets quiet for a minute. He didn't expect this. "Cristina's pregnancy is none of your concern," he finally says.

I look at him and think about the pictures I saw of Mom and him when they were younger—the one in Laura Poitier's yearbook where they were at the acting studio together, when the world was still his to conquer, and when his dreams of becoming a director were still intact before his father gutted them in the pursuit of TriCPharma's profits.

I'm counting on something—Billy never had the chance to become the person he wanted to be or to discover who he might have been. His healthy narcissism was never mirrored as a child, which caused a narcissistic injury. I recognize it because of the many patients I've had to reparent through the years, acting as a conduit for the cheering parent on the sidelines of a soccer field they never experienced.

"What if your grandson wants to become a director?" I say. My voice sounds more uneven than I'd like, revealing my nerves. "Will his dreams be snuffed out like yours were for your father's company's bottom line?"

He drills me a look, but it doesn't stop me. There's no getting out of here unless I do what I came here to do.

"Don't you have enough money?" I ask. "Or are you the billionaire at the slot machine in Vegas, trying to squeeze out one more quarter, even if it comes at the cost of dead bodies, including your daughter's mother? Haven't enough children lost their moms in this cynical game?"

He stands up from his desk and walks toward me with a menacing look, clenching his jaw tightly.

I instinctively get up from the couch, backing toward the door. The numbness I felt since Eddie left me at the hospital yesterday vanishes. A life force suddenly bubbles up inside of me.

My back is to the door. Billy keeps walking toward me. I have one of my hands behind me on the doorknob. I can feel the lima bean charm pressing against my wrist, imprinting my skin.

"If you don't set Cristina free, I'll go to the press and tell the entire world the truth about what happened to Sally," I say. "I'll cause TriCPharma more headaches than you could ever dream of until none of your board members, shareholders, whoever, want you around anymore. And I'll do it until my last dying breath."

He looks at me like a lion holding up an antelope with its mouth agape right before he's about to devour it. "Did it ever occur to you that it might not be a good idea to come into my home and threaten me?" he asks.

Yes, I want to say . . . when I realize something.

I'm in his office threatening him without any cameras around, where he could do anything to me and throw money at people after to make me disappear, but he hasn't touched me.

"I don't think you want me to die," I say, realizing it as the words come out of my mouth.

He stares at me for a long while but doesn't respond.

"I remind you of her, don't I?" I say.

He still doesn't say anything.

"I saw you with her once when you picked her up from our house. I never saw her look at any man that way except my father."

It seems Billy is all out of words now.

"You loved her, didn't you?" I ask him.

He releases his clenched jaw.

"And she loved you," I say.

I hear his breath, uneven and shallow.

"I never meant to hurt her," he says quietly. "I gave her the pills because my dad told me they were safe and would help her with anxiety. I never dreamt she'd become addicted to them or that he'd threaten me with her addiction to take Sally away . . ."

I look at Billy. He looks smaller, like a scared young man with his pregnant college girlfriend in too deep. It seems Billy, like my mom, isn't who I thought he was either.

"Or that Sally could die because of them," he whispers.

"If you cared about my mom, then why didn't you tell her the truth about what happened to Sally?"

"My dad told me if Irene ever found out, she could file charges against him. He threatened me with her safety, and later yours and your dad's. But once Margot found out, I had no choice but to tell her."

"Is that when I saw you when you came to our house to pick her up, and she came home crying after?" I say.

He nods.

"It was before the congressional hearing. Your mom hadn't planned to testify because she knew it could put your dad and you in danger. The two of you mattered to her more than anything in the world. But after she learned the truth about Sally's death, she was blinded by her anger. I tried to stop her. I was terrified she'd bring up Sally in her testimony, and your entire family would be taken out. I even hired someone to rough her up in New York to intimidate her."

So Mom wasn't mugged, as I suspected. And this is why she testified despite the risk it posed to Dad and me. She found out her first daughter died because of this family's drug empire and didn't want it to happen to others.

"Getting roughed up didn't stop her from testifying, but it scared her enough not to bring up Sally," Billy continues. "By then, it didn't matter. My aunt and uncle had found out that Margot had told your mom about Sally, and they let my dad know. He knew Irene could bring the company down, so he went after her, threatening your life and your father's. When your mom was the victim of the hit-and-run accident shortly after, my dad had his suspicions about whether she had died, but she had disappeared from her life, so he was no longer worried about her coming forward. That's all he cared about. I'm sorry. I wish things could've turned out differently."

"If you feel so badly about what happened, why did you go after her again now? Your dad isn't even alive anymore. You could've turned yourself in and finally told the truth about what happened to Sally. But you didn't, and now my mom is dead because of you." I choke on the words.

"If I did, I knew . . ." He hangs his head. "I knew Quentin would go after Cristina as retaliation."

"Your *brother?* Cristina's *uncle?*" I say, stunned.

"Even though I was named after our dad, Quentin's the one who took after him. He's ruthless and calculating and has dangerous partners who've infiltrated TriCPharma. They'll do anything to hold onto power and money. When he found out the Feds were looking for Irene after Margot's boyfriend gave his testimony, they wanted to search for her to see if she was still alive because they knew she could bring TriCPharma down. I wanted to protect Irene, so I told Quentin I'd hire a PI to find her. When I found out she was alive, I thought we could arrange for her to disappear again, but he and his partners said it was too risky to let her live. So I started being evasive about where she was, telling him my PI said she was on the move. Then they hired their own PI, who found out I was lying—and retaliated by murdering Maria."

"Quentin had your ex-wife killed?" I say in disbelief. "Why haven't you gone to the police?"

"I'm scared if I do, he and his partners will go after Cristina," he whispers. His face looks ashen, like all the blood has been pooled out of it. "They're the ones framing Cristina for Maria's murder. At least *your* mom's still alive."

"What?" I gasp.

He nods. "My old PI took some of her hair from a brush and planted it in the woods near the last town she lived in. He stopped working for me after Quentin and his partners started targeting his family. But I had an old contact at the FBI who owed me a big favor, and I asked him to write a report about Irene's remains. It was a ruse so they'd think she died," he says.

"Where is she?" I demand.

"She was teaching psychology at a senior center up north. I was nervous about her having an outward-facing job, but it was too risky for me to have direct contact with her to warn her since they're on my trail. So I paid the center to let her go due to 'budget constraints.' She picked up and moved a few towns over to Lucia Beach. I fear it's only a matter of time before he finds her."

"What name does she go by now?" I say.

"Sally Beans," he says.

I open the office door. Mom's bracelet catches on the knob, but I don't stop. I run out of Billy's house as fast as I can.

CHAPTER

56

Day Six

I DRIVE TO NORTHERN California on the I-5, the ugly way, which is the fastest way. The way that gets you there in roughly seven hours if you don't stop. And I don't.

The drive is straight and flat, except for the twenty-minute stretch of the "Grapevine." Cows, smog, and faded Larry Elder for Governor signs are the only views during daytime hours, but it's night.

I focus on the road ahead. Every mile I clock is one mile closer to seeing my mom. My precious mom. The person that loved me the most on the planet, who I'm going to save before this criminal family takes her down. This time, I'll hug her so tightly that I'll never let her go.

After seven hours, I finally reach the San Geronimo Valley and continue heading north until I arrive at Lucia Beach. It's Sunday morning.

I pull over and quickly Google the local senior recreation center. If she taught psychology at the center in the other town where Billy got them to let her go, there's a good chance she got a job doing the same thing here.

I keep driving until I reach a small one-story building perched on a foggy hill surrounded by large trees. I park in front and step inside. A group of seniors is playing Scrabble in the main hall.

I walk up to the information desk, and a young woman greets me with a warm smile, freckles covering her nose and cheeks, and a name tag on her shirt with *Mandi* handwritten.

"Are you here to pick up one of your parents?" she asks.

YES! I want to shout.

"Not exactly," I say. "I'm wondering if you offer any psychology classes here."

"We did, but funny enough, the teacher just quit. She said she had a family emergency. We're hoping to find someone to replace her."

The tears start flowing. I haven't slept since I returned from New York. I don't remember the last time I ate since I was discharged from the hospital.

I sit on a beige metal fold-up chair next to the information desk and weep. Weep for every hole left inside of me since Mom was forced to disappear from life when I was fifteen.

"Are you okay?" Mandi asks me.

"No," I say. "I'm trying to find my mom, and I think she might've been teaching a psychology class here, but she's gone."

"Oh, you're her daughter?" she says. "She might still be here. She just left a minute ago through the back." Mandi points to a door in the back of the center. "A man came to speak with her, and then she packed up quickly—"

I don't wait for Mandi to finish. I run down the hall and swing open the door to a gravel road. But I don't see Mom.

I watch from behind as an elderly woman with a short gray bob that probably just finished a round of Scrabble is about to get in her car.

But when the woman opens the driver's side to step inside, our eyes meet.

It's her.

She stops and drops all the papers in her arms onto the white rocks below. Her curly brown hair is gone. She has aged in the decades since I last saw her, with wrinkles and sunspots, but then she smiles at me. And I'm transported back to a time when I was a young girl, and I'd come home after school and tell her all about my life.

"Beans?" she says.

I'm unable to speak, frozen, unsure if this is really happening because it doesn't feel real.

She runs toward me and hugs me, and that's when I know: This is real. Her love envelops me like a superpower. A superpower that had always made me believe I could do or be anything in this world. Something I thought I'd never experience again in my lifetime. I hug her back tightly and don't let go.

"My little Beans," she says, a sudden sob escaping her.

I break down too, and we stand there, in each other's arms, weeping and speechless. "Mom . . ." I finally manage, breathing a sigh of relief.

"Billy just came here on his helicopter and told me I need to leave the country," she says hurriedly.

"What?" I say, pulling out of our embrace.

"He's turning himself in and telling the authorities the truth about Sally and Quentin's role in Maria's death. Quentin and his partners will be angry, and if they find out I'm still alive, they'll retaliate the same way they did with Maria. Right now, they think I'm dead, because of the false remains. It has to stay that way for everyone's safety, including yours."

"Take me with you," I say, grabbing her hand.

She shakes her head. "If you come, they'll assume you fled to be with me and that I'm alive. Your safety will always be in jeopardy. I won't let that happen. That's why I left in the first place . . . to protect you."

I start crying. "But I can't lose you again."

"You never did," she says. "My love for you only deepened through the years. You're my biggest blessing, what I always hold onto, especially when I feel sad or alone."

I can't stop crying.

"I'm sorry. I never meant to hurt you," she says. "As parents, we want to protect our children from the most dangerous corners of ourselves, but sometimes we fail. I'm sorry my mistakes as a young woman cost you. I didn't want you to learn about what happened to me in college the way you did. I had always planned to talk with you about it when you were older, but then I was forced to leave."

"Where have you been all these years?"

"When I first left, I went to Maine—the farthest point from California on the US mainland. I knew I needed to be as far away from you as possible, or I would be too tempted to reenter your life, which would've put you at risk. Eventually, I made my way back west again. I wanted to feel closer to you, but I also knew I'd be tempted to reach out if I was in Southern California, so I settled north. Your dad and I kept in touch for as long as we could, meeting yearly. He pretended he was seeing his college buddies until that became too dangerous."

"Wait, Dad knew you were alive all along?" I gasp.

She nods.

I feel my cheeks flush with anger. "So he lied to me for over a decade?"

"He did it to protect you," she says.

"No," I say, my blood boiling. "He betrayed me and let me struggle for all those years, thinking you were dead when he *knew* you were really alive."

"He wanted to tell you the truth. He said it to me more times than I can count—he hated lying to you. But I wouldn't let him. It was too dangerous for you to know. What if you had tried to find me and been killed?"

I quietly take in her words. After everything I've been through the last few days, she's probably right. I would've been in danger if I had tried to find her, and I wouldn't have been able to stop myself. It now hits me—the burden Dad had to carry, lying to me all those years. But he did it to protect me.

"Do you know about what happened to me?" I ask. "Did he tell you?"

She nods. "I always found a way to follow your life from a distance. I know you struggled with anorexia. I know you became a psychologist. I know you were married and had a miscarriage. Dr. Larsen and I were in contact through the years. She, like me, marveled at your bravery."

"I don't feel very brave," I say. "I have, or had, a boyfriend that I love, and he has a daughter, Sarah, who I'm crazy about. But I've always been too scared that I won't measure up as a mom."

"Sarah would be lucky to have you. You may not believe that yet, but I do," she says, taking my hands in hers. I notice the charm bracelet on her wrist. She sees me notice it.

"Billy said you dropped my bracelet at his house," she says. "Do you want to keep it?"

"Take it with you," I say, blinking away my tears. "Where will you go?"

She shakes her head. I know she won't tell me.

"I love you, Mom," I say.

"I love you more," she says. "Draw strength from this. Let it give you the courage to love others because you were and will always be loved. I need to go now."

She hugs me tightly one last time, pulls out of the embrace, and swallows hard.

She picks up the papers she dropped on the ground, gets in her car, and turns on the engine, smiling at me through the window with tears raining down her cheeks.

I wave goodbye and watch her drive down the gravel road into the thick fog until she's gone.

I DRIVE BACK TO LA the long way, the pretty way, but not because I want to take in the beauty of the Pacific Coast. I need time to think about what just happened.

She isn't who I thought she was. She was an addict that got entangled with the wrong guy and family and lost her first daughter due to an addiction.

Yet she still gave herself the grace of a second chance at motherhood. She took that risk. And I'm thankful she did.

I was born, and I was loved. That was my privilege.

How many patients have I encountered in my career who didn't have that? Most.

Even though she wasn't perfect, she tried to protect me. That was her legacy. And I will model her and do what I must to protect Sarah, which means being committed to my recovery if Eddie will still allow me to be a part of their lives.

When I get back to LA, I'm going to his house to fight for that chance. Dad gave Mom one despite knowing about her past. He still married and thought she was worthy of becoming a mother again—because she was.

I pray Eddie will feel the same about me. But even if he turns me down, and I hope he won't with every cell of my being, I know I'll be okay.

For too long, ED made me believe I wasn't worthy of being anyone's mom because of my miscarriage. But he no longer has that power over me. I finally feel deep inside me that I deserve to be someone's mother.

I'm roughly two hours from LA, nearing the Four Seasons in Santa Barbara, where Eddie and I celebrated our first anniversary a year ago.

My phone vibrates against the cup holder in the car. I glance down at it. A text from Sarah: *Hi Beans. I'm near you. Say hi please.*

I pull over to the first empty shoulder off the freeway, turn the engine off, and look on the Life360 app. It shows that she and Eddie are at the Four Seasons in Santa Barbara. I guess Eddie took her there. He probably couldn't get a refund for our anniversary weekend and didn't want it to go to waste.

I text her back: *See you soon.*

My mind starts to spin. Does Eddie know she got ahold of his phone again like she did when she texted me in New York? What if he's angry that she contacted me? What if he doesn't want anything to do with me?

I push those thoughts out of my mind and hop back on the freeway because this is my chance—to make my case about why I'll be a good mother to Sarah.

I take the first exit ramp to Santa Barbara and drive to the Four Seasons. I pull up in front of the entrance. A valet gives me a parking slip before whisking my car away.

I step inside the hotel, walk toward the outdoor restaurant in the back, and look around, but I don't see Eddie or Sarah anywhere.

I leave the restaurant and walk toward the ocean. They're up ahead, standing on a blanket on the sand in front of the water. Eddie smiles at me, which is a relief. I guess he's not mad about Sarah contacting me.

I start running toward them, and we hug each other. When we pull out of the embrace, he takes both of my hands in his. "I was going to reach out to you this week, but Sarah saw you passing nearby and texted you. We had a chance to visit the hotel's jewelry store this morning."

I look at him confused.

He turns to Sarah, "May I have the ring box, please?" he says.

Ring box?

She hands him a small shell box. He opens it, and I see a gold band with a solitaire diamond. He gets down on one knee and turns to me.

"Beatrice Bennet, when I first met you, I knew you'd be the perfect addition to our family because of your kindness. I've since learned that you're also brave. I know you know what's most important in life and that you'll always fight to be there for Sarah and me."

I look at him with tears, grateful for his words, the second chance he's giving me, and his grace.

"Will you marry me?" he asks.

"Yes," I say without hesitation.

He smiles widely.

"Under one condition," I add.

He looks confused.

I turn to Sarah. "I know I'm not your mom and can't fill her shoes, but I hope you'll let me be someone you can always count on in your life, just like your dad. Before I say yes to him, I want to make sure you're okay with this."

She hugs my waist tightly, burying her head in my stomach. Eddie joins in.

A couple standing nearby, watching the scene unfold, start clapping.

Sarah sneaks out from beneath us and starts running toward the ocean. Eddie and I chase after her.

The three of us stand in the water, wet sand between our toes, waves crashing around our ankles, as the neon pink sky swallows the orange sun above us.

PART IV
Coping aka Living

Everything can be taken from a man, but one thing:
the last of the human freedoms—
to choose one's attitude in any given set of circumstances,
to choose one's own way.

—Viktor Frankl, *Man's Search for Meaning*

58

Six Months Later

B ILLY TURNED HIMSELF in to the authorities like Mom said he would do. He agreed to provide them with evidence in their case against TriCPharma in return for a plea agreement to lessen his sentence and to secure protection for himself and Cristina from Quentin and his partners, who he identified as responsible for Maria's murder and framing Cristina for her death. Quentin was arrested shortly after.

TriCPharma stock nosedived after Billy left as CEO. With an avalanche of impending litigation and many top employees facing charges, it's not likely the company will survive.

After the evidence bore out as Detective Thompson and Special Agent Jason said it would, Cristina was cleared of all charges. A couple of weeks ago, she invited me to her baby shower, an outdoor brunch at the Polo Lounge in the Beverly Hills Hotel. We all sat at a long table in the backdrop of the hotel's iconic pink and green colors and banana leaf motif.

As everyone ate and congratulated her, I could tell her joy was tempered by her mother's absence. She left an empty seat at the table to honor her. Maybe that's part of why she wanted me there, someone who understood the particular pain of being a motherless daughter.

As for me, soon after Eddie proposed, I moved in with Sarah and him and quickly adjusted to the daily mom routine of lunch prep and school carpool lines. Eddie and I alternate drop-offs and pick-ups, but sometimes we get her together after school and go to the library to read her books or take her to Starbucks to get her a Foamaccino.

About a month ago, we had a low-key wedding with close friends and family in his parents' backyard. I invited the women from my recovery group because when I said my vows to Eddie, swearing my commitment to him and Sarah, I also wanted a symbol of my commitment to my recovery.

We're now on our honeymoon with Sarah, sitting on the Spanish Steps in Rome, waiting for her to come back with gelato. We gave her some euros to get us a triple scoop from a street vendor nearby for all of us to share.

I look around, thinking about how this place was the last trip Mom, Dad, and I went on before she had to leave us. I think about the picture she always carried in her wallet of the three of us sitting together on these steps, eating gelato. I imagine her looking at it now and the joy and pain it must bring her.

Sarah walks back to us, trying to tame a triple scoop cone in her hand that looks like it could topple over at any second. I remember doing the same thing with Mom and Dad.

She's standing before us and lifts her other hand, the one without the gelato, holding up the money we gave her.

"A lady paid for the ice cream," she tells us.

"That was nice of her," Eddie says.

"She also gave me this bracelet," Sarah says.

There's a lima bean charm dangling from her wrist.

I gasp, recognizing it's *Mom's* bracelet.

"She said I reminded her of her little bean. Isn't that funny, Beans?" Sarah asks me.

I immediately turn my head in each direction, scanning the steps, trying to find Mom's face in a sea of tourists, cell phone cameras, pigeons, and breadcrumbs.

It's as if she's everywhere and nowhere, all at once. She was here, and now she's gone again.

Sarah looks worried. "Did I make you sad?" she asks me.

"No," I tell her. "Not at all."

She smiles, relieved. Her saucer blue eyes sparkle again.

I stare at the lima bean charm on her wrist, my initials and birthdate engravings, and the tiny scratch in the left-hand corner.

But for the first time, I realize it isn't a scratch—it's a small *s*. For Sally, Mom's other bean. The daughter she never had the chance to know.

Eddie takes my hands in his, realizing what's happened.

"She'll always be with you," he reminds me.

I'm overwhelmed with emotion. And on cue, ED starts whispering all his greatest hits in my ear. Telling me I'm worthless. Telling me Mom abandoned me again because of the gelato I'm about to eat. Telling me if I don't do what he says, my life will fall apart.

No, I'm not worthless.

No, she didn't leave me because of what I eat or don't eat.

No, my life won't fall apart if I don't listen to you, so take a hike!

I beat him back and imagine him melting into a pile of water, just like Dr. Larsen first taught me to do when I was fifteen years old. She was a mother figure who stepped in when I needed one the most, the same way I get to be one now to Sarah, who's still standing in front of me, holding the cone with purple berry gelato dripping down its side.

"Wanna bite?" she asks me.

I flash to the first birthday party I went to for one of her classmates, how out of place I felt among the other moms, how I didn't feel I deserved to be there, and how I turned down her bite of cake, wishing I could be who she needed me to be.

This time I say "Yes."

ACKNOWLEDGMENTS

Thanks to my friends and family who read early drafts of this book and told me to keep going: Richard Leland, Charlotte Gordon, Traci Bank Cohen, Yoanna Binder, and Pam Pages.

Thanks to Zibby Owens and all of the authors she interviews on her podcast, *Moms Don't Have Time to Read Books,* for being my cheerleaders as I wrote this book.

Without the belief of my brilliant agent, Dana Newman, this book wouldn't have been published. And without my singularly talented editor, Jess Verdi, it wouldn't have soared. I'm deeply thankful to both of you.

Thanks to the entire Crooked Lane team for working tirelessly on making *Since She's Been Gone* the best it could be: Matt Martz, Rebecca Nelson, Madeline Rathle, Dulce Botello, Mikaela Bender, and Thaisheemarie Fantauzzi Perez.

Thanks to Anna David, whose podcast, *On Good Authority,* inspired my marketing efforts and to Leigh Stein for her fantastic TikTok class.

Thanks to Enzo Cesario for selflessly supporting me with everything technical. Thanks to Kristen Weber for the astute guidance. Thanks to Paulina Agrawal for the thoughtful insights.

Thanks to the wondrously talented authors who took time out of their busy lives to read and blurb my book, including J.L. Hyde, Matt Witten, Laura Lippman, Lara Prescott, Brendan Slocumb, Zibby Owens, and Marcy Dermansky. And thanks to the authors who blurbed my book after I turned in this acknowledgment section. I'm grateful beyond measure to *all* of you.

Thanks to all of the TikTok and Instagram creators I've connected with who championed *Since She's Been Gone* in its early days, with a special shout-out to Kristyn Fortner and Stephanie Mitropoulos. I'm in awe of what you do for authors, readers, and books.

Thanks to my husband, Rob, and daughter, Nina. This book wouldn't exist without either of you.